The Last Battle of the Revolution

the LAST BATTLE of the REVOLUTION

Daniel Boone and the
War for American Independence
on the Kentucky Frontier

A Novel

JEFF WINSTEAD

ISBN-13: 9798790193484

Cover detail from the painting *Daniel Boone at Cumberland Gap*
by Haddon Sundblom, 1968.

jeffwinstead.com

To Rachel

1776

ONE

The pursuers were exhausted and growing short on patience, although only John Floyd had the nerve—or ignorance—to verbalize his aggravation. The broken sapling he'd just tripped over didn't help matters; he and the seven other men in the party had been weaving through the thick woods at an unreasonable clip since leaving the trail several miles back, resulting in many a scrape.

"This is all kinds of wrong," Floyd said after regaining his footing. He'd been muttering under his breath for the better part of an hour, but this latest stumble raised the volume on his irritation. "Should have veered north back at that creek. The girls could be dead by now, and we're lost in the woods, heading God knows where." He ducked suddenly to avoid a low-hanging branch, a practice he had to undertake twice as often as the other men on account of his height.

Floyd cut a striking figure; he was lean and poised with dark, mysterious features. Someone had once told someone else who spread it around that Floyd's mother was half Catawba Indian, although Floyd himself had never made mention of it. His brow cast a shadow over his cold, black eyes, giving the impression of a calm, contemplative nature, which the young surveyor generally exhibited. But all men have their limits, and Floyd had reached his.

"John, for the love of . . ." Nathan Reid began, brushing his chestnut-colored hair from his eyes. At twenty-three Reid was three years younger than Floyd, three inches shorter, and a good bit skinnier, although his frame suggested it was built to carry more weight than its current burden. He'd been trudging through the forest alongside Floyd for the better part of two days and shared his friend's frustration, but had no interest whatsoever in being associated with his outburst.

Reid, Floyd, and the majority of the men looked a sight, running through the woods as they were in their Sunday best, or what used to be their Sunday best prior to the clothes getting ripped and ruined by the hazards of the forest. Critical moments had already been lost by the time they'd learned the girls had been abducted, and there'd been no time to change into attire better suited for pursuit.

Reid turned from Floyd to focus on where he was headed, which meant, unfortunately, staring again at the wide frame of William Bush. Reid was plenty sick of looking at Bush's backside, but it was preferable to seeing the man's bearded face, as that would mean Floyd's complaining had attracted Bush's attention.

Bush, for his part, was perfectly fine with the boys griping some, so long as they did it quiet-like; they were young, deficient in patience and abundant in energy, and letting them burn a little fire now might mean calmer heads when they caught up to conflict. But Floyd was in danger of working himself into a frenzy, and Bush figured it best to nip the drama while it was still manageable. He was none too happy about having to do so; it was struggle enough to keep pace with the man leading them without having to waste what little breath he had scolding miscreants.

"Stop that tongue-wagging before I shoot the both of you," Bush said over his shoulder.

Bush had an intimidating way about him, and an admonition from the man would normally set a fellow back on his heels. Floyd had built up too much steam to be stopped now, though, and had a chip on his shoulder besides; he was an educated man and had a difficult time not showing it, and thought sure frontiersmen like Bush resented the fact. As it happened, Bush admired Floyd's book-learning; he only wished that, if the boy felt led to talk, he'd at least speak on a subject he had knowledge of.

"He's leading us in the wrong direction, Bush. We should have crossed the Indians' trail a half hour ago," said Floyd.

Bush spun around and thrust a finger in Floyd's face. "How you figure that, boy? You a master woodsman and nobody bothered to tell me?" He retracted the finger and threw his thumb over his shoulder in the direction they were headed. "The day you know more than that man up there about the ways of the wilderness is the day I . . ."

Bush faced forward. The woods here were so heavy with brush that it was impossible to see more than a few feet in front of one's own nose, and he didn't want to lose sight of the fellow he was following himself. Besides, he was confident that his chastising had gained firm hold of Floyd's attention.

Reid shook his head. He knew certain a rant was coming, and swatted Floyd on the arm for being the cause.

"Why, I carved the road through the wilderness with that man," Bush continued, spitting the words out in clumps between labored breaths. "Watched him pick out the trail by smelling the wind and tasting the dirt. Seen him rassle a bear with his bare hands, and what with one of them hands previously injured in a scuffle with a pack of wolves." Bush shook his head. "Of all the no good . . ." Then he pushed through a patch of thick scrub and vanished.

Floyd's pride reared. He was a surveyor, for pity's sake—the best in the territory according to anyone you asked—and had spent more time in the wilderness than most.

"I may not be a master woodsman to your way of thinking," Floyd responded as he started through the scrub himself, "but I know a thing or two about Indians, and I know lost when I—"

Floyd's shirt sleeve caught on a collection of brambles; annoyed, he jerked it free and stumbled out of the brush and into a clearing. He squinted; the noon sun, previously obscured by the dense canopy of the forest, was blinding. He struggled to make out his surroundings. A handful of figures were standing in a half-circle around another man, himself standing over a large heap on the ground. Floyd finally managed to make out William Bush, who was closest to him. Bush took a deep breath, stiffened his back, pointed to the man in the center, and flashed Floyd a wide grin.

"Then I reckon you don't know Daniel Boone that well, do you, boy?"

Floyd's eyes slowly adjusted to the light. Standing behind Boone were the other members of the rescue party; Samuel

Henderson, Billy Bailey Smith, and the two companions of Bush's they'd happened upon that first evening—Jacobs and Tolliver, Bush had called them—backwoodsmen who'd been building cabins deep in the wilderness as a means of laying claim to the land. Floyd realized just then that, despite having traveled and camped with the men these past two days, he hadn't caught their full names; the mood of the group was serious, circumstances being what they were, and there'd been little interest in idle chatter.

Henderson was fair-haired, well-constructed, and typically sported a devil-may-care attitude, but now shuffled foot to foot with pent-up anxiety, occasionally scratching the whiskers on the left side of his face; he'd been smack in the middle of his weekly shave when he'd heard the girls yelling out from the river and ran to help, leaving his face smooth on one side, bristly on the other. He was a mess of ragged nerves and had been since the ordeal began; Betsy Calloway, one of the victims, was his fiancée.

Henderson wasn't the only man behaving out of character; Bailey Smith, known to be the most boisterous and energetic man on the frontier, had become downright sedate. Billy was nearly as tall as Floyd and about a decade his senior. He took nothing seriously including himself, lived as much for adventure as the embellished retelling of it, and was always smiling—except now.

Daniel Boone crouched to examine the heap, which Floyd saw now was a dead buffalo calf. It'd been shot between the eyes, a quick, clean kill, and the meat of its hump carved off with a hunting knife.

Boone struggled to focus, working to tamp down his overpowering concern for his daughter. He needed every scrap of time he could capture, and there was little left before the kidnappers crossed the Ohio River and entered Indian country where their numbers would be overwhelming. He tried to force from his mind thoughts of what the Indians had done to his son James three years prior; tried not to think of how they'd ripped the nails from his hands and feet until the boy begged for death, tried not to think of the same happening to Jemima.

Tried but failed.

Boone took a breath. The girls were alive, certainly; if the Indians had been intent on murder, they'd have killed them immediately. That one of the girls was Boone's daughter likely worked in their favor; Boone had powerful friends among the frontier Indians, although, admittedly, they'd been less friendly of late, what with tensions between the Indians and settlers bubbling over thanks to the encouragement of the British. Still, the captors might be reluctant to treat the girls poorly for fear of retribution from their own.

He had enemies among the Indians as well, although it served no purpose to dwell on that now.

The men waited in silence, wanting to give Boone time for his pondering and, although none would have admitted it, appreciative for the chance to catch their breath; Boone was nearly forty-two but moved through the woods with the speed and dexterity of a man half his age—better, apparently, since even the youngest members of the group were just now recovering from the brisk pace the man had set.

"It's a fresh kill," said Boone after a time. "They'll stop to cook at the first water they come to, which isn't far distant. If the Indians spot us, they'll tomahawk the girls and fight rather than give them up, so no man fires until I give the signal." Boone stood, then looked over his shoulder in the general direction of Floyd and Reid.

"And no more talking."

TWO

Betsy Calloway wasn't well. She sat close to the cooking fire, knees drawn up to her chest, head hung between them. Her hair surrounded her face; she'd dropped her combs some ways back to mark the trail for a rescue party she now knew wasn't coming. She'd developed a chill that morning, and shivered despite the afternoon heat. The youngest of the Indians, who had grown sweet on her, had given her his woolen matchcoat for warmth. It wasn't helping. She was only sixteen, but felt ancient and feeble.

Her younger sister Fanny sat beside Jemima Boone on a downed tree a few yards away. The girls were bleary-eyed with fatigue and sat shoulder to shoulder to keep from falling over if one or the other of them nodded off.

Their kidnappers paid them little mind. The girls were hungry and exhausted from the two days of forced marching, and it was obvious to both captor and captive that they didn't have the energy to attempt an escape. Jemima knew one of the Indians, a Cherokee chief called Hanging Maw, named unimaginatively for the pronounced, forward-jutting jaw that drooped open at all times in a predatory grimace, as if the muscles of his face weren't strong enough to hold the massive slab closed. Jemima couldn't guess at his exact age, but he was certainly over thirty and the elder of the group.

The rest were strangers to her, although Jemima had spent enough time around Indians in her thirteen years to guess that one other was also Cherokee, and the remaining three Shawnee.

The second Cherokee had been assigned the low task of gathering firewood, which he clearly resented. Jemima caught sight of him dallying at the stream, skipping rocks across the water and into the thick cane that lined the opposite bank.

The scariest of the Shawnee prepared the meat from the buffalo calf they'd killed earlier; Jemima was unsettled by his skill with the knife and the zeal with which he went about the task. He was shirtless and fit, his face painted for war, and had a regal bearing. He rarely spoke, preferring to nod or point his instructions to the other Shawnee, who deferred to him in most matters.

The youngest guarded the camp from a small mound beneath a large tree that faced back toward the trail, although he wasn't giving the assignment his best effort. The further they traveled from Boonesborough, the more confident the Indians became that they'd outsmarted and outmaneuvered any pursuit.

The last Shawnee sat by the campfire a few feet from Betsy, mending his moccasins and leering at her after every stitch. He smiled often, but the gesture was more threatening than pleasant, and he had proven to be short on temper. He wore an old, ratty, white man's hunting shirt that he'd acquired by trade or murder. He teased the girls frequently, and although they'd learned to be watchful when he was close, fatigue, illness, and the dancing flame of the fire conspired to dull Betsy's senses, and she was taken by surprise when his hand shot forward and grabbed her hair.

Overjoyed that he'd finally managed to snag his prey, he exploded to his feet and was beside Betsy in a flash. He flung his moccasins to the side and leaned down over her, pulling her face closer to his. Betsy strained to pull away, turning her head as far over her shoulder as she could manage. She felt the Shawnee's hot breath on her neck. She reached back and clawed at the ground, trying to get enough of a grip to pull herself away. The Shawnee smiled.

Then he howled and began hopping around the camp. Betsy's fingers had found a sheet of bark which she'd grabbed, plunged into the fire, withdrew loaded with hot coals, and dumped on the brave's bare foot.

She loaded the bark with more coals and sprang up; the Shawnee was in pain now, but would surely retaliate once he recovered. The guard, the wood gatherer, and Hanging Maw heard the man's screams and came running, then watched as the moccasin mender dropped to the ground and began blowing on his burned foot. The three turned to Betsy; they assessed the scene, pieced together what must have happened, then began laughing so hard it brought tears to their eyes. They pointed, jeered, put their hands on each other's shoulders, then pointed and jeered again. Hanging Maw in particular disdained the moccasin mender, and he graced Betsy with an exaggerated bow to show his appreciation.

"You can drop that, " Hanging Maw said to her, pointing to the bark in her hand as he wiped his eyes. "You made the squaw dance enough for today."

Then the three Indians were laughing, jeering, and pointing again. The mender hopped to standing and glared at them, sullen. Betsy tossed the bark into the fire.

The Shawnee leader approached, carrying a spit holding the skewered buffalo meat. The others stopped laughing. The wood gatherer cleared his throat, hustled to the fire, and began using his club to drive the two Y-shaped branches that would serve as the spit's uprights into the ground. The mender hobbled over at his best speed to help. The guard hustled back to his tree.

Hanging Maw offered Betsy his hand. She accepted. Placing his free hand on her elbow, he guided her to join the other girls. Amused though he was, he figured it best to keep the three of them together; they'd exhibited impressive ingenuity at every turn, marking the trail by breaking branches and digging their heels into the dirt, and this latest episode illustrated the importance of watching them with a keen eye.

Fanny and Jemima were standing, having jumped to their feet when the commotion started. Hanging Maw gestured to the downed tree and the three girls sat, Betsy between the younger two. They scooted close to her, and she put her arms around them. Hanging Maw sidled over to Jemima and patted her on the head.

"Don't worry, little Boone—you are still my favorite," he said, his jaw hanging open in such a way that he resembled a grinning catfish.

Hanging Maw's involvement confounded Jemima; he knew her and her family well. The Cherokee was too unreliable for her father to consider the man a true friend, but they were certainly well enough acquainted to expect the Indian not to kidnap one of his children.

"Why do you do this?" Jemima asked. "Has my father not been kind to you? Has he not always treated you with respect?"

Hanging Maw put a hand over his heart, feigning injury at her words. "Have you not been treated well? Have I not protected you?" He leaned close to her.

"When you said these were your sisters so the others would think you all Boone's daughters, did I not keep your secret?" he whispered. "When we came upon the old pony in the woods and you pretended to be unskilled at riding—you, a child of Daniel Boone—did I betray you?" He pointed at each girl in turn. "And when I saw each of you mark the trail—yes, I knew—did I speak? It was not because of me that the others finally noticed."

Hanging Maw pointed at his chest. "Also—two Cherokee," he said, then nodded toward the fire. "Three Shawnee."

He shrugged.

Jemima turned from him and started picking at her fingernails. "Hanging Maw, the great Cherokee chief, afraid of the Shawnee," she said.

Hanging Maw's back stiffened. He crossed his arms and snorted. "I fear nothing. But numbers are numbers." He turned on his heels. What had he to prove to a little white squaw?

Jemima's temper flared and she turned to let him know it. "And what will you do when my father catches you?"

Hanging Maw chuckled. "Yes, yes—we have done pretty well by old Boone this time," he said, being sure to speak loudly enough that the other Indians would hear; they spoke English to varying degrees, but even if they missed a word or two they'd grasp the sentiment. Then Hanging Maw walked from the girls and joined his companions at the fire.

Fanny was a year younger than Jemima—a big year as maturity is measured—and had reached her breaking point. She began to cry. Betsy pulled her close.

"It's hopeless now, isn't it?" Fanny asked.

Betsy suspected as much, but could see no profit in saying so. "Shhh. Don't despair, Fanny. Don't despair."

Jemima reached over and grasped Fanny's hand. "Our fathers will save us, I know they will. You'll see."

Betsy turned to Jemima, surprised. It sounded as if Jemima actually believed what she'd said.

She did. She had to. Her parents had educated her honestly in the ways of the frontier, and she knew what possibilities awaited her and the Calloway girls; they'd either be taken to the Shawnee village of Chillicothe where they'd be adopted into the tribe and forced to marry, or sold to the British as political prisoners where they'd be kept in deplorable conditions and brutally treated.

Jemima understood bits of both the Shawnee and Cherokee languages and, although she hadn't mentioned it to Fanny or Betsy, overheard one of the Indians say they'd killed a farmer the very same day they'd snatched the girls from the river. It was likely the farmer would turn out to be someone the girls knew, as the number of settlers on the frontier was small. So, while it was true that the kidnappers had treated them decently up to this point—to the extent kidnapping could be considered decent treatment—knowing the Indians had murder in them didn't suggest to Jemima that the best interests of the girls would be considered when deciding their fate.

Jemima again chastised herself as she'd done over and over for the past two days. Her father had told her never to paddle too far downriver—she hadn't listened. He'd told her never to wander too far from the fort without bringing her older brother and a rifle along—she hadn't listened.

She closed her eyes and promised herself that if she and the Calloway girls were rescued, she'd never ignore her father's words again.

She heard a snap in the distance and opened her eyes. No one else seemed to have noticed. Careful not to draw attention, she slowly turned her head east and caught sight of a figure slinking through the brush several dozen yards away.

Jemima smiled.

Boone saw her looking and, peering through the tall grass and brush, put his index finger to his lips.

Hanging Maw had tired of watching the meat cook and was walking to the stream when a slight breeze kicked up and tugged at his attention. His eyes darted to the woods. He saw nothing. He glanced at his companions; they seemed undisturbed. The moccasin mender and wood gatherer chatted by the fire, tending the meat. The guard was walking toward them, rummaging through his pouch for tobacco to pack his pipe. The Shawnee leader had vanished.

Fanny's head was in Betsy's lap. She stared toward the campfire. She half-noticed the Shawnee guard lighting his pipe, although her vision was blurred by tears and she was focused on nothing in particular. Still, she was aware enough when red mist spurted from the guard's chest. She flinched a half second later when the sound of the shot that killed him reached her ears and the Indian fell face-first into the flames.

THREE

Looking down the sights of his long rifle, John Floyd watched the Shawnee guard leave his post and make for the campfire to light his pipe. Floyd's heart jumped—the Indian had walked off and left his musket leaning against the large shade tree. The time to strike was now. Why hadn't Boone signaled? Had he not noticed?

It seemed to Floyd that Boone had crawled dangerously close to the camp; the Indians were certain to spot him at any moment. There was also little chance that the camp's one guard would abandon his position, weaponless, a second time.

Sweat ran down Floyd's forehead and dripped into his eyes. He curled his index finger around the rifle's trigger.

The guard, smoke now rolling from his pipe, turned to walk back to his post. Just to his right, Floyd heard William Bush whisper, "Patience, boy . . . patience," but Floyd pulled the trigger anyway, whether by instinct or conscious decision he never recollected.

If Boone was surprised by the shot no one would have known it; he was on his feet before the Indian hit the ground.

"Down!" he yelled to the girls.

Rifles barked as the rescuers fired into the camp. The Indians scattered, all save the Shawnee leader, who appeared from nowhere, Tomahawk drawn. Jemima dropped to the ground, reached up, grabbed Fanny's hand, and pulled her into the grass. They huddled against the log. It took Betsy an instant longer to react, time enough to feel the breeze of the leader's tomahawk whizzing past her ear before it embedded itself in a tree not far in front of her.

Boone fired a running shot and the leader spun as the lead ball tore into his side. Still running, Boone tossed his spent rifle and unsheathed his hunting knife. The leader staggered, caught sight of a musket on the ground that one of his companions had left behind, and hobbled toward it. Boone slid to a stop in front of the man then threw himself to standing, plunging his knife beneath the leader's chin as he did so, the force of the blow lifting the Shawnee from the ground. Boone shifted his hold on the knife to a reverse grip and shoved his arm forward and down, driving the dead man to the dirt.

The remaining rescuers swarmed into the camp, not wasting time to reload, hooting and hollering as they entered the clearing to make it seem as if they were greater in number than they actually were. The ruse worked, and the remaining kidnappers kept running, dashing into the stream and across to the security of the overgrown canebrake that lay beyond. Hanging Maw laughed all the while, then paused on the stream's opposite bank.

"Boone! That you, Wide Mouth?" he yelled, his hands cupped to his face. Then he resumed laughing and sprang into the cane. "Almost got the better of you this time, Wide

Mouth! Almost," he said, the sound of his laughter trailing off as he bobbed and weaved through the stalks.

Jacobs ran as far as the campfire, then, seeing the Indians had already crossed the stream, crouched to reload. He was a big man and up in years, and it was obvious he had no chance of catching the young braves, but a lead ball from a long rifle just might. He coughed, struggling to get a fresh breath, then realized the stench of burning flesh coming off the Indian whose face was in the fire was making that impossible.

He reached over, flipped the body from the flames, and caught a glimpse of movement from the corner of his eye. He turned to see an Indian they must have missed—or had he simply miscounted?—rushing straight for him. Only it wasn't an Indian, it was Betsy; the matchcoat, her free-flowing dark hair, the dress the Indians had torn at the knees so she could walk faster all conspired to convince Jacobs—who'd never met her—that she was one of the kidnappers.

Jacobs jumped to his feet and flipped his rifle around, clutching it by the barrel like a club. He reared back, closed his eyes, and swung with all his might as someone grabbed his wrist and brought the swing to an abrupt stop.

"God's sake, don't kill her after all we've done to save her," said Boone, his tone gentle despite the white-knuckle force he was exerting to hold back the man's arm.

Jacobs looked at Boone, eyes wide, then looked again at Betsy. All energy drained from him suddenly, and his face went white.

"God help me, I thought she—" Jacobs began before choking on whatever words he intended to follow.

Boone released the man's wrist and put a hand on his shoulder.

Samuel Henderson rushed past Boone and Jacobs to Betsy and grabbed her up in his arms. He pulled her close. After a moment Betsy lifted her head from his shoulder, got a good look at his face, then ran the back of her hand against his unshaven cheek.

"Could you not be bothered to remove your whiskers before you came calling, Sam?" she said, smiling. Everyone near began to laugh except for Jacobs, whose mind was still trapped in imagining the damage he'd nearly inflicted on the girl.

"See there, Jacobs? All is well," said Boone in an attempt to console the man, patting him on the back. Then he sensed movement behind him and turned.

"Jemima," he said as she jumped and wrapped her arms around him, nearly knocking him over. She pressed her face tightly against his chest.

"My girl. I feared I'd lost you."

"I should have listened, daddy, but I let my guard down and I'll never do so again, I swear . . ." She began to cry.

Tears came to Daniel as well as he put his index finger beneath her chin and nudged her face up to look her in the eyes. "Ah, but you made up for it in cleverness, didn't you, little duck. Without your sneaky clues we'd never have found you." He used his thumbs to wipe the tears from her cheeks.

Jemima sniffled. "I knew you would. I knew it."

Nathan Reid walked up with a blanket and put it over Jemima's shoulders. He gave her a gentle squeeze and smiled. "Ah, you should have seen your old dad guiding us though. No rest for us until you were safe, no missy—"

"I think this one here is chief Blackfish's boy," said William Bush as he crouched beside the man Boone had killed. Boone's knife was still stuck in the underside of the brave's jaw. Bush grabbed the handle and gave it a good pull; the weapon jerked free. Then he wiped the blade clean on the brave's breechclout.

Boone walked up beside Bush and stared down at the body of the Indian. Bush handed Boone his knife. He tucked it into its sheath, then leaned down and managed a close look at the Shawnee for the first time. Bush was right. It made an already ugly situation all the more complicated, and Boone wondered what the whole affair would mean for their already tattered relationship with the tribes. There was nothing to be done about the matter now, though, so he pushed the question to the back of his mind.

Boone straightened. He turned back toward Jemima and saw she was well-tended; the men were bustling about, fetching water from the stream, ripping strips from the bottoms of their shirts to repurpose as bandages, and generally doing whatever they could think of to ensure the girls' comfort. Boone noticed many a wet eye among the rescuers; the angst of the past several days being what it had been, he didn't begrudge them in the least. Still, he was surprised when he looked to his side and saw even the cantankerous William Bush was touched with emotion. Boone slapped the big backwoodsman on the shoulder.

"Go ahead and get it out," Boone said to the men, smiling. "But let's not make an afternoon of it—I suspect these girls are hungry, and since the Indians went to the trouble, we might as well eat before starting home." Bush grimaced and shoved Boone's hand away. Daniel laughed.

Jemima waved for Floyd. He walked over and mussed her hair, smiling. He glanced toward Boone, who was working with Bush to carry the body of the Indian Floyd had shot away from the campfire so as not to spoil everyone's appetite. Boone caught Floyd's eye, held it a moment, then turned back to the task at hand. If Boone disapproved of Floyd firing that first shot into the camp before being told to do so, Floyd never knew it. Perhaps the success of the affair spoke for itself. Floyd was content not to press the issue.

FOUR

The party made good time on their return to Boonesborough and were within a few miles of the fort by early the next evening.

Having their first meal in nearly forty-eight hours went a long way toward boosting the energy and spirit of each of the girls. The Indians hadn't been out to starve their captives, exactly; they'd offered them jerked buffalo tongue several times during their forced march, but—knowing the girls would find the pungent organ too repugnant to eat—the gesture was mostly in service to their own amusement.

Fortified, the group started home at a comfortable but steady pace. It wasn't long before exhaustion caught up to the girls, though, and camp was made just after sundown. Betsy, still fevered, spent the majority of the trek that first day carried on Sam Henderson's back. He didn't mind.

They all slept well and were on the move by early morning, refreshed and exhilarated. Around noon the group happened upon the same old pony the girls had pretended they couldn't ride just two days prior, falling off repeatedly in an effort to slow the progress of their kidnappers; now Jemima and Fanny took turns riding the animal with such practiced skill that they occasionally nodded off as the horse navigated the rough wilderness terrain.

Billy Bailey Smith, his default high-spirited nature restored, rushed ahead to announce the news of the rescue to the settlers at the fort, and by the time the rest of the party emerged from the woods nearly everyone in Boonesborough, about one hundred in all, had gathered on the riverbank opposite to cheer them home. The settlement's lone canoe waited, captained by Smith, to ferry the group across three at a go, starting with the girls. Sam Henderson couldn't stand to be separated from Betsy for a single minute and stripped off his shirt, handed it to Betsy after she'd settled into the canoe, and swam the width of the river beside the craft.

As they closed in on the bank, Jemima jumped from the canoe, splashed into knee-deep water, and scurried up the bank straight into the arms of her mother, Rebecca, who burst into tears. It was the first time Rebecca had cried since the ordeal began; it wasn't in her nature to cry in the midst of strife, only when it ended, whether the outcome was good or bad.

Fanny rushed to her parents. Elizabeth Calloway dropped to her knees to embrace her; although not Fanny and Betsy's birth mother, Elizabeth cherished the girls and had raised them as her own. Richard Calloway was too shocked by what he was seeing at the river to pay Fanny much mind.

Sam Henderson burst from the water and, dripping wet, scooped Betsy out of the tiny craft and carried her to the bank, her arms wrapped around his neck. Richard Calloway's face flushed with anger and embarrassment, partially at his daughter's behavior, but mostly at the fact that his neighbors were there to witness the spectacle. Sam lowered Betsy gently to her feet and she ran to her father, a bit unsteady at first; her chills had passed, but she was still weak. Richard's temper melted somewhat and he hugged her, then held her at arms length and gave her a once-over.

"You look a sight, but thank Providence you're unharmed," he said. "You are unharmed, aren't you?" She certainly seemed to be, the expected scrapes and bruises of four days in the wilderness aside.

Betsy smiled. "I'm well, father. Much better now we're home."

Richard's greatest fear—indeed, the fear among many in the settlement—had been that the Indians would force themselves on girls. That didn't seem to be the case, though, at least as best Calloway could tell by the behavior and appearance of his daughters. His power of observation would have to suffice as proof, for he could never bring himself to ask directly.

Calloway turned his gaze to Daniel Boone and his eyes narrowed. Boone was in the midst of a mob anxious to hear his account of the rescue. Daniel smiled and nodded, patting folks on the shoulder as he politely pushed through the crowd to rejoin his family.

It was Boone who had suggested Calloway lead a group of riders to the crossing of the Licking River at Blue Licks where they might cut off the Indians if Daniel's party didn't overtake them beforehand. Calloway and his men arrived and waited, and waited some more, then made a quick return to the fort, hoping for the best. But the more Calloway considered it, the

25

more he suspected Boone's aim had been to get him out of his hair.

He was right.

Experience had taught Boone that Calloway was arrogant, hot-tempered and ill-bred for respecting any counsel but his own. The two had met sixteen months prior, Calloway having signed on with Richard Henderson's Transylvania Company, joining Boone and a small crew of axemen as they cleared a trail through the Cumberland Gap to lead pioneers from North Carolina to the unsettled frontier. Calloway, a decade Boone's senior and a militia colonel (Boone was a mere captain) assumed he'd be in command. But Boone was the natural leader; the wilderness was his element and the other men, most of whom were also experienced woodsmen, respected him. Calloway was outraged, but had no grounds for pulling rank on a civilian expedition. He settled instead for stewing in his resentment, questioning Boone at every opportunity, and behaving as an all-around contrarian.

If that had been the end of the friction Boone could have let it pass, but Calloway became even more insufferable when the settlers named their new home in the promised land after Boone. From that day on the colonel stomped about, flaunting some perceived authority which the residents roundly ignored. On the rare occasion the independently-minded settlers sought guidance, they turned to Boone. And seeing there was nothing he could do to bring Calloway around, Boone decided limiting his dealings with the man was the best course of action.

Boone made slow progress as he worked his way through the hugs and handshakes of his neighbors. The situation brought to mind an Indian rite white men referred to as the gauntlet, where a captive would have to run through a throng of men, women, and children as they pelted him with fists and rocks. Boone's current pelting, though, was delivered in the form of questions and congratulations—hardly worthy of complaint by comparison. He laughed to himself. Life on the frontier was a constant stream of troubles, and any victory that stemmed the flow, even temporarily, was just cause for celebration.

Daniel's children queued up behind their mother to greet Jemima one by one, taking measure of their sister's fragility so as not to overwhelm her, until noticing that not only did she seem hale and hearty, but the more she talked—she was speaking quite a lot, and vigorously so—the more her spirits seemed to rise.

"Stop talking long enough for me to have a decent look at you," said Susannah, Jemima's older sister, as she stepped forward to embrace her. Susannah was just shy of sixteen, strikingly beautiful, and already had a family of her own— her husband, a young Irishman named Will Hays, and their newborn daughter, Elizabeth. Will leaned down and kissed Jemima on the cheek, cradling his sleeping daughter in his arms. He doted on Elizabeth, which he could hardly be blamed for; as the first child born in Boonesborough, she was treated as something of a princess by all the settlers.

Levina, Susannah and Jemima's ten-year-old sister, was struggling to keep hold of a burden herself—Jesse, the girls' little brother, who'd just turned three and was wriggling something fierce to free himself, not understanding that the holding was preferable to the resultant fall were he successful.

Jemima laughed, kissed Levina on the forehead, then took possession of the rambunctious Jesse. Now unencumbered,

Levina wrapped her arms around Jemima. She was immediately joined by Rebecca, the youngest of the sisters, who, although two years Levina's junior, could pass for her twin. All of the girls shared similar characteristics, most notably the jet-black hair they'd inherited from their mother, and were never mistaken for anything other than Boones.

"Jemima," shouted Daniel Morgan, seven, as he rushed from out of nowhere and embraced his sister. He adored Jemima and, of all the children, was the most outwardly distraught over her kidnapping. Now that he saw she was safe with his own eyes he jumped up, kissed her on the cheek, then ran off to chase a frog he'd spotted in the grass not far away.

Daniel smiled; it surely was a heartwarming sight. Then his brow furrowed. Where was Israel? What could his oldest be up to that was more important than his sister's homecoming?

Someone touched Daniel's hand. He turned expecting to greet yet another of his neighbors but found his wife looking back at him instead. She shot him a wink; she was on a rescue mission of her own. She gave his hand a squeeze and started to walk him through the crowd until Daniel planted his feet and gave her arm a gentle tug, pulling her close. He kissed her. Their neighbors laughed and cheered and gave the couple some breathing room. Then the two started hand-in-hand toward their children.

Levina and little Rebecca ran up and wrapped themselves around Daniel's legs. He kept walking, keeping his knees stiff as the girls held tight and laughed.

"Don't burn through your stories all at once," Daniel said to Jemima, pointing to the children standing on his feet. "Parse them out to entertain these young ones at bedtime."

Then he noticed Jemima was staring right past him; her eyes were locked on Flanders Calloway, Richard Calloway's fair-haired nephew. The young man's eyes widened when he noticed. Jemima waved at him. Flanders waved back enthusiastically, then saw Daniel watching and threw his arm back to his side. He then hurried off to greet Betsy and Fanny.

Daniel had suspected for some time that Jemima and Flanders were sweet on each other and considered this solid confirmation. It was a shame the boy was a Calloway, although Boone didn't hold him to account for that any more than he did Betsy or Fanny, both of whom he was quite fond of. Still, he was none too keen on a union that would forever bind him to Richard.

As Flanders passed from his view, Daniel caught sight of Israel standing in the distance. The boy kept looking down at his feet, shuffling between them as if contemplating movement but unable to commit. Israel was seventeen and just turning the corner on his awkward phase; he'd shot up like a sprout in the past few months and was now taller than his father, but lanky—he just couldn't manage to eat enough to keep up with his growing. Food was in short supply on the frontier; few crops had been planted due to frequent Indian raids, and so many men had been attacked and killed by braves while hunting that the rest were reluctant to venture deep into the woods where game was most plentiful.

Israel avoided looking at his father, but could feel the man's criticizing gaze, or at least imagined he could. Then, as if shoved by an invisible hand, Israel suddenly lunged forward and walked within a few feet of Jemima, who was laughing along with their mother and Susannah at something Will Hays had said.

Israel wished Hays would go on somewhere—he needed to speak with Jemima alone. The presence of his mother and Susannah made it difficult enough, but at least they were family; Israel hadn't warmed to Will as such. The qualities in Hays that most folks found charming, Israel found annoying. His father seemed to have particular affection for the man, treating Will like a son even before he and Susannah were married, and apparently had insisted Hays not join the rescue party so there'd be a man around to watch over the family. Israel's family.

"Israel," said his mother, noticing the boy from the corner of her eye. Jemima turned. The two siblings stood for a moment looking at each other. Israel's eyes shot again to his feet. Then he scratched his head, rushed forward, and hugged Jemima.

Daniel wondered at the cause of all Israel's hemming and hawing, but decided there were no answers to be found pondering the subject and swept it from his mind; he rarely understood his son's behavior when it came to most anything. At least the boy had finally turned up.

FIVE

As afternoon moved into evening and evening into night, the story of the rescue spread through the fort like dandelion seeds on a breeze, with Boone's actions, in particular, growing increasingly Herculean with each telling.

A banquet was prepared (such as the provisions of the poor settlement could provide), followed by abundant dancing and drinking. Having spent many weeks isolated in the woods, William Bush and his fellow cabiners enjoyed the festivities with particular relish, and Bush's laughter could be heard at every corner of the fort. Music accompanied the affair courtesy of a man named Monk, a slave belonging to James Estill, who was a right good fiddle player.

Boone crossed the courtyard where Monk was playing and they exchanged nods. The two men were well acquainted; when Monk was first brought to Boonesborough, he and Daniel had got to talking on the best means of producing gunpowder. Powder was the most essential commodity on the frontier, and if you didn't know how to make it yourself you'd soon do without, as there was no means of acquiring it otherwise. Boone and Monk worked together to produce several batches, and Boone was impressed enough with Monk's technique that he adopted it as his own from then on out.

Boone scanned the crowd for Jemima. He'd made a habit of doing so several times per hour since they'd returned; he knew she was there in the fort, knew she was safe, but confirming it visually at regular intervals was the only way to cement the fact in his mind.

She was easy to find this time; a crowd of children—there weren't many in the settlement, so Boone figured it was just about all of them—surrounded a stump upon which Jemima stood, her cuts bandaged and wearing a clean dress. She was gesticulating wildly, no doubt regaling her friends with tales of the tribulations of the past few days. Boone knew she was dog-tired—Fanny, he was told, had been tended to and tucked into bed immediately after having her supper—but holding an audience captive by oration had energized Jemima. She was a natural storyteller, apparently, just like her father.

Boone smiled and shook his head. Then it occurred to him that the sounds of the fort had changed; Monk was still playing, his neighbors were still conversing, but something was missing. After a moment he realized he hadn't heard Bush's laughter for several minutes. He scanned the crowd and found Bush huddled with John Floyd and Nathan Reid in what looked to be weighty conversation. He walked to join them.

"William. Boys," said Boone. They turned to him. The faces of all three were painted with concern.

"Just heard Nathaniel Hart's place was set upon," said Bush. He smelt strongly of whiskey but his eyes were clear and sober. "Indians burnt it to the ground. Cabin, crops, and all."

"His orchard?" asked Boone.

"That too. All five hundred trees."

That was a particular blow. New apple trees could be planted, but it reset the clock on the years it would take before seeing any fruit.

Floyd stepped forward. He'd been in a state of change since firing the shot that killed the Indian and set the rescue in motion, which concerned Boone. Killing reshaped a man, but it molded each man differently, and there was no way of guessing at the final form of the reborn Floyd until the transformation had run its full course.

"I'll write Colonel Preston, tell him what's transpired these past few days," Floyd said. "Perhaps once Virginia has a complete picture of our situation . . ."

Floyd's confidence in his words withered even as they left his mouth. It was in part the look on Boone's face that did it, part Floyd's own realization that no help would be forthcoming no matter what he said or to whom he said it. Floyd was the best connected man on the frontier, his skills as a surveyor having made him invaluable to the wealthy and influential in the colonies who looked to claim large swaths of this new land with coin rather than sweat. Such men could afford the gamble that the frontier would eventually be wrapped in Virginia's protective arms and become a proper county, particularly since they were the very same men who made such decisions. Floyd made a regular habit of expressing the frontier's need for support, need of militiamen and supplies, but no help from Virginia ever followed. Perhaps resources were too thin; or perhaps those in power considered the prize of the frontier worthy of their small ante, but too much a risk to bet real money on.

Boone patted Floyd twice on the arm; he could see the man needed comforting.

A crowd of rowdy men surrounded Boone and his group a second later, all of them drunk or well on their way. Bush's companions were among them, along with Billy Bailey Smith, who was holding a sloshing, near-empty whiskey jug which he thrust in Floyd's direction. Floyd tossed the men a feeble smile, the halfhearted nature of which their senses were too dulled to notice, then took a swig. The men cheered.

Bush shot Boone a somber look followed by a grin and a shrug. There'd be time enough for fretting in the days ahead; best enjoy the moment now before them. He then reached out his meaty hand and snatched the jug from Floyd, which was no great effort since Floyd had no desire to keep it.

"Boys, Black Betty and myself have been too long apart," Bush said, just before throwing the jug back and taking a long pull.

"What are you on about?" said Bush's friend Jacobs. "You done polished off a whole jug on your own not ten minutes ago." All the men laughed, including Boone as he turned to leave.

"Excuse me, fellers, but it appears Rebecca has need of me," said Boone. Bush snickered at the lie and waved to him as a couple of the other men scanned the area for Rebecca and spotted her a good ways off, chatting with a group of neighbors—she hadn't signaled for Boone at all. The two men looked at each other, scratched their heads, then resumed their frolicking.

Daniel crossed the courtyard, walked up behind Rebecca, and put his hands on her shoulders. She didn't look back, just placed her hands on his. The group's attention was centered on Samuel Henderson and Betsy Calloway, who were holding hands and gazing at each other moon-eyed as they answered questions from the folks around them without looking at the person doing the asking. Despite being thoroughly mesmerized, Samuel somehow managed to spot Boone out of the corner of his eye. The boy lit up and rushed toward him, pulling Betsy along by the hand.

"We've decided to marry as soon as can be arranged, Daniel, and we'd be happy if you did the marrying," said Samuel in a burst.

Betsy laughed. "What he means to say is, we'd be honored if you'd officiate the service, seeing as how you're responsible for us having a future together at all."

All eyes turned to Boone and he flushed. It took him a moment to find his voice.

"Why, it'd be my pleasure, Betsy," Daniel said. It occurred to him after he said it that her father would be none too pleased, but this bothered Boone not a whit beyond the thinking of it. "Although I'd get a good night's rest before agreeing to take this young man's hand, I were you," he continued. "I have it on the good authority of his hunting companions that he's a powerful snorer. You might be signing up for a lifetime of sleep worse than what you had when traveling with the Indians."

Everyone had a good laugh, including Samuel. Betsy reached up and tousled his hair. Daniel took the opportunity to kiss Rebecca on the neck before placing his lips against her ear. They were near the same height which made them a good fit for whispering, an advantage they availed themselves of quite often. It seemed to all who knew them, particularly their children, that Daniel and Rebecca shared many delightful secrets.

Daniel pointed across the way toward Jemima, who was still holding court with no detectable loss of energy or enthusiasm. She caught them looking and threw her parents a big wave.

"Told you I'd bring her home safe." Daniel whispered to his wife.

"You surely did," Rebecca said, turning to him finally, taking his face between her hands, and kissing him.

Daniel smiled at her. Then he cut his eyes left to right, saw the others were still laughing and carrying-on, winked at Rebecca, and slowly backed away before pivoting and starting for the gate of the fort. There was no need to explain; Rebecca understood. Daniel enjoyed the company of others right up until the moment he didn't. It was how he was made, as sure as he was made to walk upright. It had been three days since he'd spent more than a moment alone with himself, which Rebeca knew was well past her husband's fill.

Israel watched as his father swung open the fort's wide wooden gate. He considered running to join him, to talk with him, but immediately thought better of it.

"That's right, isn't it, Israel?" said the freckle-faced boy sitting on Israel's right as he nudged him with his elbow.

"I reckon," Israel responded, not even knowing the question.

Israel and his friends were sitting on two logs on either side of a bonfire. There were five of them, all teenaged boys, sneaking sips of whiskey from a shared cup. They weren't tipsy, although it wasn't for lack of trying; the only liquor they'd managed to scrounge up all evening was a quarter-full jug one of them had pilfered from an unobservant adult.

They were hunting companions, and indeed had been out hunting and camping when Jemima and the Calloway sisters were abducted, not even learning of it until returning the next day. This disturbed Israel in a manner he hadn't been able to shake; he felt guilt that he wasn't part of rescuing his own sister, and guiltier still that he was more bothered that he missed out on the adventure of it and the accolades that followed.

He hadn't exercised much care in hiding his sulking, which Daniel questioned him on after dinner that evening. Although reluctant to discuss the matter with his father, Israel made a fumbling attempt at trying, leaving out the part that made him sound selfish. As he expected, Daniel didn't understand; instead, he laughed and assured Israel that it was of no consequence, that time passed and shrank the importance of such things.

"Why, I was on a hunt so long that I actually missed Jemima's birth, and she's never held it against me a day," Daniel told him. He neglected to mention Rebecca's feelings on the matter.

A loud cheer snagged Israel's attention. He and his friends turned to see John Floyd thrust into the air and lifted onto the shoulders of his drunken companions. Near everyone in the fort turned from their own conversations and joined in the cheering, figuring Floyd's part in the rescue was what was being celebrated. Monk even stopped the tune he was playing midstream and starting up a new one more appropriate to the moment.

As Israel clapped and whistled, he scanned the crowd and spotted each of the available young women in the settlement, easily done as there were only a few, and found them to a one staring up at Floyd doe-eyed as if the young surveyor were a modern Achilles. Israel didn't begrudge Floyd a bit of it— hell, he'd long idolized the man—and the fact that Floyd didn't let on that he was enjoying it made Israel admire him all the more.

Boone pulled the gate closed behind him, then popped his head back into the fort and politely reminded the two guards to bolt it shut once he'd left. Although both men were drunk, Daniel assessed neither as too far gone to shove a spike through a latch.

He took a deep breath of the fresh air, then walked across the gently sloping field to a large elm that stood alone fifty yards distant. The tree was the first true landmark of the settlement; it had been singled out for its impressive canopy as the site for the first convention in the region, where a few loose rules of the new society had been more or less agreed to.

Boone leaned against the trunk and looked back at the crude fort. Even the sight of it was stifling. Most of the folks within lived on their own land in regular times, separated from their neighbors by multiples of acres, but the constant threat of Indian attack had driven them to the relative safety of the shoddily constructed, half-finished stockade. They'd have to prioritize finishing the fort now, and do a decent job of it—the Indians were making that plain enough. It was the Cherokee who'd sold this land to the settlers of the Transylvania Company in the first place, even though both parties knew the tribe didn't have a particular claim to the country. The Shawnee didn't either, although that didn't keep them from being sore when they learned of the transaction. If the

Shawnee were willing to look past that now to work with the Cherokee against them, it meant the worst kind of trouble.

Boone gazed up at the stars and tried to quiet his mind. There'd be no escaping into the forest for hunting and exploring any time soon.

He heard hoof falls in the distance, moving through the woods at a quick pace up the narrow trail that led to the fort. He concentrated. Only two horses. They weren't trying to hide their approach, which likely meant the riders had no ill intent, but he wished he'd brought his rifle with him all the same. Careless. His knife would have to be enough if he'd figured wrong.

As the riders broke from the trees, Boone knew immediately from their manner of riding that they were white men. But what could be so important it was worth galloping at night through dark woods likely thick with Indians? Boone hustled up the slope. The riders reached the gate first, and both sprang from their mounts. One cupped his hands, and began yelling.

"You at the gate! Open up! You'll want to hear this news!"

Boone hoped the guards weren't so drunk that they'd start shooting before he got there to advise on the situation. As it happened they took the opposite approach, flinging open the gate with no caution whatsoever just as Boone reached the riders. He recognized one of the young men . . . Thomas, was it? The eldest son of a family who were part of the original group he'd led from North Carolina. They'd moved on to the Hinkston settlement, a good thirty-five miles off. How long had these boys been riding? They had quite a few miles under them at this stretch, if the panting of their horses and dust on their faces was any indication.

Thomas saw Boone and his face lit up as if the hunter's arrival was the fulfillment of a prophesy.

"Captain," the lad exclaimed. "Here, sir; read this to them. They'll appreciate hearing it in your voice rather than mine."

Thomas slapped his companion on the shoulder and the man thrust a rolled document into Boone's hand. Boone looked down at it, then up at Thomas, then to the other man Boone now recognized as a fellow named Jasper. They stared at Boone expectantly. He undid the leather thong that held the document closed and unfurled what turned out to be a copy of the *Pennsylvania Evening Post,* dated July 6. The first sentence was printed in large type. Boone read it silently to himself. The excitement of the boys, palpable as it was, hadn't prepare him for what he was seeing.

They'd gone and done it. The colonies had declared independence from England.

He gave the rest a quick read, looked up, and saw near about everyone in the fort had suddenly gathered at the mouth of the gate, watching him in silence. He'd been engrossed in the text longer than he thought. He glanced again to the two riders; they smiled back at him and nodded. Then Boone looked at the crowd, cleared his throat, and started reading aloud.

The residents were silent until he'd finished, and silent for a moment after. Then another. Then one of the men let out a whoop, and in a snap the crowd was alive with chatter. Folks began hugging each other. Men laughed and slapped the hats off of other men's heads. The celebration of the rescue, which had been winding down to its natural conclusion, was instantly reborn and repurposed. The settlers moved back into the courtyard of the fort, excitedly discussing the possibilities and meaning of what they'd heard. A woman stepped forward, took one of the young riders by the elbow, and guided both men inside the fort for a drink of water, no doubt followed by something a mite stronger. Two children took the horses by the reins and led them to a trough for a pull of their own.

Nathan Reid pushed through the tide of the crowd to Boone, who handed him the newspaper. Reid scanned it.

"Shoo wee," Reid said without looking up. He read some more, then slapped the paper with the backs of his fingers and said again, "Shoo wee."

Reid was suddenly aware that Floyd was standing beside him. The tall man leaned over and gave the paper a quick once-over. Satisfied, Floyd turned and strode with purpose back inside the fort.

He'd be gone by morning, without a word to anyone.

Seeing that Daniel's feet were firmly planted, Rebecca walked through the gate to join him. He put his arm around her waist.

Reid kept reading, jumping from point to point, too excited to read the text straight through. Finally, too worked up to read at all, he handed the newspaper back to Boone.

"How about that?" he said to Daniel and Rebecca. Then he took off toward the fort.

Israel Boone was leaning against the gatepost, and as Reid passed the boy he tapped him on the arm and repeated, "How about that?" as he trotted into the courtyard to join his peers and make plans. Israel followed.

This is it, thought Israel. *This is how I'll make my mark.*

Daniel carefully rerolled the paper; the document's meaning was plain enough, and reading it again wouldn't change the ramifications for his family and neighbors. Battling the crown in the colonies meant whatever small flame of hope existed that Virginia would send reinforcements to the frontier was now extinguished. Worse, if Reid's enthusiasm was any measure, it meant losing many of the young men on the frontier to the war effort. It also meant increased ginning up of the Indians against the settlers by the British. Declaring independence was all well and good, but for the Kentuckians it meant the hell they were living now was just a taste of the hell that was coming.

1782

SIX

Few men could stir a crowd like Simon Girty, and no man basked in the ability more. So impressed was Girty with his current effort—for barely an effort it was, the words flowed so easily—that he was beginning to buy into his own rhetoric.

Girty stood above his audience on a hastily erected stage consisting of a plank laid across two barrels of British gunpowder. He watched the sun dip below the tree tops, bringing at least the promise of relief from the day's heat to Chillicothe, the Shawnee village on the bank of a river named after the Miami, in a country named by the Iroquois. Orange and gold reached up from the horizon into the Ohio sky and out over the water's glassy surface.

Warriors from six tribes had gathered in the village; Delaware, Mingo, Miami, Cherokee, Shawnee, and Wyandot. A war party of over eleven hundred. It was by far the largest gathering any among them could recall or had even heard their elders speak of, and nearly large enough an audience to satisfy Girty's ego. His words could reach into their minds and mold their emotions in any manner he desired. Mirth or melancholy. Anger or angst. Fear and hate was what he was serving now, though, and he was just getting to the meat of things.

"Brothers," Girty continued, raising his hands to get the crowd he himself had whipped into agitation to quiet down. "Brothers. The Long Knives have overrun your country and usurped the hunting grounds of your fathers. They have destroyed the cane, trodden down the clover, killed the deer and the buffalo, the bear and the raccoon. The beaver has been chased from his dam. Was there a voice in the trees of the forest, it would call on you to chase away these ruthless invaders who are laying the country to waste."

The facts of it were true enough; white men now claimed most of the Kentucky country, hunting grounds that had been designated as such by centuries of tradition and treaties among the Indians. The tribes were not without culpability, however; each had betrayed the other, selling to the whites what they figured none owned anyway—how could anyone own the land? That the whites were willing to give them goods in exchange for ephemera was both amusing and profitable.

But the settlers spread through the meadows and woods like wildfire, and with equally devastating results; they cleared the land for building cabins and forts, for planting crops, and for grazing animals. A handful of white hunters one day became scores of families and clans the next, and by the time the Indians were awake to what had happened the flame was too vast to easily snuff out.

Simon Girty was a white man himself, but only in the way that mattered least. As a child, he was kidnapped along with his two brothers by the Delaware. The boys were soon separated, with Simon given to the Seneca where he was adopted as a son of chief Guyasuta.

Simon found he had a gifted ear, and quickly absorbed both the language and culture of his new family. The tribe embraced the boy. He thrived. He grew tall and strong and respected. His fair Irish skin aside, he blended well with the Seneca thanks to his dark hair and eyes so brown they read as black. Seven years later, the boys were reunited and returned to their mother in Pennsylvania as part of a prisoner exchange, but all three were Indian now and preferred it that way.

Girty dressed in near-parody Indian fashion and often went shirtless, partly to intimidate—he was impressively lean and muscular for a man of forty-one—partly to play to type; the more vividly he painted the image of himself as a white savage, the more money civilized men were willing to pay for his services. And seeing as how he spoke ten Indian languages, his services were in high demand these days. His employers called him a translator; an inaccurate description, but one they found palatable. There were any number of white men or women who had been adopted into tribes, or even trappers who traded with the Indians regularly, who could perform that simple task. No, Girty's unique skill, the thing for which they were willing to pay such a hefty price, was his power of persuasion.

"The enemy is at hand," Girty continued, blending Shawnee with Cherokee with nods to the languages of the other four tribes to maximize his pandering. "Darkness will come upon them, and the earth will cover them. Let us go forward together and hasten their destiny."

Theatrically, he threw both hands into the air and looked up at the dark red sky. The warriors cheered. The last rays of the setting sun felt cold to Girty compared to the warmth of their adoration.

Private Frederick Ellis refused to look away from Simon Girty; not because he was in awe of the man's speaking prowess—Ellis had no idea what Girty was saying—but because he felt taking his eyes off the man, even for a moment, would be equal to turning his back on a wildcat. Although his post at the river bank was nearly a hundred yards from the gathering, he could sense the energy of the crowd and its raw, emotional response to Girty. It was enough to make Ellis' blood run cold. So cold, in fact, that he stepped from beneath the canopy of the large sycamore at the river's edge to stand in the last rays of the setting sun.

"What you think he's saying to them?" Ellis asked, more or less rhetorically.

"Doesn't rightly matter, does it?" Private Becker responded. "So long as it steers that lot in the direction of the rebs."

Becker leaned against the tree's trunk, tossing one stone after another into the river, paying no attention whatsoever to the whoops and cries from the rally behind him.

Ellis glanced quickly toward Becker; then, feeling certain Girty was about to ambush him, swiveled his head back toward the village in time to see Girty jump from his makeshift stage and into the cheering crowd.

"That's the question, ain't it?" said Ellis. "They say Girty sided with us over the rebels on account of them not paying him the five Spanish dollars they owed for some scouting he'd done. If he would do that over a trifle, he could turn them savages against us," Ellis turned back to Becker momentarily to deliver a dramatic snap of his fingers, "just like that."

"It was fifty dollars," responded Becker as he crouched to collect more stones, "and he'll be getting whatever the crown has promised him, you can bet. Caldwell holds the purse, and he'll be sure an Indian lover like Girty gets his quid. Peas in a pod, those two."

Ellis turned quickly to Becker, his eyes wide. "I'd tread carefully I were you," Ellis whispered. He then took a single, broad step which brought him closer to Becker and back under the protective cover of the sycamore. "You weren't there at Pipe's town. You didn't see what Caldwell let those Indians do."

Ellis didn't want to speak on the matter further and knew he didn't have to. So gruesome was the story that it was passed from soldier to soldier to shopkeeper, shopkeeper to wife, wife to neighbor, taking root in the souls of all who heard it. Ellis was certain the tale had reached Fort Niagara where Becker was previously stationed in the two months since the event occurred.

In a last-ditch effort to end a rash of Indian raids against settlers on the frontier, the Continental Army sent Colonel William Crawford and a militia of five hundred men from Pennsylvania to destroy the Indian villages in the Ohio Country from which the attacks were launched. Simon Girty got word of this—he had a vast network of spies, acquired over many years by favors, fear, and intimidation—and sold the information to Major DePeyster at the British Indian Department in Detroit.

DePeyster, who'd near singlehandedly coaxed the regional Indian tribes to side with the British against the Americans, sent Caldwell and his group of Butler's Rangers, along with braves from multiple tribes, to the Sandusky River to ambush Crawford's force. Girty accompanied them.

After two days of intense fighting, the Pennsylvanians were routed. Many died on the battlefield, but most escaped. The rest were taken prisoner and force-marched to a town led by a Delaware chief know as Captain Pipe. The lucky among the prisoners were killed quickly; the unlucky were tortured for a time, then killed; the damned were brutalized for hours and made to beg for death. Ninety-six Delaware had been massacred by a Pennsylvania militia three months earlier—men, women, and children, all Christian converts, no less—and this was retribution.

Crawford knew his fate would be the most terrible. He'd already been stoned by the women and boys of the village, and his bloody face was painted black as a sign of his pending execution; Captain Pipe had done the job personally. Crawford was then thrown to the ground, his hands and feet bound, and made to watch as the tribe danced in celebration as they prepared a pyre.

Girty sat nearby. Crawford rolled as close to him as he was able and, through swollen, torn lips, asked the white Indian to shoot him. Girty picked up his rifle, examined it, then tossed it to the ground just in front of Crawford's nose.

"How can I shoot you?" Girty said, his face expressionless. "I have no gun."

Crawford was scalped alive. An elderly woman then poured hot coals on his exposed pate. Other tortures followed. When he finally died, his body was burned at the stake.

Ellis had witnessed it all, running outside the camp to vomit twice, only producing dry heaves the second time.

Many of his comrades were equally horrified and watched the proceedings play out in stunned silence. Colonel Caldwell, though, seemed to barely notice; he ate, conversed, and smoked his pipe as though he were sitting by the hearth in his own home, enjoying a pleasant evening with guests.

"Thing of it is," Ellis began, swallowing hard to force his stomach back to its proper place, "Crawford and his men weren't the ones what killed those Christian Indians. They weren't even there," said Ellis.

"What does it matter," Becker said. "Rebs is rebs. Savages is savages. Whatever gets the job done, eh?"

Becker reached into his palm and found he was again out of stones. He crouched to collect more. "This is some outfit, though—I'll give you that. All the officers either taken up with a native woman or gone half native themselves. Not very prim and proper for English gentlemen, eh, Ellis? But what does one expect of men in a savage land. Why, what I wouldn't give to be back in New York, enjoying a feather bed and a fair-haired—"

Becker rose and barely had time to register the figure standing beside him before the stones he'd just scooped up were smacked from his hand. He turned to see Simon Girty smiling at him.

The wildcat had pounced.

Whirling, Becker saw Colonel Caldwell and a half dozen Rangers standing behind the petrified Ellis. The green coats worn by the Rangers grounded them to the woods, making the standard-issue red garments worn by Becker and Ellis seem ridiculous by contrast. Becker cleared his throat and hastily stood at attention.

"If this is the way you performed your duties in New York, Private Becker, it's little wonder you were exiled to this wilderness," Caldwell said. His voice was calm, almost melodic, a sharp contrast to his hard-edged features, as every facet of his face looked as if it were chiseled from stone. He was only thirty-two but read a good ten years older despite being fit and attractive.

"Colonel, you see, I—" began Becker.

"Many of these frontier rebels are as stealthy as we," continued Caldwell as he stepped forward. "Were we them, why, the entire company would have been ambushed as a result of your dereliction of duty. You see, you are right about one thing, Private; the adoption of Indian ways is the secret to survival here."

Caldwell stopped beside Becker. He then turned and put an arm around his shoulder.

"Have you not heard of Simon Kenton? Daniel Boone?" Caldwell leaned in close to Becker's ear, pointed to the woods, and whispered. "Boone could be out there now, amongst the trees, you in his sights. It's said his rifle has a name—Tick Licker he calls it. Do you care to guess why?"

Caldwell stepped away. He began pacing back and forth in front of Becker, his fingers laced behind his back. Becker swallowed, his throat so dry he nearly coughed, but he dared not.

"No?" Caldwell continued. "Well, the story goes that Boone is so accurate with his long rifle that he can flick a tick off of a bear's snout at a hundred yards." Caldwell snickered. "Preposterous, really. Humorous, but preposterous. Still, the spirit of the myth is likely true enough. And men such as that make men such as you a liability."

A shaft of light from the dying sun pierced through the trees directly into Becker's eyes. He squinted. He blinked, and sweat ran from his forehead into his eyes, stinging them. He tried to focus as Caldwell turned and walked back toward the Rangers.

Becker heard a click and flinched.

"Has anyone seen Private Becker today?" Caldwell asked his men.

They stood in silence, staring at Becker. Then each man turned and put his back to him.

"No one?" Caldwell asked. "A deserter, then. A shame."

"Sir, please," Becker began, stammering. "There are regulations. The British army has rules . . ."

Caldwell turned and pointed his pistol at Becker.

"Ah, this isn't England. Or the proper colonies. As you said yourself, Private Becker—this is a savage land."

The pistol barked. Birds fled from the branches of the tall sycamore.

Caldwell turned toward his men and waved the smoking pistol toward Becker's body. Two of the Rangers rushed forward, one to Becker's feet, the other his head, and bent to lift him. Girty caught their attention and motioned for them to stop. They dropped Becker unceremoniously and righted themselves.

Girty grabbed a sleeve of Becker's coat. He gave it a forceful jerk, spinning the body face down into the grass. A second tug removed the coat entirely. Girty examined the item, then slipped it onto his naked torso and chuckled. The two rangers watched as Girty smiled and admired his new attire. Girty looked up, his smile turning into a scowl, and motioned for the men to carry on. They picked up the body and started toward the woods. Girty resumed his preening as Caldwell and the remaining Rangers started back toward the village.

Caldwell glanced back. He resented that his superiors forced redcoats into his ranks as disciplinary action for their breaking some rule or another (although Private Ellis had at least proven capable of menial tasks), but the uniform repre-sented a hierarchy, a tradition to which Caldwell had dedicated his entire life. Watching Girty make a mockery of it turned Caldwell's stomach. His every instinct was to turn and forcibly remove the coat from the smug savage, but he tamped down the impulse. No, Girty had no love for the crown or its cause, but he was, for the moment, an invaluable asset. Setting his jaw, Caldwell turned away and resumed conversing with his men.

Girty brushed the dust and grass from one sleeve, then the other. Then he turned to Private Ellis, who stood, dumb-founded, in the same spot Caldwell and company had found him. Fear stabbed Ellis at the base of his skull. Girty nodded, directing Ellis to approach him. Ellis did so, and began dust-ing the back of Girty's new coat, Girty smiling all the while.

SEVEN

Thursday, August 15

He saw the lights of the bonfire and lanterns a good ways out; looked to be he was arriving in Boonesborough in time for a right decent celebration. He supposed there had just been a wedding; that would be the most obvious reason for merry-making and the only one that made any sense, conditions in Kentucky being what they were. He figured the matter confirmed when he was close enough to hear fiddle playing coming from inside the fort. Feeling it uncouth to walk a packhorse loaded with pelts into a wedding reception, he dismounted his lead horse, a stout bay, and tied both animals at the trough outside the north gate.

A lantern hung close by. In the dim light he caught his rippled reflection in the trough's water as his horses had a good pull. He rubbed a hand over his chin and examined his face. He looked a sight; scraggly beard, hair slathered with bear grease, plaited and clubbed, clothes torn and dirty. His distinctive features were buried beneath—long, slim nose, tight mouth, sharp cheekbones, deep-set, cold blue eyes—but he looked nothing like the clean-shaven, well-kept man who'd set out two months prior.

He grinned.

He turned to see a young boy staring at him—the Jacobs boy, if he recollected correctly. The child had probably gotten bored watching the adults frolic and wandered off to explore.

"Mind my horses till I get back, and you can peel off a beaver pelt for your trouble," Boone proposed.

Young Jacobs examined the packhorse, stretching to the tips of his toes to better assess the situation; he noted the substantial, tight bundles of furs strapped to the animal, then looked back at Boone and nodded. Boone nodded back; perhaps the task would keep the boy from wandering too far from the fort. Then he pulled the wide brim of his felt hat low over his eyes, turned, and headed for the gate.

In the high season he would've ridden out and returned with three loaded down packhorses, but this was summer, and summer wasn't the best time for hunting and trapping. He'd missed out on hunting in the fall and winter, having spent those months twiddling his thumbs in the legislature in Virginia. October had rolled around and Cornwallis had surrendered at Yorktown and there was all manner of carrying on in Richmond as if that meant the war was over. Boone knew different, as did all the representatives who lived further inland; there was a clear correlation between how close to the coast a man lived and his degree of ignorance on the matter.

By the time the session was over and he'd returned home in the spring, it was nearly time to lay in the crops. He found farming uninspiring and wanted nothing more than to grab his rifle and dogs and head into the woods; after all, he had children old enough now who could handle the planting. That would have been unseemly, though, so he resigned himself to the task and set his rifle aside for a few more months.

He reached the gate and found it neither locked nor guarded; he'd expected as much when he saw the Jacobs boy outside. Careless. He left the gate open a crack on the chance young Jacobs needed to rush inside in a hurry, and proceeded in himself.

He gave the fort a quick once-over. It wasn't much to look at, but it had four solid walls that would hold; they'd proven as much when the Shawnee sieged the fort just two years after the rescue of Jemima and the Calloway sisters.

A platform had been erected for dancing, with lanterns hung from ropes strung from the posts at each corner. The fiddle playing Boone had heard earlier was coming from a little girl Boone recognized as Hannah, youngest of the Clements clan, who stood at the edge of the stage. She was pretty good; certainly a better fiddle player than the residents were dancers, and just as good as old Monk, who was now a free man with a family of his own and had moved on.

It was late enough in the evening that most of the older folks were tired out and the dance floor was populated by the young. Boone knew from experience that they'd dance and carry on until late at night, then return to their cabins and fall asleep instantly and soundly as young people are gifted to do. The adults sat around the dance floor, some the bonfire, conversing and laughing while passing around jugs of whiskey, certain among them happy to use the occasion as an excuse to overindulge.

The sound of a face-slapping popped from the platform. The dancers parted; Boone looked past them and spotted

Susannah and William Hays. Will was rubbing his cheek and doing his best not to laugh. Susannah was yelling at him, the reason for which Boone couldn't hear over the sound of the fiddle, Hannah Clements having the good sense to keep right on playing; Susannah and Will had public rows often enough that it was best not to let them be cause for distraction.

Will couldn't hold it in any longer and burst out laughing. Susannah glared at him and put her hands on her hips. Will bent forward and kissed her forehead. A moment passed. Then she jumped into his arms and kissed him hard on the lips as he threw his arms around her waist. Suddenly they were dancing again, oblivious to the fact, or uncaring, that they'd given everyone a show. The others on the dance floor looked at each other and laughed or shrugged or both and resumed dancing themselves.

Boone grinned and shook his head; at least the argument had kept folks from noticing him so he could continue with the fun he had planned. As he passed the dance floor he saw Susannah and Will's children—Elizabeth, Jemima, and William—sitting to the side and laughing at their parents. Elizabeth, now six, caught sight of her grandfather. Her laughter stopped and she stared at him quizzically. Daniel wasn't sure if she recognized him or not through all his scruff, but he put a finger to his lips anyway to instruct her to be quiet. She mimicked the gesture, then smiled. Daniel winked and pointed to a group standing by the bonfire as if to say *watch this.*

Rebecca Boone was at the center of the group, fielding questions from the friends and neighbors ringed around her; she was well-liked by near everyone in Boonesborough, and her day-to-day presence had been missed since she and the

Boone clan moved from the village that was their namesake and established Boone Station six miles northwest.

Rebecca was now forty-three and as striking as ever, taller than average for a woman and above averagely built. The rhythm of her black hair was broken by the occasional strand of white, which, rather than aging her, simply added texture to her beauty and mystery. Of all Daniel Boone's accomplishments, that he'd managed to convince a woman as resourceful and fetching as Rebecca to marry him was his most admired, and the only of which he bragged.

She was wearing a new blue dress—Daniel remembered she'd finally gotten around to starting it just before he'd left, using fabric they'd brought back from North Carolina three years earlier. He marveled that she'd found time to finish it while he was away, what with summer days being long and there being so much to tend to both indoors and out. Then he reminded himself that circumstances were different now than they'd been in the early days when he'd go off exploring and Rebecca would be left to wrangle their young children along with the crops, chores, and cooking, oftentimes having to do hunting of her own to put meat on the table. Nowadays, what children they had living at home were old enough to pitch in, aside from their youngest, Nathan, who Daniel noticed was sleeping soundly in a vegetable basket at Rebecca's feet, oblivious to the activity about him, swaddled in his mother's scarf.

Rebecca's pregnancy had been a surprise to everyone, Rebecca and Daniel included. When their last child, William, died shortly after birth in 1775, the couple swore off having another. As the years passed it began to look as if the pain and difficulty Rebecca had gone through while delivering

William had left her incapable of conceiving again regardless. But nature, as it turned out, was only taking a pause.

Facing the bonfire, Rebecca had half finished answering a friend's question when she suddenly felt a hand at her waist. Shocked, she smacked the hand and spun full around, then looked up to see the hand belonged to a dirty, grizzled old hunter whom she didn't recognize, his hat low over his eyes, half his face concealed in deep, dancing shadows created by the light of the fire, the other half lit unnaturally by the same. He put his other hand on her waist and held her tight, smiling at her in a too-familiar manner; clearly, he'd had several pulls of whiskey too many. She squirmed and tried to push him away.

"Get your——. Sir, I'm willing to forgive your drunkenness, but——"

She kicked him in the shin. Wincing, he turned her loose and hopped back a few paces while rubbing his leg.

"Lord, woman," he said. Then he righted himself and chuckled. "Madame, don't deny me a dance. Why, you have danced with me many a time on nights such as this," he sprang close to her and whispered, "observed and alone."

Rebecca recognized her husband immediately upon hearing his voice. She punched him in the chest, then hugged him and kissed him on the lips. The stunned onlookers could scarcely believe what they were seeing; Rebecca Boone kissing a dirty old woodsman. A handful, however, were beginning to catch on. Laughing, Daniel turned to address the crowd.

"Friends, I realize I'm hidden under many a layer of wilderness and time," he removed his hat, "but don't force me to prove my identity with an exhibition of my lackluster dancing."

EIGHT

Boone found himself surrounded a moment later; turned out there were more people at the fort than he initially thought. He soon learned why—they were celebrating a double wedding rather than a single one, the couples apparently combining ceremonies to avoid placing undo strain on the meager provisions of the settlement. Boone was impressed by such practical thinking, which he figured boded well for the success of the marriages.

He congratulated both couples, all four of whom he knew—everyone knew most everyone in Kentucky. One pair he and his neighbors had expected to marry; the other came as a complete surprise. Humorously, it was the second couple Boone felt was better suited to each other, although one could never tell with such things.

He was careful not to get too close to the brides to avoid dirtying up their freshly-sewn dresses. He attempted to keep his children at arm's length as well, although they were having none of it. Jesse, now nine, Daniel Morgan, twelve, and little Rebecca, not so little now and fourteen, ran up to their father and gave him a combined hug. Levina pulled out a handkerchief, made a show of rubbing it in a circle over a small area of Daniel's cheek, then kissed the spot.

Susannah and Will's children appeared next as their parents waved from further back in the crowd, figuring on greeting Daniel properly once they returned to Boone Station.

A three-year-old girl toddled up to join the Hays children. Elizabeth took her by the hand to help her along. Daniel scooped the little girl up and pressed his nose against hers. She giggled.

"Pa," Jemima scolded him as she approached. "Her dress."

Daniel handed little Sarah to her mother. He couldn't get over the child's hair; she was the only fair-haired Boone he'd ever heard tell of. But then again, she was also a Calloway.

"How do, Daniel," Flanders Calloway said, extending a hand to his father-in-law. Daniel gave it a shake. Flanders had his and Jemima's newborn, John, flung over one shoulder. The infant was asleep with his thumb in his mouth.

"Flanders. Where's your cousin and Holder?" Daniel asked. Fanny Calloway and her husband, John, lived at their own station several miles upriver.

"We expected them to make it in but ain't seen them. Could be John arranged to get himself distracted, which would've made Fanny none too happy."

Jemima kissed her father's cheek on the semi-clean spot Levina had provided. "We saw you arrive but spotted the mischief in your eyes and didn't want to spoil your fun."

Her father chuckled.

Rebecca and Daniel managed a dance and a half before their neighbors grew too interested in hearing of Daniel's time in the woods to leave them be. Before being near dragged from the dance floor, Daniel told Rebecca that he made straight for their cabin on his way out of the wilderness, then decided to continue on to the fort when he found no one there.

"I'd've had to bring down the pelts for trading sooner or later anyways," he said.

"Had I known you were coming, I'd have sent the others along and stayed behind," Rebecca whispered, before grabbing his earlobe gently between her teeth.

Most men on the frontier engaged in long hunts, but none ventured as far into the woods or lived in them for as long a stretch as Boone—especially alone. He'd been gone two months this time out; far from his longest excursion—he spent two years exploring Kentucky before leading the first group of settlers into the new land—but a good length of time, particularly when taking current hazards into account. He always returned with stories of danger and adventure revolving around bears, severe weather, and Indian encounters. Folks were particularly interested in the latter considering the increased number of attacks on outlying homesteads, and his neighbors, most of whom had been cooped up in and about the fort for months, were thirsty for the knowledge and entertainment.

Boone took a seat on a well-worn tree stump near the fire, indulged in a swig from a jug he'd been handed—it was a celebration, after all—and cleared his throat. Everyone circled around; it was late enough in the evening that even the young folks had had their fill of dancing. The newlyweds had excused themselves, the only people in the settlement disinterested in Boone's storytelling, and understandably so. Hannah began to play her fiddle in soft accompaniment as Boone sank into the rhythm of his tales. They developed a rapport after a time; Boone would signal the girl when arriving at a particularly riveting moment in his story, and she'd give her wrist a quick flick to make the fiddle squeal in punctuation and shock the audience.

Israel Boone had heard his father's hunting stories countless times and enjoyed them immensely. In this instance, however, the twenty-three-year-old recognized his father's storytelling as an opportunity to steal a few moments alone with April Calloway. April stood with her back to the wall of the northeast corner blockhouse, facing the bonfire several dozen yards distant. Israel stood in front of her, one hand on the wall, the other on his hip. They were full in the open, in clear view of anyone who cared to look, but hidden in a practical sense as everyone had their backs to them, facing Daniel and listening attentively.

Israel had grown into an attractive young man, taller and less stocky than his father with unruly hair that paired well with his playful, bright eyes. He was a Boone through and through, charming and easy to like (although a mite on the cocky side) helpful to anyone who needed it, confident in his abilities but quick to laugh and congratulate an opponent whenever someone bested him, which was such a novelty that he enjoyed losing almost as much as winning. Israel was so appealing that April had the good sense to conceal the full measure of her interest, which had the effect of heightening Israel's interest in her.

"Don't you want to hear of your father's exploring, Israel?" April asked.

"I live with the man," Israel responded. "I'll get around to it. At the moment, I'm much more interested in hearing what you thought of the weddings." He smiled at her.

"Why, they were lovely, I'm sure, for those that get swept up in such things," April said, looking at her nails as she pushed herself from the wall, forcing Israel to step aside. Confused but entertained by her coyness, Israel darted in front of her, walking backwards to match her slow march toward the bonfire.

"What do you mean by that? I thought the couples looked mighty happy and content, aside from Joseph, who looked so dazed I was concerned he was suffering from a blow to the head," said Israel. "But the girls seemed relieved to have locked down their men, no longer fearful other women might recognize their value and snatch them up." Israel coughed. It was a comfortable night for August, but still plenty warm. However, even as they inched closer to the fire, Israel felt cold.

"Joseph is a nice boy," April began, "but he can't hunt and can't fish. His one skill is carpentry, but it only seems like a skill because he's so bad at everything else." She stopped. She looked up at Israel and caught her first clear look at his face now that they were closer to the light of the fire.

"Are you well, Israel?" she asked. Israel put a hand to his forehead. It came away wet with sweat.

"Fit as Hannah's fiddle," Israel said. He began to dance with an imaginary partner, still walking backwards. Then he collapsed, crumpling straight to the ground as if his spirit had suddenly been yanked from his body.

Daniel saw April Calloway running toward them, trying to draw his attention. He couldn't make out what she was saying. He stopped talking and stood, which caused Hannah to stop playing and everyone else to turn and look. Daniel caught a glimpse of a figure on the ground. He knew Israel was stuck on April, had noticed now that the boy was missing from the crowd, and took off at a run. As Boone reached April he spun her about and continued toward his son, figuring reaching him quickly and April's telling of events were of equal importance.

"We were talking and walking to the fire and he passed out. I think he's got a fever," April said. That she was able to stick to pertinent details in a moment of stress impressed Boone; most would have stammered through it and wasted time. Despite April being Richard Calloway's niece, it may have been that Israel had good instincts letting his eye fall on the girl.

Daniel skidded to a stop and dropped to one knee beside his son. He rolled him onto his back and took his head in his hands; the boy was hot as coals. Others from the crowd were close behind, Rebecca leading. An instant later she was beside Daniel, brushing the hair from Israel's forehead.

Boone heard a belch and turned. There was a wagon just a few yards away; in his concern for Israel, Daniel hadn't noticed the figure sitting on the ground in front of it, the man's back against one of the large wooden wheels, a whiskey jug cradled in his lap. Half his face was darkened by shadow, but Boone recognized him even so as Hugh McGary.

"Dammit, man," Boone spat. "You mean to sit there while my son lies face down in dirt?" He couldn't figure why McGary had come all this way from Harrodsburg, then remembered that one of the grooms was a relation of Hugh's late first wife. McGary must have fancied the wedding a grand opportunity for socially acceptable consumption of vast quantities of other people's whiskey.

With a good deal of effort, McGary forced his head from the wagon wheel. He lost hold of the jug and it rolled from his lap. Empty. He was only thirty-eight but looked far older, a significant amount of hair having fled his head, leaving behind a motley crew of dirty, dingy-colored survivors. He hadn't shaved for several days. He peered at Boone through slit eyes, struggling to focus. Then he noticed the crowd. He knew everyone was staring at him, disgusted. He was suddenly aware that the seat of his pants was wet, but he was too drunk to muster any embarrassment. That would come with morning.

Boone went to lurch toward McGary but felt Rebecca's hand on his arm and stopped.

"Daniel. Leave him be."

Boone calmed instantly. He wasn't often quick to temper, and most always quick to cool-headedness in those instances where his blood got up.

Jemima kneeled down on the other side of Israel and slapped him somewhat gently across the face several times.

"Hey, beanpole—you want to wake up? You're making a spectacle," she said.

Israel began to stir. Daniel scooped him up.

"I can walk," the boy whispered groggily.

"Let's not test it," responded Daniel.

"Our wagon's by the south gate," Rebecca told him.

Boone started off in that direction and the rest of the family hurried after. Flanders and Will Hays rushed forward to help Boone carry Israel, but Daniel waved them off. Rebecca turned to their neighbors before following.

"We'll get him home and into bed and send someone down in the morning to report on his condition," She said.

Then she looked directly at April and winked. "He'll be fine."

April forced a smile. Her concern for Israel was plain to see, which touched Rebecca.

Some folks headed back to the fire. Most read the situation as a cue that the evening's festivities had come to an end and started saying their goodbyes. The young men who were peers of the grooms grabbed a couple of whiskey jugs, figuring to go around to the cabins of the newlyweds and drink and taunt them from outside, as was tradition. It was the part of the evening they'd most looked forward to, unsupervised by their elders and unbound by the manners required when women other than the brides were around.

As the crowd dispersed, Hugh McGary rolled forward onto his hands and knees and crawled for his jug. Perhaps he'd have saved himself the effort had he remembered he'd already emptied it. He eventually managed to stand and slink away, stumbling, swinging the jug as he went. No one saw and no one cared.

NINE

They made the six-mile trip to Boone Station in a rush, Daniel weighing the need to get Israel home quickly against the comfort of the ride. Even being mindful, the trail made for rough going; everyone was buffeted to-and-fro, particularly the children in the bed of the wagon, which didn't much bother most of them, although midway through the journey Israel popped up from the straw he was lying in, tugged on his father's shirt sleeve to get him to pull up on the horses, and leaned over the side of the wagon to clear out his stomach. Elizabeth Hays and Jesse Boone looked at each other and scrunched and pinched their noses. Israel's fever broke soon after, although he looked green the remainder of the trip.

In normal conditions, Daniel would've recommended against making the ride at night—had Israel not fallen ill, the family would likely have lingered at Boonesborough until daybreak—but he'd traveled this way just a few hours earlier and saw no Indian sign. All the same, Will and Flanders rode horses of their own as armed escort, Will taking point, Flanders the rear.

Levina rode beside the wagon on Israel's horse, proud to have graduated from the wagon bed, at least for a time. Jemima rode in Levina's spot to keep an eye on Israel. Rebecca sat beside Daniel on the bench at the wagon's head, holding little Nathan who was now awake but seemed quite amused by the ride. Susannah sat beside her mother, holding Jemima and Flanders' son, John.

Boone Station was a lightly fortified compound of storehouses, outbuildings, and a dozen cabins in various stages of completion. Daniel settled the family in the area after returning to Kentucky from North Carolina three years earlier, figuring the spot ideal for trading and safety, situated as it was at the crossroads of Boonesborough, Lexington, and Bryan Station.

It was also the case that living in Boonesborough again had been out of the question, as Daniel had little desire to reside in a place, even one named in his honor, where some had accused him of treason.

Fifteen families lived within the station's palisades, along with a good number of single men looking to discover their fortunes on the frontier. Many of the residents were related to Boone, others were friends or simply folks who'd chosen to throw in with Boone by dint of the man's reputation. Jemima's family had their own cabin within the fort, as did Susannah's. Daniel had built a good-sized place for himself and Rebecca, although in retrospect he should have made it larger, seeing as how it also had to accommodate their now six younger children, at least one of whom he figured would have married by now. Israel was well-liked by a number of young ladies, however, which didn't do much for lighting a fire under the lad to settle.

Daniel pulled up on the horses directly in front of the cabin. Flanders swung Israel's arm over his shoulder and helped him from the wagon, up the steps of the porch, and into the cabin's large main room. Jesse and Daniel Morgan rushed ahead, clearing the way of obstacles. Their father's hunting dogs ran up, beside themselves with excitement at the sight of the family, as Daniel had been their only company for the past two months. The boys had no choice but to run and play with the hounds to keep them from getting underfoot.

"Lord, what's happened to him?" asked Rebecca's sister from the doorway of the next cabin over. Martha favored Rebecca, only she was a bit shorter and had a narrower frame. She was also the widow of Daniel's younger brother, Edward. Martha's eleven-year-old daughter, Sarah, stood behind her, rubbing sleep from her eyes.

"Fell ill at the party," Rebecca answered as she rushed up the porch steps.

"Goodness," said Martha. She knelt down beside Sarah. "Everything will be fine, dear. Go on back to bed now." Sarah made a groggy pivot on her heels and stumbled back into the cabin. Martha hurried after Rebecca.

Flanders half dragged Israel to one of the small bedrooms and eased him onto the bed. It was Levina's room, but since Israel typically bunked on a pallet in the rafters above the kitchen and hoisting him up there was an impracticality, they'd have to switch for the night.

Flanders backed away and Rebecca sat down on the bed beside Israel. Martha appeared with a basin of water, moving quickly but steadily to avoid spills, and set it on the bedside table. She had a cloth draped over her shoulder which she grabbed, dipped into the water, wrung, and handed to her sister. Rebecca gave the cloth a gentle shake then put it to Israel's forehead.

"You'll likely be fine come morning," said Daniel, standing at the foot of the bed in front of the room's open window. He didn't know how to make himself useful and settled for patting Israel awkwardly on the foot. "I brought back plenty of bear I need you to help me make bacon of, seeing as you'll be eating most of it."

"I don't know, Pa," Israel mumbled through a groan. "I'm feeling pretty sick."

"Ah, if you think this is sick you ain't never been," Daniel responded.

Rebecca cleared her throat. "Forgive me for saying so," she dipped the cloth back into the bowl and gave it a good wringing, "but now that we're indoors, Daniel, and you're standing in the path of the breeze . . . well, appetites hereabouts might be stronger once you've had a bath." She looked over at him and smiled.

Daniel debated putting on a show of being hurt, but he was too tired; he'd spent most of the day trudging out of the woods, and the effort of it was finally catching up with him. He remembered the Jacobs boy suddenly and wondered if the lad would keep vigil over his haul through the night and take good care of his horses. If so, Boone owed him a pelt larger than a beaver's.

Daniel lifted his arm, tucked his nose beneath it, and gave an exaggerated sniff. "Can't say as you're wrong," he said, turning his head and wincing. "Might as well come along, Rebecca. You can check my handiwork."

Jemima rolled her eyes. She extended her opened hand to her mother and Rebecca handed her the cloth.

"I'll watch Israel and little Nathan," Jemima said. "Levina will help." Then Jemima glanced to the chair in the corner of the room and saw Levina slouched there, sound asleep.

"Or perhaps not," Jemima said.

Martha laughed. "I'll stay awhile."

"Have Jesse or Daniel Morgan fetch you fresh water and whatever else," Rebecca said. She placed a hand on Jemima's shoulder, glanced down at Israel, then turned to Daniel and said, "I'll get the soap," as she left the room.

Daniel followed and Jemima made a point of holding her nose as he passed. Seeing her, Israel managed a meager chuckle. Daniel leaned down and scrabbled the boy's hair.

"Oh, just think, son," Daniel said. "If you survive til morning, I can tell you all the hunting stories you missed hearing while you were making time with the Calloway girl." He turned to Jemima and winked, then followed Rebecca out the door.

TEN

Daniel stripped, strode down the bank, and waded into the creek, walking until he was submerged to his chest. The water hadn't managed to cool much from the heat of the day, but he found it soothing all the same.

Although the creek itself wasn't far from the station, Daniel and Rebecca had a particular spot they favored, a private spot that was well worth the few extra minutes of trekking. As they walked along the bank, Daniel was reminded of how much he loved this land. Even still, he suspected they wouldn't stay forever; the war would eventually end and more settlers would arrive, and Boone, although he valued the company of other men, valued the space between himself and them more.

He brought along a clean hunting shirt and moccasins for after his bath, skipping the pantaloons, figuring he'd be so tired by the time he finished that he'd walk back to the cabin, kick off the moccasins, and fall right into bed. He hadn't decided on whether his grimy hunting clothes could be salvaged or had to be burned.

As Daniel bathed, Rebecca sat beneath her favorite tree at the edge of the bank, her toes in the grass, dividing her attention between her husband and the night sky. The moon, though only a crescent, was bright, its position in the sky letting her know it was well past midnight. She hadn't been up this late in ages. She knew she'd pay the price come morning, since the responsibilities of a new day showed up regardless of when a person blew out the candle on the previous. But it was a beautiful night, her family was reunited, and Israel's illness didn't appear to be serious.

"The boy sure gave us a right scare," said Daniel as if responding to Rebecca's thoughts, scrubbing his torso vigorously with soap. "Not sure what befell him. I'm half-hoping it's just that he's allergic to the Calloway girl."

Rebecca sighed. "April's a fine young lady, sharp and pretty, and hardly a Calloway at all in the way it concerns you— Richard's cousin's girl or some such." Since Daniel seemed intent on getting around to the subject of Richard Calloway, she figured it best to cut straight to it rather than let it linger.

Daniel held his tongue for an admirable moment. "First Jemima goes and marries one," he said, "now Israel's sick over another . . . I can't be rid of them." He rubbed the bar of soap though his matted hair; it was his third go-round, the bear grease used to hold his locks in place being particularly tenacious.

Rebecca picked up a pebble and threw it at him. "Now I can't take you seriously. You're quite fond of Flanders and everyone knows it," she said. "Let it go, Daniel. Richard Calloway has been dead over two years now."

Daniel sunk beneath the water and stayed there for a time. After the girls were kidnapped, Calloway had set his mind on building a ferry on the river behind Boonesborough—the lack of an easy method of crossing had slowed the pursuit of the rescuers that day, proving the need for one—and was brutally killed by a party of Shawnee during construction. A man who'd seen the body, passing through Boone Station on his way to Lexington, told Boone that Calloway was the worst barbecued man he'd ever seen. The hatred Richard held for the Indians was clearly mutual. Boone wouldn't have wished that fate on any man, even one who had tried to have him court-martialed. That said, the spirit of distrust that poisoned many of the residents of Boonesborough against Daniel largely died with Calloway, and each day that passed was added antidote to the man's spiteful legacy.

Daniel decided he'd had his fill of thinking on Richard Calloway. He unspooled the tangle of thoughts from his mind, imagined them drifting downstream in the slow current, then popped up from the water and took a satisfying breath of the night air.

Rebecca studied him as he wiped the water from his eyes; they were working together without saying so to chip away at his melancholy. The hull of it had been removed, and it was now time to get to the nut.

"Go on and tell me what you didn't tell the others." She nodded toward the forest. "What it was you saw out there that concerns you."

He considered the question. "I'm not certain. I usually brush against an Indian party or two on a hunt this long, some friendly, others not so. But neither type this time."

He lifted a foot from the water and began scrubbing it. "This pact between the British and the Indians—it's not apt to be broken anytime soon. Even knowing Cornwallis surrendered, the soldiers and agents the British sent west have no interest in seeing the war ended; not if it means them losing. The Indians don't see it much different. The Cherokee in particular, and I've had several of them tell me so more than once, prefer war time to peace, as war offers superior profit."

"Oh? When did they tell you this?" Rebecca asked.

Balancing on the one foot, Daniel looked up at his wife and smiled. "You can learn a lot from Indians raiding your camp and stealing your pelts a time or two. When it's five or six of them against the one of you they don't see you as a threat, and if you have a jug to share with them, why, it's quite conducive to loose talk." He put his one foot down and lifted the other.

Rebecca stood. "Since you broached the subject, I think it's time we discussed you not leaving me for so long on these hunting excursions." She put her hands to her chest and began removing the pins that held her dress closed. "But perhaps I need to be in a better position to make my argument."

The dress dropped to the ground. She undid her stay, slinked from her petticoat, then pulled off her shift. As she stood, naked, her fair skin magnificent in the moonlight, Daniel stared, admiring her shape, then her scars, of which she had several. Life on the frontier was rough, injury common. Each scar triggered a memory in Daniel that formed the tapestry of their life together.

He tossed the soap onto the bank. Rebecca slowly walked into the creek. When she reached him he looked into her eyes, dark and mysterious and impenetrable, before his attention was grabbed by a tiny pool of water that had collected in her clavicle. He felt her arms wrap around his waist beneath the water.

"Remind me—what did the Shawnee call you when you were living with them?" Rebecca asked, smiling.

"When I was a hostage, you mean," Daniel responded.

"Yes. When you were a hostage."

"You know. I've told you many times."

"Tell me again."

Boone paused. "*Sheltowee*," he said finally.

"And what does *Sheltowee* mean?" Rebecca teased.

"You know, woman."

"Tell me."

Boone shook his head and fought back a smile. "Big turtle."

Rebecca threw back her head and laughed. Daniel broke and laughed himself. Then she kicked away from him, swam a short distance, spun around, and shot him a look he knew well.

"Come to me, my big turtle, " she said.

And he did.

ELEVEN

Anne Morgan sat up in bed and looked up through the rafters into the darkness above. *God keep me from killing the man,* she thought. Her husband's constant fretting over imagined Indian raids was irritation enough in the daylight, but waking her from a comfortable sleep in the middle of the night was taking it too far.

"Anne, I'm serious," said James, standing beside the bed and pulling on his breeches in a rush. "I heard something." He sloppily tucked in his nightshirt, then slipped on his moccasins and grabbed the cradleboard that hung on the wall beside his rifle.

"James—you are not waking that baby and taking him traipsing though the woods at this hour," Anne said, throwing her hands to her forehead.

James laid the cradleboard on the bed, then took two large steps toward the crib at the foot. The elaborately carved crib was far and away the most valuable thing they owned and the only furniture they'd brought with them to Kentucky; it had been Anne's as a child and her mother had handed it down to them. James smiled down into it—he couldn't tell in the dark if Thomas was asleep or awake, but it didn't hurt to project a cheerful demeanor just in case—then he reached in and gently lifted the child. He brought Thomas' face close to his own and squinted. Good. The boy was sleeping like a log. Then he carried the baby to the bed and hurriedly tucked and laced him into the cradleboard.

Anne's green eyes widened. "God almighty—you're serious," she said, flinging back the blankets and swinging her feet to the floor. There was no arguing with him when he got this way. She was wide awake now, and the quickest way of getting back to sleep was to let the man play out his imaginings. Besides, the fresh air might be good for the child, and help him sleep a little later into morning.

James lifted the cradleboard, gave it a gentle shake to insure the boy was secure, then spun it around and put his arms through the leather straps. The flat of the board settled onto his back. He walked to Anne's side of the bed and crouched beside her. He brushed a lock of curly red hair out of her eyes and placed it behind her ear. Through the darkness, Anne saw his face clearly for the first time, saw his resolve, and accepted, fearfully, the idea that he might be right.

"Dress, then get under the bed," he said. "Stay there until I get back. If it is Indians, we'll have to move quickly."

She rose and gave him a peck on the lips. "Be careful."

James turned and paused for a moment so Anne could kiss the baby. Then he walked around and snatched the rifle from the wall. As Anne gathered her clothes, James strode out of the bedroom, stopped in front of the cabin's door where Anne could see him, and tapped the door with the rifle's muzzle.

"Bolt it," he said. "Then . . ." he pointed at the floor beneath the bed with his free hand. He grabbed the doorknob and turned it slowly. Then he pulled the door open slightly and peered out. Nothing. He opened it further, just wide enough to squeeze himself and the cradleboard through, then walked out into the night, pulling the door shut behind him.

James was an experienced hunter and knew how to navigate the woods, even at night, in relative silence. The baby lacked that experience but was managing all the same, at least for the moment; James was never more happy that Thomas was an exceptionally sound sleeper as babies go.

Father and son hadn't ventured far—James could still make out the shadowed mass of the cabin behind him—when he heard a snap on his periphery. He turned toward it, squinted into the distance, and saw the silhouette of a man relieving himself against a tree. Beyond the man, further off, was the flickering light of a small fire.

James pivoted and moved with practiced stealth back toward the cabin, running the next series of events through his mind. He knew this day was likely to come and had prepared; the horses would be quick to saddle, the prepacked provisions were close at hand. That the Indians hadn't found the cabin before nightfall meant they had a chance of escaping.

He'd only taken three steps when he saw them; half a dozen braves creeping toward the cabin, each from a different angle, tomahawks drawn, rifles at the ready. He was suddenly aware of the weight on his back; Thomas was waking, shifting, and making gentle noises that would within moments turn into crying. James froze, watched as the Indians crept closer to his home, watched as their silhouettes melted into the silhouette of the cabin and vanished. He held his breath. Then he heard pounding against the cabin door, once, twice, thrice, then the sharp crack of splintering wood. He heard a shot. Anne's rifle. He hoped she'd missed; the Indians were less likely to kill her if she hadn't killed one of their own. There were sounds of a scuffle, Anne screaming, then silence.

TWELVE

Hugh McGary leaned against the cabin door, only it no longer latched and he fell through the threshold and landed face-first onto the packed dirt floor. He heard his horse snort and felt sure it was the animal's way of laughing at him. McGary pondered picking himself up, but couldn't think of a reason to bother—the floor here was no more dirty than the floor in the empty bedroom.

He hated that room. His wife spent three long years dying in it, consumed by grief.

McGary had married Mary, a widow, and taken in her three boys. He figured he came out ahead in the bargain; although physically frail, Mary was strong-willed and had a knack for managing McGary's tempers, which folks around them were plenty thankful for. The boys proved to be capable farmers, and William, the youngest, was particularly appreciative to have a new father. He and Hugh had developed quite a strong bond before the boy was killed by the Shawnee.

William's murder shattered Mary's spirit. She was far along in a difficult pregnancy at the time, and when baby Hugh was born several months later, she showed the child no interest or affection. She never left the bed and rarely spoke.

McGary focused all his efforts on consoling her. He built the cabin he was now lying on the floor of so she could be closer to friends and relatives in Boonesborough. Few visited, though, and those that did only did so once on account of McGary's belligerence, which ran rampant in the absence of Mary's influence. His drinking didn't help matters.

As the days passed, his sympathy for Mary evolved into frustration, then devolved into anger and self-pity. He began to take up with other women and was none too discreet about it. One of those women was Caty Yocum, whom he married within a few weeks of Mary's death. Caty was just as disagreeable as McGary, which made for a combustible union. It was Caty who was raising his son and was now waiting for him back in Harrodsburg.

She'd have to keep waiting.

McGary coughed, then realized his cheek was wet; he must have passed out. He ran his fingers through the goop, then put them to his nose. There was little scent, so he determined it was drool rather than vomit. He could barely muster being thankful for the distinction; if Boone were to walk in and see him now, he'd look down his nose at him with the same contempt either way.

It hadn't always been this way; time was when the two were hunting companions. Hell, they'd explored Kentucky together years before Boone led the first families into the territory. But that was a lifetime ago. In the years since, Boone had transformed into something more than mere flesh and blood in the eyes of other men; McGary, on the other hand, was an insubstantial shadow.

McGary heard a sound and opened his eyes. He'd passed out again. He lifted his head, which was somewhat easier to do than the last time he'd tried—some time must have passed and perhaps he was sobering up—but saw nothing in front of him. He propped himself up on an elbow, which caused his head to throb, pivoted onto his side, then looked down toward his feet, which were blocking the threshold and preventing the cabin door from closing. Two chickens were standing there, pecking at the dirt floor.

"G'outta here, stinking birds," McGary slurred. He made half an effort at shooing them away, stopping short of a full effort since the half one caused his head to ache badly enough. He flopped down onto his back and stared up at the rafters. He could see the night sky through the multiple gaps in the roof, the moon bright. For a moment, he was at peace. Suddenly, an upside-down face filled his vision. McGary spun quickly around, kicking himself closer to the cabin door and away from the sheet-enshrouded figure that was standing before him. He could see clean through the apparition's body and into the bedroom. It was his stepson, William, draped in the sheet Mary had given McGary to wrap the boy's mutilated body in for burial.

McGary flailed about, kicking with his legs to push him-self through the cabin door, but when he reached it found it was now closed. Had he kicked it shut in his panic, or had William shut it? William stared at him, scowling with re-proach; reproach for McGary's unfaithfulness to his mother, reproach for his unchecked rage, reproach for the life he was wasting.

The specter had visited McGary before, always after a night of heavy drinking. Despite the regularity, though, McGary was as frightened as ever and began to whimper, burying his tear-filled eyes into the crook of his arm.

"I know, I know," McGary repeated over and over. He knew that he deserved his stepson's scorn and whatever punishment the wraith cared to dispense, but he was too cowardly to face either with open eyes and dignity.

Darkness overtook him.

He woke before daybreak, slumped against the cabin door. The apparition was gone. Of the events of the previous evening, the visit from William was the only one he remembered clearly. It was certainly the one that felt most real.

McGary collected his horse. It had wandered to a stream near the cabin, still saddled.

Before leaving, McGary burned the cabin to the ground.

THIRTEEN

Tired as he was, Daniel couldn't sleep. He was happy to have Rebecca beside him, but otherwise found the cabin stifling after having spent two months sleeping in the open wilderness. He stared at the rafters, feeling as if they were conspiring with the walls to suffocate him. He had the same trouble every time he returned from a hunt for the first couple of nights; he knew there was an adjustment period, although knowing didn't make it any less frustrating. He wondered why he never had trouble making the transition in the other direction.

He sat up and slowly swung his feet to the floor, trying his best not to wake Rebecca, although he figured he'd already been keeping her from sleeping soundly; she'd always been sensitive to his restlessness. She turned on her side and patted his hand, which he knew meant *go ahead, get up, I'll join you in a bit*. He placed his other hand on hers for a moment, then stood and stretched.

He stepped to her side of the bed, looked into the cradle against the wall beside it, and was surprised to see Nathan staring back at him. The boy was wide awake, yet hadn't made a sound.

"Taking in the rafters yourself, huh, boy?" Daniel whispered as he scooped up the child. Nathan put his fingers on his father's bare chin; Daniel was thankful Rebecca had convinced him to push through his tiredness and shave while at the creek.

He rested Nathan against his shoulder and walked out of the room. He crossed to the next doorway and peered inside; Israel looked to be sleeping peacefully finally. Jemima was asleep in the chair across the room, a blanket pulled up to her shoulders. She'd sat with Israel all night, even after Daniel and Rebecca had returned. Daniel took a step inside and placed his palm on Israel's forehead. It was damp and warm, but not the inferno it had been a few hours earlier. Relieved, he stepped out.

Tiptoeing into the main room, careful to avoid floorboards he knew to be creaky, Daniel stepped over one child after another sleeping on pallets on the floor. There was no way around it—he'd have to go ahead and build that addition to the cabin before the weather turned. He stepped stealthily around the large kitchen table to the cabin's main door, opened it slowly, and slipped outside.

He stood at the porch railing and took a deep breath. Aside from the occasional whinny of a horse, the station was calm and silent. Looking out at the horizon, beyond the station's palisades, Daniel could vaguely make out the hemp and corn fields. They weren't the best cared for, but considering tending a field—or doing anything outside the walls of the fort—meant a good chance of getting killed, it was a wonder they'd been planted at all, let alone that they hadn't been burned by Indians in the meantime. Both crops would be coming in soon; Daniel reckoned he'd have to stay close to home for the harvest. Matter of fact, the more he looked around—at the fields, pastures, stables, fort walls, porch, and home behind him—the more work he saw for himself. He sighed and eased himself down into one of the porch's two chairs. Nathan was breathing deeply and steadily; evidently, the child had fallen back to sleep. Daniel looked beyond the fields, stared at the silhouetted tree line of the forest, then fell asleep himself.

A shift in the air woke him; not a sound so much as his surroundings making space for something that wasn't there a moment before. Instinctively, smoothly, Daniel switched Nathan from his right shoulder to his left, stood, and reached to his waist for the hilt of his hunting knife before realizing he hadn't strapped it on—hell, he hadn't even put on pants and was still in his nightshirt. He was about to slide to the other end of the porch for the broom he hoped was in its usual spot in the corner when he heard a whistle. He relaxed, allowed himself a breath, and eased his grip on little Nathan, who was still fast asleep.

"How do, Raven," Boone said into the darkness.

A couple of seconds later he heard moccasins crunching on twigs, then a man emerged from the shadow of the next cabin over, rifle in hand. Boone didn't bother wondering how he'd gotten within the fort's walls.

The Indian stepped onto the porch. Boone squared up to him. The man was close to Boone in age but a good head taller, dark-skinned and lithe with wide shoulders.

"Daniel," the Indian said.

Both smiled. The Indian shifted the rifle to his side and Boone stepped forward and embraced him. The man returned the hug and slapped Boone twice on the back with the flat of his massive hand.

He was Savanukah, the Raven of Chota, Cherokee chief.

The two men had known each other for years and were hunting companions when the Boone family lived on the Yadkin River in North Carolina. Boone found the Raven to be a skillful woodsman with an agreeable disposition, essential qualities in a man who might be your only company in the wilderness for days or weeks at a time. It didn't hurt that Savanukah was feared by the Catawba, who were less than fond of white hunters. For that reason, Boone found it head-scratching that the Catawba had now sided with the Americans against the British, but he supposed it proof that the tribe's decades-long feud with the Cherokee, who were British allies, ranked higher than their dislike of the settlers.

The Raven spoke better English than any natural-born Indian Boone knew, and Daniel credited himself with improving the man's hold on the language by reading *Gulliver's Travels* aloud around their campfires at night. Boone, in turn, had a right solid command of Cherokee thanks to the time he'd spent in conversation with Savanukah, building on the basics he'd picked up as a boy hunting with members of the tribe in Pennsylvania.

Later, Savanukah was one of three Cherokee chiefs who signed papers ceding a large swath of the Kentucky country to Richard Henderson's Transylvania Company, the outfit that employed Boone. The Cherokee claim on the land was dubious, but the paperwork gave the deal the veneer of authenticity which was to the benefit of both parties—or at least seemed so at the time. The Transylvania Company got a deed to land they desired, and in exchange the Cherokee received money and goods for a commodity they didn't feel any could own in the first place. But the deed would prove worthless when the Virginia government rejected its validity, the tribe's enthusiasm for the goods fleeting even as their increased reliance on such things compromised their autonomy, and in the end neither party would have much to show for the bargain they'd struck.

At the time, however, there was much cheering and backslapping, and Henderson ordered beef slaughtered for a feast to feed the hundreds of Cherokee who had gathered for the signing and subsequent divvying of the goods. While everyone was celebrating and congratulating themselves, Savanukah and Boone shared a pipe.

"Brother, we have given you a fine land, but I believe you will have much trouble keeping it," Savanukah said.

Boone was the last man who needed the warning. He'd already lost a son in the attempt to settle Kentucky, murdered by Indians, at least three of whom were Cherokee.

Boone's mind now flashed on the image of his James' body, shot full of arrows, his skull bashed and scalped.

"New grandson?" Savanukah asked, the question pulling Boone back to the present.

The Indian put his hand on Nathan's head. Boone chuckled; even a man like the Raven, whose life it was to be one with nature, could still be surprised by its mysteries.

"Nope. Mine and Rebecca's," Boone responded.

"Say," Savanukah said, indeed surprised. He gave Boone a congratulatory pat on the back. As the man stepped closer, Boone saw his injuries for the first time; minor cuts and bruises, but many of them. He'd obviously been in a note-worthy scrape, and recently.

Boone peered over the Raven's shoulder and made a show of looking for something he knew wasn't there.

"No horse?" Boone asked.

"Psh. I'm not anxious to be shot from a horse by some fool kin of yours. Safer on foot. Faster most often besides," said Savanukah.

Boone couldn't quibble the point. Tensions were such that both parties, white man and Indian, tended toward trigger happy. On top of that, Savanukah had been involved in more than one skirmish with frontier militia, so taking a shot at him wouldn't be judged as unwarranted.

"Well, take a seat," said Boone. "I don't reckon any kin of mine would shoot you off my porch."

The Raven considered it; he was visibly anxious, his eyes moving constantly, scanning the shadows. After a long moment, Savanukah finally eased himself into one of the porch chairs, laying his rifle across his lap.

"What happened to your good one?" Boone asked, pointing to the rifle as he lowered himself into the other chair. Savanukah had won a fine long rifle years ago in a target contest at a community gathering on the Yadkin—Boone was off hunting at the time, or he figured he'd have won it himself.

The Raven looked down at the gun that lay across his legs and realized suddenly that he was clutching it with such force that his knuckles were white. He relaxed his hands. He lifted the rifle slowly as if it were many times heavier than its actual weight, then leaned it against the wall between the two chairs.

"Lost it some time ago," he said.

Boone figured that unlikely; it was the man's prized possession. But rumors had been circulating that Savanukah had fallen out of favor with his people—either because he was too peaceable toward the whites or too warmongering, Boone couldn't recall—and was fighting to maintain his position as First Beloved Man of the tribe. Had there been a coup? Was the Raven in exile or on the run?

"A real shame. It was a fine rifle," Boone said.

Savanukah had obviously rushed to the station with urgency but, for whatever reason, was reluctant to say why. Boone worked at coaxing it from him.

"What brings you around, Raven?" Boone asked. He nodded toward the rifle. "It sure ain't hunting, not with that thing. Hunting's gotten pretty thin around here anyways."

Savanukah took a deep breath. With noticeable effort, he peeled his eyes from the woods and hills and turned to Boone.

"You remember the time we were tracking a large buffalo bull through that ravine on the Clinch?" he asked.

"You, me, two of your braves," responded Boone. "You and the others thought sure the tracks were fake, that it was a Catawba trap."

"We pressed on anyway, prepared for ambush," Savanukah continued, "then saw—"

"A giant pile of fresh buffalo dung," interrupted Boone.

"Yes. And you said—"

"Tawba no make this."

Both men laughed quietly, then seriousness crept back into Savanukah's face. He leaned in close to Boone and looked him in the eye.

"That is what you say. If they say I was there, you tell them it is bullshit."

Boone stared at him.

"Okay. So you weren't there." He had no idea what the man was talking about, but figured the details would come soon enough if he kept his mouth shut and let Savanukah get to them in his own time.

"This morning, a rider will arrive. He will tell you of an Indian attack in a settlement to the south," Savanukah said.

"Hoy Station?" Boone asked.

The Raven nodded. He turned from Boone and resumed sweeping the shadows with his eyes.

"I'd been hunting, alone, on the Upper Blue Licks," he began after a time. "Two days ago, I heard shots. Many of them. I followed the sound to a stream where I saw militiamen in an open meadow taking fire from braves hidden in the woods. The whites were outnumbered and retreating. I counted four dead, one wounded. I did not know any of the white men, but one referred to the man who ordered the retreat as captain."

Captain John Holder most likely, thought Boone. The location suggested it, and it explained John and Fanny's absence from last night's wedding celebration at Boonesborough.

"The Indians separated afterward. I spotted a man I knew. Cherokee," Savanukah said, then interjected quickly, "but not of my tribe."

Boone nodded.

"I caught him alone," Savanukah continued. "He told me the party had set upon the station, Hoy Station as you say, four days earlier. They captured two boys—I did not see them—to force pursuit and draw those that followed into the ambush."

The Raven paused, and again Boone waited.

"I encouraged him to tell more, and he said this was only the beginning." Savanukah looked down at the planks of the porch floor. "That was the end of the talking."

He looked up and turned to Boone. "There are more coming, Daniel. Many more. Perhaps they are already here— already in Kentucky."

Boone sat back in his chair. "Likely putting yourself in a predicament coming here and telling me this," he said.

Savanukah's eyes darted to the door of the cabin.

"Nothing I can't handle."

The Raven stood and faced the door. Three seconds later Rebecca emerged, holding a cup of coffee.

"Don't think you can leave without a hello to me," she said. She extended the cup to Savanukah.

He leaned down, kissed her on the cheek, then took the cup.

"Rebecca. Lovely as ever," he said. She blushed a little, which she almost never did. This made Daniel smile as he stood and switched Nathan to his other shoulder.

"Good to see you, Raven," she said. Then she turned, walked back toward the door, and looked over her shoulder at Daniel. "You can come get your own coffee," she said with a wink, before disappearing into the cabin.

"Suspect she's going to grab you some grub," Daniel said. He watched Savanukah take a sip. The look on the man's face suggested it was the best thing he'd ever tasted. The two men stood at the railing together and stared out toward the woods.

The door creaked open a few minutes later and Savanukah turned, expecting to see Rebecca.

"Jemima," he said.

Jemima smiled, walked to Savanukah, and hugged him.

"How long's it been?" she asked.

"A good while," he responded. He put his hands on her shoulders, leaned back, and gave her a once-over. "You look fine, little Boone. How are your children?"

"Growing," said Jemima. "Oldest is about the age now I was when you and I met."

"Hard to believe," he said.

Daniel was warmed by their reunion. His older children had grown up in the company of Indians, much as he had in Pennsylvania; it was through no effort on Boone's part, just the nature of life in the Yadkin Valley. Whatever tensions existed between a tribe and the settlers as a whole, good relations between individuals was the norm. In the years since Jemima had met the Raven, she'd been abducted, her father taken captive, her home sieged, friends and neighbors killed—all by Indians. Yet Jemima didn't hold Savanukah to account for that any more than he held her to account for the harm done to him and his by other whites.

That way of thinking was dying now. Clear lines had been drawn, hatred and distrust stoked by powers that benefited from the resultant havoc with little cost to themselves.

Jemima and the Raven spoke for a few minutes before she went back inside. Soft noises could be heard within the cabin, other members of the family beginning to stir. Rebecca stepped back through the door with a bundle of hard biscuits and bear jerky and handed it to Savanukah. He nodded his appreciation.

"Best be going," he said. He went to hand Rebecca his empty coffee cup, but she slipped past it and gave Savanukah a hug he was unable to return, both his hands being occupied.

Then she released him, took the cup, and headed back into the cabin.

Figuring he'd already had his hug, Daniel reached up and slapped the man on the shoulder. He couldn't think of anything to say that hadn't been said already.

"Be seeing you, Daniel." Savanukah clasped Boone on the shoulder. Then he turned and stepped off the porch, disappearing into retreating shadows fighting a losing battle against the rising sun. Boone knew Savanukah could fend for himself; *Raven* wasn't a name—it was a title; an honor held by the most skilled hunter, tracker, and scout of his tribe. The best of the best of the greatest woodsmen known to man.

Even so, Daniel couldn't shake the feeling that he'd never see his friend again.

FOURTEEN

Of all their children, Susannah reminded Daniel most of Rebecca. She was spirited, sharp, beautiful, and vivacious. Daniel and Susannah shared a birthday, November 2, at least according to the New Style calendar that had been adopted in 1752. He didn't give the change much thought, leastways not until Susannah was old enough to be tickled that she and her father had the date in common, at which point he was glad of it.

As she came of age, Susannah became the object of affection for every young man on the Clinch River in Virginia where the Boone family lived at the time. Although it was true that there were only a handful of eligible young women in the area, it wouldn't have mattered if there'd been a thousand; Susannah had a thirst for life and a vibrancy that was as intoxicating as it was rare. Predictably, her positive outlook was so foreign to some that it first engendered confusion, then jealousy; certain in the community began to spread rumors, pointing to Susannah's gregarious and admittedly flirty demeanor as evidence of more unbecoming behavior.

Unsurprisingly, such rumors did little to diminish her popularity with the boys.

That being the case, when Susannah accepted a proposal of marriage from William Hays there was collective disappointment among the bachelors in the area and a general sense of surprise; Hays was a likable enough fellow, but introspective and bookish—hardly a match for Susannah's unbridled personality. But the girl unlocked something in Will; once she entered his life he became a romantic adventurer, a passionate daredevil. The couple had a fiery affair, particularly incendiary when they squabbled, often publicly, usually raging at each other one minute, bursting into laughter and kisses the next. Especially heated arguments became solid predictors that a child would arrive nine months or so after.

For Boone, it was a pleasant surprise to discover he'd gained not simply a son-in-law, which were easy to come by and not of particular value in and of themselves, but a pretty fair bookkeeper. Boone had dabbled in several business ventures over the years, most failing when he grew bored of the record keeping necessary to keep them afloat, so he immediately put Hays to work. Will also had a gift for writing, a quality Boone admired in a man almost as much as skill at hunting, as reading was his favorite pastime. Although Boone could write well enough himself—exceptionally, even, by frontier standards—there were occasions where more finesse and precision than Boone could muster were required.

For his part, Will greatly respected Boone, which was common both among men who knew the frontiersman and those who didn't—Boone's exploits became well-known and mythologized once the story of the girls' rescue spread to the colonies. Of course, the same qualities that engendered admiration in some men bred hate in others, and Boone, like all men of consequence, had to contend with the envy that accompanied notoriety.

As Boone walked toward the open cabin door he could see Hays, standing with his hands on the kitchen table, staring at a collection of loose papers and shaking his head. Will was so engrossed and perplexed by whatever it was he was examining that he seemed oblivious to Daniel's approach.

"Those aren't my papers causing that wrinkle in your brow, I trust," Daniel asked from the doorway, knowing the answer.

Without looking up, not in the least startled by Daniel's arrival, Hays waved Boone over and began continuously poking an item on one of the pages with his index finger.

"What in God's name is this supposed to be?" Hays asked.

Daniel walked over, put an arm around Hays' shoulders, and looked down at the scribble in question.

"It says, 'tree with kidney-shaped knot at base marks north edge of property line,'" Daniel answered. He snapped his fingers. "Ah. These are my notes on the Abrams claim." One of Boone's dabblings was hiring himself out as claim locator for folks who held warrants for purchasing land on the frontier.

Will gestured in the general direction of the woods beyond the station. "And just how many hundreds of trees are out there that fit this description?"

"Why, I don't see how that matters none," said Daniel. He put his index finger on the page. "This is a note about a particular tree. I can find it again whenever I need." He righted himself and slapped Hays on the back.

"It's not important that *you* can find it, Daniel; it only matters if a judge or magistrate—" Will broke off and starting sifting through the hodgepodge of papers. "And did

Abrams even pay you? This is from two years ago, and there's no notation—"

Will turned to Daniel, who was looking at him with raised eyebrows; it was clear the man had no interest in the topic. Will threw up his hands, grabbed his empty cup from the table, and walked to the stove to pour himself more coffee. "Never mind. How's Israel this morning?" he asked. He grabbed a fresh cup from the shelf above the stove.

"Don't know," Daniel answered. "Still sleeping. Suspect he'll be fine when he wakes. Susannah about?"

Will poured coffee into the cup and handed it to Daniel. "Letting her and the children sleep in. Too much frolicking last night. They were plumb tuckered." Will nodded toward the table. "Besides, I'll have to clean up this mess of yours before she can start in on breakfast."

"Don't spoil the girl too much, William," Daniel said, knowing as everyone did that spoiling Susannah was Will's highest calling in life. Susannah and Will had married just before Daniel's crew set out to hack the wilderness trail, and Will had signed on. So Susannah spent her honeymoon on the rough journey, cooking and keeping camp for the men along with a slave woman. Will vowed at the time to make it up to her, and had spent every day since in the trying.

"What brings you around, Daniel?" Will could tell there was something on the man's mind.

Boone placed his cup on the table and began straightening the papers. "Something's stirring. It'd be wise to set up a patrol. Perhaps ten men at a time, working in shifts."

"I'll grab a few of the boys and head out straight away," Hays said, springing to attention as if he'd placed his hand on the hot stove.

101

"Not just yet," Daniel said. He wasn't in the least surprised that Will was raring to go without even asking for specifics, which was as concerning as it was amusing. Boone held up a hand to put Will's enthusiasm in check. "I have a letter to write first, and need your help to ensure the language is flowery enough for a major."

It felt to Boone that the sun was reluctant to rise, but it finally got around to doing so as he made his way back to his cabin, passing neighbors who were now setting about their chores. It turned Boone's stomach to see so many people living in the station; not because he craved more elbow room, although he wouldn't turn it down, but because it was unnatural for folks to be forted up this way, mentally and physically exhausted from life lived under constant threat, having to choose between dying by tomahawk while working a field, or dying from starvation to avoid the tomahawk.

Yet most people remained pleasant somehow—downright courteous, even. A representative from every household Boone passed waved and asked after Israel. Boone waved back, said how do, and told each of them that the boy was fine, just fine, as he kept walking, careful not to get drawn into conversation; Will would be along shortly, and he'd let everyone know of the concern for trouble as he rounded up volunteers for patrol.

There wasn't much else that could be done in the meantime. Riders from Hoy's would have already reached stations to the south to warn them, and sending word to Major Todd in Lexington now, before a rider arrived at Boone Station, was pointless; there was no way for Boone to explain how he knew of the incident without placing Savanukah in harm's way, and Todd would view the Raven's information as secondhand and untrustworthy besides. No, if Boone knew Todd, there was no way the man would take action before receiving word directly from Hoy's.

Best to spend the next few hours with his family and managing his own affairs, Boone figured. There were plenty of chores that needed doing, fences, crops, and livestock that needed checking up on, tedium that was at least good for letting him think on what might happen next.

He was also plenty hungry.

FIFTEEN

Daniel poked his head in the open cabin door and yelled for Jesse, Daniel Morgan, and little Rebecca to come with him to do the milking. They looked at each other, dumbfounded at the idea that their father apparently planned to do the chore with them, then shrugged and hurried after him.

Twenty minutes later, Rebecca watched through a window as the group walked back toward the cabin, her husband laughing and carrying the pail of milk, their children skipping beside him. Rebecca smiled and shook her head. She knew when she married Daniel that domesticated life didn't suit him—it didn't hardly suit her—but she always enjoyed watching him play at it.

Daniel shooed the children in the direction of the chicken coop to collect eggs, then strode through the cabin door and set the pail on the table. The smell of Rebecca's bread baking in the hearth hit him as he entered. That was one of life's pleasures that couldn't be found in the woods, and it made him happy to be home.

*

The Boones had a satisfying breakfast of fresh milk, bread, eggs, bear bacon, and coffee, all while the tableful of children—minus Israel, as Rebecca and Daniel thought it best to let him sleep as long as he could manage—took turns updating their father on the goings-on in their lives while he'd been away. Each took a leisurely time with the telling, as the longer they chatted the longer they could put off their chores.

Jemima brought her family over for the meal, and Daniel tasked Flanders with riding to Boonesborough to trade the pelts and furs he'd left behind, bringing back his horses, and seeing if there was news of Captain Holder and Fanny.

"Folks there have likely been told of what happened at Hoy's," said Boone, "but go ahead and let them know if they haven't. Tell them you crossed paths with a friendly Indian on the way there and learned it from him. Whatever you tell them, keep it simple."

Flanders agreed; Jemima had told him of the Raven's visit, so he knew there were things that needed doing before the relative calm they were enjoying now came to an end. It was possible Boone Station would escape attack, but very likely many of its men, himself included, would be called up for militia duty if the attack on Hoy's proved not to be an isolated incident.

But if Flanders felt a strong need to hurry along, Daniel couldn't see it; the man had an uncanny talent for eating considering how skinny he was, and was taking his sweet time in the effort. Daniel cleared his throat every so often in a vain attempt to pull his son-in-law's attention from his plate. He gave up finally, figuring instead to lead by example.

"I'd best get to it," Daniel said as he stood from the table and stretched. "I want to give the station walls a thorough going-over."

"You'll find them in good condition," said Flanders between forkfuls.

Daniel kissed Rebecca, put on his hat, and headed for the door.

"Well, if it isn't Sleeping Beauty," Daniel heard Flanders say behind him. He turned to see Israel shuffling into the kitchen.

Israel's hair was sticking up here and there from his fitful sleeping. It reminded Rebecca of when her son was a young boy, small and vulnerable.

"Feeling better?" she asked.

"Yes, ma'am," answered Israel. He put a hand to the base of his skull. "Only my neck aches like the dickens."

Daniel poured a cup of coffee and handed it to his son.

"This will fix that right up," Daniel said. "Drink it down, have something to eat—not too much, mind, as your stomach's likely still unsettled—then come find me."

"Well," Israel began, looking down at the floor, "I thought I might go with Flanders, give him a hand with the horses."

Flanders snickered but kept eating.

Daniel understood now why the boy had finally popped out of bed; he'd overheard there might be opportunity to visit the Calloway girl. He smacked Israel lightly on the cheek. "Eat, then come find me," he said. "Flanders can get one of Martha's boys if he wants company." Then he looked around the table at the other children. "Well, one of you that's finished get up and give your brother a chair."

Jesse stood with mock frustration. Everyone laughed, even Israel. Daniel kissed Rebecca again and walked out as Israel took a seat.

Daniel walked the perimeter of the station, figuring he'd get a better look on foot than horseback. Flanders was right, the walls didn't look half bad; he and the boys had done a decent job of upkeep. As Daniel rounded the last corner, coming back around to the main gate, he spotted Israel heading toward him.

"I tried to get out sooner, but Ma wasn't having it," Israel said to answer the question his father hadn't yet asked, and perhaps wouldn't have, although Israel knew he was thinking it.

"That mother of yours," Daniel said. "She intended to tuck you back into bed, I suppose."

"She didn't go as far as that, likely knowing your reaction," Israel replied.

Boone did think his son looked rather ill; worse than he had earlier. But perhaps being up and about would do him good.

"Come on, then. Let's check on the livestock. We'll take it easy on your account."

Although Israel was used to long periods of silence when working with his father, it didn't make them any less uncomfortable. Making matters worse, his mother had told him of Savanukah's visit and his warning, and Israel desperately wanted to get every detail he could from his pa. He'd have asked, but he'd learned that the surest way for him to not get a satisfying answer from the man was to present him with a direct question. Israel was certain his father was thinking on the situation, he just wished he'd do his thinking out loud. In some ways, though, Israel figured that he was; it was clear that the work they were doing was meant to ensure they were well fortified for attack.

They slopped the hogs, then moved on to the rest of the livestock. The few cattle, sheep, and goats they kept were in fine shape, as there was plenty of summer grass for grazing; trouble would come in winter as grain was in short supply and the station's horses would have to take priority. Of course, if Indians sieged and slaughtered the livestock between now and then that wouldn't much matter, so Daniel made note of the healthiest animals, hoping at least a few could be brought within the walls of the fort if need be.

Other folks were now venturing out. Will Hays had delivered the news of potential threat while drumming up volunteers, and the settlers intended to squeeze the good out of the time they had if there were any chance of trouble, harvesting what there was of the shabby crops, collecting water from the river, or just rolling in the grass, breathing fresh air, and enjoying a moment of life outside the prison they had, by necessity, built for themselves.

Daniel and Israel righted a couple of posts in the horse pen that were in danger of falling over, then moved on to chopping firewood. Israel couldn't figure why—chopping wood was Jesse and Daniel Morgan's chore—but it seemed his father felt driven to do at least a little of all that needed doing.

Two and a half hours or so after sunrise, with no warning, Daniel split one last log and announced they were done.

"Leave the wood. I'll send the boys down to collect it."

Israel buried the head of his axe into a stump and walked to the tree where he'd hung his shirt; the day was already hot and humid, and he'd taken it off some time ago. He grabbed the garment and used it to wipe the sweat from his eyes.

He figured his father must be expecting that rider from Hoy's round about now. But Daniel hadn't stopped because of that; he'd done so out of concern for Israel. The boy didn't look well. Rest and water might do him good.

They filled two buckets while they were at the creek and headed back to the station. As they crested the gentle slope that rose from the bank, Daniel paused. He tapped Israel on the shoulder, pointed at his own ear, then pointed toward the trail in the distance. Israel heard it now—hoof falls. They put down the buckets and hustled to meet the rider.

He wasn't long in coming. The man rode up to them at full gallop before pulling up on the reins and leaping from the saddle. Daniel and Israel recognized him—Ambrose Wilcoxon, a young man around Israel's age with a ruddy complexion that had flared up from a long stretch of riding in the hot sun.

"Colonel Boone—" Ambrose began, struggling to get his breath.

Boone held up a hand to stop him. "Take a second there, Ambrose. Easier to talk if you can breathe."

"Yes, sir," Ambrose answered. He put his hands on his knees, took a moment, then lifted his head. "Indian attack on Hoy Station," Ambrose continued. "Kidnapped William Hoy's son and another boy. Four men dead and one wounded in the pursuit."

Ambrose looked over and got a good look at Israel for the first time. "Israel? You look like a fish that's been flopping on the bank an hour or two," he said.

Boone took the reins of the man's horse, handed them to Israel, and nodded for his son to get the horse watered. "Come on up to the house. Have some food and water; you'll want to be fortified before riding to Lexington with the letter I mean for you to deliver to Major Todd."

Daniel and Rebecca sat at the kitchen table with Ambrose as he told what he was sent to tell, swallowing down cold bacon and several cupfuls of water between sentences. The details matched up with what the Raven had told them, but the couple kept that to themselves.

Daniel excused himself and left the room. Rebecca continued collecting details from Ambrose, offering him another helping when he'd cleaned his plate which Ambrose declined, not wanting to ride on so full a stomach. Boone walked back into the room and handed Ambrose a folded sheet of paper.

"Major Todd," Boone said.

Ambrose was surprised Boone could compose a letter that quickly; perhaps he'd been so engrossed in eating and drinking that he'd lost track of time. Boone stared at him, which Ambrose took to mean it was time to get going. He stood, had the last swig of water from his cup, gabbed his hunting pouch from the back of the chair, and shoved the letter inside.

"Thank you, ma'am," he said, nodding to Rebecca. "Colonel." Then he slipped on his hat and hurried out the open door.

Rebecca collected the dishes from the table and Ambrose appeared a moment later supporting Israel, the man's arm slung over his shoulder, struggling to keep him on his feet.

"He was half passed out leaning against my horse," Ambrose said as Rebecca rushed forward to help steady her son.

"Horse is fed and watered, though," Israel mumbled.

Daniel stepped in and took Israel's weight. "We've got him," he assured Ambrose. "Best go on now."

Ambrose nodded. "I hope you feel better, Israel," he said as he exited again. The Boones heard him hurrying down the porch steps.

Daniel and Rebecca walked Israel into the bedroom. Daniel saw the concern on his wife's face.

"He overdid it," Daniel said. "Fault lies with me."

"I'm fine," Israel said, his voice thin. "Just need to lie down for a minute, is all."

They lowered him onto the bed. Daniel smiled to Rebecca as he took off Israel's moccasins. "Let him rest a bit, then I'll carry him down to the creek to cool him off."

Rebecca turned to Daniel, returned his smile halfheartedly, then turned back to their son and brushed the hair from his damp forehead. Israel was already fast asleep.

SIXTEEN

Will Hays took point, riding well ahead of the rest of the patrol. He was a skilled horseman, as comfortable navigating the woods in the saddle as most men were on foot, and rode with an exuberance and abandon that some might consider reckless. It wasn't that he cared for showing off himself—at least not unless Susannah was watching—but he did relish any opportunity to show off Stoneheart.

The three-year-old filly was a purebred Andalusian, directly descended from horses brought to the continent by the Spanish over two hundred years earlier. Hays had brought a stallion and mare with him when he left the Clinch River for Kentucky, and Stoneheart was the only result of their breeding. Will would tell anyone who'd listen that she was the finest horse on the frontier, and he may have been right; she was swifter than most to be certain, but more importantly she was agile, built for navigating the dense Kentucky woods while moving at a good clip. Hays was fond of saying that the filly could make a hairpin turn at full gallop that was so smooth he could sip tea while in the saddle and spill nary a drop.

Will had named the filly Stoneheart for her striking, dappled gray coat and in reference to her unflappable temperament, a steel nerve that never wavered, even when Hays asked her to do something outlandish and seemingly impossible.

The man loved that horse.

The patrol rode northeast before making a wide arc west. Hoy Station was south of them, but Savanukah had told Boone that the Indians responsible for that attack had gone their separate ways and now posed little threat—what concerned Boone was the prospect of a party heading down from Ohio, a larger force that might already be near.

Hays and his men made the first round as a group, noting trails and crossings they agreed to be the most likely paths of attack. Hays repeatedly put too much distance between himself and the other nine riders and had to double back often to check in. Some of the men seemed bored, and Hays felt led to remind them that if they weren't out here in the relative cool of the shady woods they'd be back at the station doing whatever chores needed doing in the heat of the late morning sun.

Excitement grabbed hold of Hays as he approached a familiar clearing. He encouraged Stoneheart into a gallop. He felt the sun on his face as they broke through the tree line and the filly bolted across the wide expanse of grass. A new row of trees lay ahead, growing along the bank of a shallow creek that ran perpendicular to his path, right alongside the well-worn buffalo road that led to Lexington. The filly, having jumped the creek many times in the past, knew what was expected of her and lowered her head as she picked up speed. Hays smiled. Then his face was cool again as they hit the shade of the trees on the other side of the clearing.

Hays saw the creek rushing toward him, then Stoneheart was airborne and Will's stomach leapt into his throat and back down again as the horse landed with a satisfying jolt on the opposite bank. In a flash they were out of the shade and back into the summer sun as they cleared the trees at the edge of the buffalo road.

Then Will was airborne again, only without his horse under him this time, as Stoneheart came to an abrupt stop to avoid colliding with something Hays never even saw, throwing him from the saddle. He hit the ground, rolled, rolled, and rolled again into a patch of thick brush. Then he was on his back, looking up into the trees.

Concern for Stoneheart struck him. Will sprang to his feet, wobbled a bit, and turned back toward the trail he had been thrown across to see a group of men staring down at him, four on horseback flanking another man who had dismounted his own horse and was holding Stoneheart's bridle.

"God almighty, Captain Hays—you nearly killed us both," said Major Todd. "I could forgive my own murder out of an abundance of Christian charity, but would doubtful feel the same if your recklessness had maimed this magnificent creature." He turned to the filly and rubbed her muzzle.

Will chuckled as he dusted himself off and patted his body for broken bones. Being called *captain* was a novelty, a title only used when the militia was mustered, and then only by officers who cared about such things because they were of higher rank.

Will felt something wet running down the side of his nose. He put a hand to his forehead and it came away red. He reached for the pouch at his side, found it wasn't there, looked up, and saw the bag, his powder horn, tomahawk, hunting knife, and hat strewn along the trajectory of his rolling. He started toward the trail, picking up his gear along the way. When he reached the bag, he pulled a rag from within and held it to his forehead.

"Sorry for that, Levi," Hays said as he gave Stoneheart a once-over. "The odds of you being on this road at that exact moment . . . helluva coincidence, ain't it?" Satisfied that the filly wasn't injured, Will smiled and gave her a scratch behind the ear. "You okay, girl?"

Todd handed Stoneheart's reins to Hays. Levi was twenty-six, boyish-looking with a Scotch-Irish complexion and sandy brown hair, but his manner was that of a man who had long since left youth behind. Hays and Todd had crossed paths several times, and Hays found the man likable enough, although lacking in imagination and a bit snobbish; Todd was well-educated and had little interest in Will until learning Hays had some schooling himself. Still, Todd was a friend and colleague of John Floyd's, which was fact enough to vouch for the man's character.

"If you want to make it up to me we can swap horses," Todd said with a smile.

"Not on your life," Will responded.

One of the riders flanking Todd cleared his throat. Hays turned; he was still unsteady from his tumble and had to blink a few times to bring the man into focus.

William Ellis. The only man on the frontier more stuffy than Todd. *Too much seriousness in one place*, thought Hays. He sighed.

"Ellis. You're looking very much yourself this fine day," Hays said, smiling up at the tan, fair-haired twenty-one-year-old. Captain Ellis nodded back then looked away, annoyed, clearly signaling that this interlude was keeping the party from important business.

Hays craned his neck and looked down the buffalo road; there were more men with the major than he'd initially realized—many more. About thirty he'd guess, just over half of whom were on horseback. He recognized some of them and threw the men a general nod.

The fog cleared from Will's head, and the reason he was in the woods in the first place struck him suddenly. "Where you fellas headed, anyway?" he asked.

Todd started to answer but stopped when he heard hoof falls approaching from the woods behind them. He turned, as did his men. Some raised their rifles.

"Easy now," Hays said. "They're with me."

The members of Hays' patrol emerged from the woods seconds later. Todd lowered his rifle, then remounted. He looked down at Hays. "Indians and British have Bryan Station surrounded. A couple of riders managed to get through their lines and get word to me in Lexington. We're off to make an assessment of the situation and do what we're able while the rest of the militia is called up."

"Well, hell," Hays said, pulling the rag from his forehead. He noted the amount of blood—not all that much, really—then touched the wound with the back of his hand. It came away dry. "Boone penned you a letter just this morning, telling of an Indian attack at Hoy Station not a week ago, followed by an ambush against Captain Holder. That's why we're out here patrolling."

Todd shifted in the saddle, then glanced over his shoulder as Hays' words were passed down the line, one man to the next. "Jesus," Todd whispered. He turned to them. "One likely got nothing to do with the other, men. Times we live in, is all." He turned back to Hays, who gave him a subtle shrug by way of apology; it was clear Todd feared his men would ride off to defend their homes and families if they thought Indians were mounting coordinated attacks against the settlements.

"Seeing as how we're out here on account of Indians anyway, I'm sure a few of us would be glad to ride with you," Hays said.

Todd turned to Hays' men and gave them a quick appraisal; each was armed and looked capable enough. "Well, we wouldn't turn down strengthening our numbers," he said, "but we'd best get going." Todd raised his arm to signal his men, waved it forward, and they started up the trail.

Hays swung himself into his saddle, patted Stoneheart on the neck, then looked back at his men. "Boys?"

Hays' men exchanged confused glances. One of the men, Samuel Brannon, turned to Hays.

"I reckon we're all coming," he said, a wounded tone in his voice. He was a big man, strong but thoughtful, and known for having his feelings easily hurt.

"Alright, alright," Hays said, putting up his hands and smiling. Then he wagged his index finger at the youngest of the riders. "Not you, though, Joseph. Best ride back and tell your uncle where we've gone and why."

The seventeen-year-old Joseph was Martha Boone's eldest son, and Daniel's nephew. His father, Edward Boone, had been mistaken for Daniel and killed by a group of Shawnee two years prior, and Will had no desire to be responsible for Martha losing a son to Indians as well.

Joseph's head dropped in disappointment, but he knew Will was right; he was the youngest by several years, and someone did have to get this news to Boone Station. He raised his chin.

"Yessir," he said, and he turned his horse to start back. As he picked up speed he looked over his shoulder, smiled, and yelled, "Cousin Susannah ain't going to be happy with you."

The men laughed.

"When I return a hero," Hays began, laughing himself, "having saved the land from the damn English, I expect she'll be at peace with it."

The patrol filed in with Major Todd's militia. Hays gave the filly a squeeze and she darted to the front of the line, Hays riding alongside Major Todd, taking Captain Ellis' spot.

SEVENTEEN

They first saw the smoke from a mile or so away. The militia-men had made good time, even with a good portion of their number on foot, arriving outside of Bryan Station just after noon. It helped that they'd wasted no time making conversation; Ellis in particular was famous for his silence, and Todd, far from talkative himself, seemed to be taking the man's lead, either by example or out of honest concern for the seriousness of the situation he was leading the men into.

They paused below the crest of a hill three hundred yards from the settlement and dismounted, keeping low. A large, thick cornfield flanked the path on the right, woods on the left. Major Todd raised a hand to instruct the men to remain silent; as they were traveling the main route to and from the station, it was safe to assume the attackers had it under close surveillance. But aside from the sound of their own horses swishing their tails to shoo away flies, the men heard nothing.

The group's one advantage was the haste they'd made in getting here; the Indians and British were unlikely to expect reinforcements, scant as they were, to arrive so quickly.

Even still, this was as close as they could get to the station without exposing their position; cresting the hill to assess matters would make them easy targets.

At the head of the militia, Todd, Hays, and Ellis stared at the massive plume of smoke rising above the hill and wondered if they were already too late.

"One option, Captain," Todd said softly, "is we leave the horses, fan out, half of us through the corn, the other half the woods, and proceed with stealth on foot. If we're lucky, some of us reach the fort before the enemy knows we're here. Those of us that don't, though . . ." Todd paused.

The break in conversation went longer than Hays expected, so he turned to Ellis to see what was keeping the man from responding and found both Todd and Ellis were staring at him. Curious. Then Hays realized that Ellis wasn't the captain Todd had been addressing—he was. It was an acknowledgement of Hays' authority, as the men from Boone Station were, ostensibly, under his command and were his responsibility.

Hays cleared his throat, turned back to watching the smoke rise into the sky, and squinted. "Or," he began, "the mounted among us charge straight for the station at full gallop, taking the enemy by such surprise that we're safe within the fort before they've gathered their wits."

There was silence. Hays cut his eyes back to Todd, who looked to be pondering the suggestion. Todd twisted in his saddle, looked back at his men, then turned back toward the smoke and stroked his chin.

"That'll do," he said.

Hays nearly laughed; he'd grossly misjudged the man. Then the reality of what he'd suggested hit him, and his stomach went cold.

"Half the men on horseback will head for the gate," Todd continued. "The fewer the riders the more difficult they'll be to target. The remaining men will spread out in the cornfield. Once the shooting starts and the enemy exposes their position, we'll advance, provide covering fire, and take out as many of the bastards as we're able."

Ellis went to speak, but Hays cut him off.

"I'll lead those doing the rushing, Major," Hays said.

Todd smiled. "I'm afraid not, Captain. You've been wobbling in the saddle, likely concussed from that tumble you took, and your horse is half spent."

Hays couldn't disagree. Risking himself was one thing, but the filly? That wouldn't do.

"Hmm," Hays sighed. "The other men will have to pull straws, in that case."

The officers turned and saw that each of the twenty-seven other riders had heard them, and each to a man nudged their horse forward.

"Okay," Hays chuckled. "What say I pick half my boys based on the quality of their mounts, Major, and you pick half of yours?"

Ellis' back stiffened. He turned to Hays. "How long had your men been riding before we crossed paths?" He asked. "No, we've riders enough with comparatively fresh horses. We'll go."

Ellis was a man of contradictions. A frontier preacher, he was energetic and personable from the pulpit but aloof in fellowship; peaceable by word, but one of the most experienced Indian fighters on the frontier by deed, having fended off many a raid on his isolated, backwoods land claim. He'd escorted the five hundred members of Lewis Craig's Traveling

Church up from Spotsylvania by way of the Wilderness Road just last year, when Indian attack was just as likely as it was now. Word spread that when the group emerged from the woods surrounding the rugged trail and spied the bluegrass of the Kentucky country for the first time, many of the women began to cry. Ellis was made so uncomfortable by the display that the only thing he could think to do was ask a slave in the group known for his banjo picking to play a tune as accompaniment to the women's sobbing. The playing was so mournful, though, that it caused some of the men in the party to cry as well, which was altogether too much for Ellis; he left the group and rode ahead to scout a camp for the night, even though it was only ten o'clock in the morning.

But the most commonly known fact about Ellis, and most pertinent to the current situation, was he despised the British.

A decade ago, Ellis' father, Hezekiah, was arrested for publicly denouncing English tyranny and its local purveyor, Lord Dunmore, then Royal Governor of Virginia. Hezekiah fell ill in prison and died, shackled to the floor of a dank, dark cell. This seeded in young William a bedrock-deep dedication to the cause of American freedom that, even in his youth, those around him understood to be a fixation.

When William Ellis was in, he was in all the way.

Ellis divvied his riders into two groups. Seventeen was the number settled on for the advance party, with none of the men showing either disappointment or relief in being selected for one duty or the other. Those that were riding ahead moved forward. Those remaining behind checked their rifles. The only chance the seventeen had was to ride full-out, heads down; taking the time to raise rifles and return enemy fire would only increase their chances of getting shot.

Everything settled, Ellis and the sixteen others swung onto their horses. Then Ellis looked down at Todd. "We'll flush them out, Major. Once they've fired, you ought to be able to pick off a good number of them before they have time to reload."

Ellis threw Todd a salute. Todd was taken aback, as there wasn't much saluting done on the frontier. But he recovered quickly and reciprocated.

Hays expected he'd have found the gesture humorous, but it struck him instead as oddly necessary and appropriate; Ellis had whittled the moment down to its essence, taken hold of it, then cast it like a net that caught up the rest of them.

Stone-faced, Ellis encouraged his horse forward, glanced over his shoulder at his men, and for the first time any could recollect, smiled. Then he gave his horse a squeeze and the animal bolted over the rise. The other riders took off an instant later.

The sound of the seventeen galloping away was thunderous at first, then tapered as each in turn disappeared from view, hidden by the slope of the hill. Leading their horses, Todd and the remaining men elbowed their way into the cornfield a few yards, then cut down and at an angle in the direction of the station, spreading out as they went, ready to charge when the moment arrived. The field was so thick with stalks that one man could scarcely make out the next.

Todd and Hays waited for what they thought sure would be an explosion of enemy gunfire—and kept waiting. They turned to each other, baffled. Finally, a shot rang out in the distance, followed by a second, a third, a tenth. Both men swung onto their horses and were then able to see others in the group, dotted throughout the field, doing the same. Hays tightened his grip on his rifle, lowered his head, and went to smack Stoneheart on her hindquarter when he heard another shot, only closer and from behind. He looked to his right and saw a man crumple in his saddle and fall from his horse. Hays swiveled his head, trying to get a bead on where the shot had come from. More shots zinged around him, and he watched as another rider was hit and thrown from his saddle into the stalks, hitting the ground with a thud, still alive, though, as Hays could hear him cussing. Hays saw a blur of green on the periphery of his vision darting through the stalks; he turned toward it, then saw another.

Hell, he thought. *Rangers.*

Hays cut the filly to the right, raised his rifle, and fired into the corn in what was his best guess at the location of the shooters. Other men did likewise. They couldn't make a break for the station—the braves and Rangers between them and there were expecting them now—and couldn't stay here making like fish in a barrel. They'd have to fall back and hope they hadn't yet been surrounded.

Todd yelled out the retreat but needn't have wasted his breath, as all the men had come to the same conclusion. Hays slung his rifle into the scabbard strapped at the side of his saddle—no time to reload in the middle of an ambush—and let out a yell to let Stoneheart know it was time to move and not be shy about it. He heard the continuous crunch of stalks breaking as men and horses rushed through the field. Out of the corner of his eye, Hays caught a passing glimpse of a rider reaching down and half dragging, half pulling a man who was on foot up to share his horse, but for the most part the corn was so thick it was impossible to see much of anything, so those that had horses rode and those that didn't ran, fast as each could manage, cornstalks lashing them in the face as they pressed forward.

Finally, Stoneheart broke through the field and burst onto the buffalo road. Hays and Todd were now at the rear, and the dust kicked up by the horses that hit the trail before them was so thick Hays could barely make out the rider just a few yards ahead. He locked his eyes on the man's back as best he was able—he might ride straight into a tree otherwise—before a blur snatched the man from his saddle, leaving the horse running riderless. Hays turned and saw Todd was riding beside him and staring at him wide-eyed, then realized Todd wasn't looking at him at all but beyond him, over his shoulder. Todd's mouth moved to shout a warning and Hays twisted to his left just as an Indian smashed into his side and sent him flying. Hays hit the ground a second later, landing hard, squarely on his back, the Indian landing somewhere outside his field of vision, hidden in clouds of dust. Hays couldn't breathe—all the air had been forced from his body by the impact. Just as well, he figured, as he'd only be sucking in lungfuls of dust anyway. Gasping, nausea rising in his stomach, he reached with his right hand for the hunting knife strapped to the left side of his waist and found the hilt just as the Indian landed on his torso, pinning his right arm. The Indian's face was painted black with brilliant slashes of red running across it at a diagonal, his head plucked clean save for the crown where the hair was tied with beaded string and adorned with feathers, and raised high above his head was his right hand gripping a tomahawk. Hays reached up with his left, but the tomahawk arm was too far away so he grabbed the man's face instead, pushing it back with what little strength he could summon. Two wide, white eyes glared at him from between his fingers through swirling dust. His vision began to tunnel. Hays saw the tomahawk rushing toward him in a flash, then saw nothing.

EIGHTEEN

Hays awoke sitting upright and puking. He was being jostled something fierce, which didn't help his nausea or his throbbing head none, but at least the contents of his stomach were being left behind on the trail as the makeshift travois he was strapped to was dragged unceremoniously forward. A horse's tail swished against the back of his head. He went to turn to see whose horse was pulling him but was stopped by a sharp pain in his neck. He put his hand to his throat and felt a cloth, warm and wet. Then he noticed a large strip had been torn from the bottom of his hunting shirt— likely the scrap had been repurposed as the bandage he was now touching. He pulled his hand from his neck and it came away red.

It was only early afternoon, and he'd already spent a good portion of the day bleeding.

He laid back on the travois, tried to come to terms with the jostling, and looked up as far as he could manage without craning his neck.

"Where's my horse?" he hollered.

"She's fine. One of the men has her," Todd yelled back over his shoulder. "Don't move too much. You've lost a lot of blood. Again. I was quick enough to keep you from getting your head lopped off, but too slow to prevent you acquiring that souvenir."

Hays put his hand to his neck again. "I can't help but move, the way you're riding," he said. "You kill that Indian that was about to scalp me?"

"Didn't kill him, but I expect the butt of my rifle is the last thing he'll ever see out of his left eye," Todd answered.

"Let me off this thing," Hays said. "I'll do my own riding." He sat up and started to roll from the travois.

Todd pulled back on the reins. "I imagine the ride was worse when you were lying across the rump of my horse before we had time to stop and fashion that sled. Be glad you weren't awake for that." He whistled as he dismounted to signal the men ahead to stop. He offered Hays his hand. Will took it, and Todd pulled him to his feet.

Hays stumbled; he motioned to Todd to stay back and give him a moment to figure it out on his own. He placed his hands on his knees and took a couple of deep breaths to keep from throwing up again.

"The British among the Indians were Rangers, not regular infantry," Hays said, staring at the ground to steady himself.

"I know. I got a glimpse of one." Todd replied.

It took some effort, but Hays managed to raise his eyes to look toward the rest of the party. Aside from Todd, they were all Boone Station men. Hays felt a wave of relief. He scanned again, just to be certain. Sure enough—although they were dusty and a little scratched up—all eight were accounted for. Then the absence of Todd's men struck him and his stomach fell.

Samuel Brannon, who'd been leading Stoneheart, dismounted his own horse and walked the filly to Hays.

"Here you go, Will. Not a scratch on her," Samuel said. Hays noted the quiver in his voice; the man was clearly shaken from the skirmish.

Hays nodded, took the reins, then rubbed Stoneheart's nose with his knuckles. Mindful of his neck, he turned to Todd. "Your men?"

"Two dead," Todd said. He pulled his knife from its sheath and began cutting the ropes that held the travois to his horse. "A couple of others wounded, but they were well enough to ride. I sent them and the rest ahead to Lexington to sound the alarm. We'll need a lot more men before returning to Bryan's."

Hays felt a sting of shame; he knew his injury was bad enough that he wouldn't be going back. "Ellis and his riders?" Hays asked.

"No way of knowing," Todd responded as he cut the last rope. "I half expected you to die, which would've meant riding into Boone Station myself to deliver you to your widow." He sheathed his knife. "So I appreciate you living to spare me that discomfort, Captain, not to mention a good deal of time. My brother is in Lincoln County on business, and I'll need to get word to him as quickly as possible." He kicked the rickety travois to the side of the trail, then swung back onto his horse.

"Pleasure's all mine," Hays said. He placed a foot in its stirrup and slowly pulled himself up onto Stoneheart, careful it didn't look to the others that he was struggling.

"I'll send a messenger to Colonel Logan as well," Todd continued. "There's no chance of him and his men making it

129

to Bryan's ahead of us, but we may need reinforcements by the time they do."

Hays settled into the saddle. His vision went white. He wobbled once but managed to steady himself enough to keep from falling off. "Boone will start recruiting immediately, soon as he knows the situation. He'll meet you at Bryan's when the time comes—I'm certain of that."

Then, surprising himself, he offered Todd an earnest salute.

"Good luck, Major," Will said.

Todd saluted back, gave his horse a "snickt, snickt," and galloped down the trail.

The Boone Station men stopped at the creek Hays had jumped a few hours earlier—it seemed like days—drank, and rinsed the dust from their faces. When the others had finished, Hays undid the now crusty bandage around his neck and tossed it into the bushes; the last thing he needed was for his wife and children to see him riding into the station with a bloody rag tied around his throat. He crouched at the bank, leaned over and splashed water onto his neck to clean away the dried blood, sending red rivulets downstream. He was careful not to loosen the coagulation that had stopped the bleeding. Although he couldn't see his reflection clearly, he could feel the gap in his flesh where the tomahawk had done its work. He was lucky to be alive, and had Levi Todd to thank for it.

When he stood he didn't bother to ask the men how the cut looked—their faces told the tale. He ripped a fresh strip from the bottom of his shirt and wrapped it around his neck to conceal the wound.

Hays then sent the men ahead at the best speed they could manage—it was important to get word to Boone without delay. Only Brannon stayed behind, ostensibly to look after Hays and make certain he didn't pass out and fall from his horse along the way, although the truth of it was Hays figured the slower ride back would give Brannon's nerves a chance to settle. It seemed to work; Brannon was quiet at first, but eventually turned to talking. However, no matter how hard Hays tried to keep the conversation focused on horses and rifles, Brannon would tack back to talk of the ambush. His eyes welled with tears when he spoke of the two dead men they'd left behind.

Just before entering the clearing that led to the station, Hays brought Stoneheart to a stop. He reached over and placed a hand on Brannon's shoulder.

"Samuel. You don't have to go back to Bryan's," Hays said.

"Oh, I'm going back. I'm going back," Samuel said, talking more to himself than Will as he dabbed his eyes and nose with the sleeve of his shirt.

"Alright," Hays chuckled. "Well, dry up, then, and let's ride in and see if any young ladies fancy a hero." He slapped Brannon on the back.

"Samuel smiled, and they headed into the clearing. They saw figures in the distance, milling about inside the station's opened gate. Hays picked out his wife's silhouette, saw she was wearing her hair down, which was how he liked it, and the aching in his head eased up a little. He leaned forward in the saddle. Stoneheart got the message and took off like a shot across the field. Brannon didn't expect they'd be galloping in, but he took Will's cue and followed close behind.

131

The crowd heard the horses running and turned, which was Will's intention, and when he was just outside the gate he signaled Stoneheart, and she slowed and proceeded at a regal canter through the open gate. Hays smiled; he'd spent a fair amount of time training the filly to perform, and he enjoyed getting the good out of it. Brannon's horse slowed and followed, minus the fancy footwork, and the men rode into the station looking every bit like a knight attended by his squire.

Susannah Hays ran toward them. As the filly continued at a steady gait, Will swung his right leg over the saddle and executed a running dismount, landing with perfect form before being overtaken by dizziness and stumbling to the ground. He sprang up a moment later, dusted himself off (which, he thought to himself, had become almost as much a habit today as bleeding), and was nearly tackled by Susannah. Will looked at her eyes, her mouth, and the world surrounding her blurred—not from his being lightheaded, but because that's how the world always looked to him when she was close. She grabbed him tightly, stroking his hair, careful not to touch his neck; Will figured the other men, having arrived half an hour or so earlier, must have told her of his injury. This was quite a relief; he'd been dreading delivering the news himself. Still, he was looking forward to a time, well outside of the emotions of the moment, when he could entertain his wife and children with dramatic retellings of how he'd acquired what would then be a quite impressive scar.

"Lord, Will—what have you gone and done to yourself?" Susannah asked, although not exactly a question, glancing first at her husband's neck then at the cut on his forehead, which was so minor by comparison that Will had completely forgotten it.

"Done to myself?" Will repeated, straightening his back, feigning that he'd taken offense. "This here is the work of a professional," he said, pointing to his neck. The wound had opened some and a red stain was spreading slowly across the bandage, but Will didn't know it. Susannah's hand went to her mouth. Seeing fright in her eyes, he pointed to the cut on his forehead. "Now this," Will began, "well, this one I did more or less do myself, yeah."

Susannah half smiled, then kissed him. Their girls, who'd been running to catch up with their mother, ran up and each took one of their father's hands. Susannah turned and started walking, and the girls began leading Will after her, pulling him at a good enough clip that Will had to skip a time or two to keep up.

"The filly . . ." Will began. He tried to look over his shoulder at Stoneheart but the pain in his neck prevented it.

"I'll take care of her, Will, don't you worry none," said Thomas Boone, Susannah's fourteen-year-old cousin, bursting with excitement as he rushed past the Hays family toward the horse. Will knew the boy had a way with horses and a genuine affection for Stoneheart, so he decided he'd allow it.

Several neighbors patted Will on the back as they passed. Will spotted Daniel standing with the other members of the patrol, but when he planted his heels to get the girls to stop, Daniel shook his head.

"We'll talk later," Daniel said as the girls dragged Will past. Boone understood the potential seriousness of a wound to the neck, having been shot in his own during the Boonesborough siege.

Susannah grabbed Will's arm to help the girls pull him along. Will figured it best not to argue—he didn't have the energy for it anyway, and was pretty sure he was about to pass out and would just as soon do so closer to his bed. He glanced to his opposite side and saw Jemima and Israel. Israel looked pale and clammy, and for some reason was shirtless and looked to have a woman's apron draped over his shoulders.

"You look terrible," Will said to him as they passed and continued on toward the Hays family cabin.

NINETEEN

Israel's sleep had been restless—his father had led him to the creek to cool him down, which had worked some, but he was still too achy and the room too stuffy to be comfortable—so when he heard the commotion of horses galloping into the station he forced himself out of bed, walked to the window, and saw members of the patrol racing into the courtyard, only without Will Hays. Israel slipped on his moccasins and hurried out. By the time he shuffled into the common area most everyone in the station was there, circled around the riders, listening as they told Daniel of the siege at Bryan Station. His mother was hugging Susannah, who was crying, as the men had just been telling of Will's injury and near killing by tomahawk. Daniel turned and conscripted a group of children to fetch the men water and tend to their horses.

When Israel learned his father had asked Will to organize the patrol, he didn't shed any tears over missing out. It sounded to him a boring assignment anyway, and, had he not been ill, his father would certainly have volunteered him to go along.

Now he was hearing that the patrol hadn't done much patrolling at all but had instead been involved in an Indian skirmish. Israel couldn't believe it; he'd missed out on adventure again, sidelined by happenstance. There was no dialing back the clock—the opportunity had been lost. He'd never be part of the story and never part of the attention his father was paying to its telling.

"Israel?" He heard Jemima say behind him. "Should you be up?" She put her hand on his shoulder. "You're shivering."

Something caught Israel's attention beyond the station's gate. "I'm fine," he said, staring into the distance. He watched as two riders approached through the clearing.

Jemima untied her apron and draped it over her brother's shoulders.

Will Hays and Samuel Brannon rode into the station, Will making a show of it as Israel expected he would. He was glad to see it, as it meant Will's injuries weren't as bad as everyone feared. Samuel was glassy-eyed and appeared to be in something of a befuddled trance.

Will stumbled during his performance yet somehow managed to not look a fool. Folks rushed to Samuel, shaking his hand, offering him water, and pelting him with questions.

Even Samuel Brannon gets to be a hero, Israel thought, and hated himself for thinking it.

Hays' men didn't complain. Boone knew they were tired and hungry, but servicing those concerns would have to wait; he needed them to tell again what they knew while it was fresh in their minds, both what they'd experienced firsthand and what they'd been told by Major Todd regarding the situation at Bryan Station. Ringed by a crowd of their neighbors, the men sat three to a log facing Boone, who was sitting on a stump in front of them. One man would tell part of the story then pass it off to another so he could add what he knew, then another would chime in with a detail the others weren't aware of, and on down the line. Occasionally, someone in the crowd would pipe up with a question, and Sam Boone, Daniel's older brother, would shush them. If Daniel happened to find the question relevant, he'd hold it in his mind and repeat it himself at the next opportunity.

Finally, Daniel stood. "Alright, boys," he said, satisfied now that he had a clear picture of the situation. "This surely wasn't the day you were expecting when you got out of bed this morning, but you weathered it well. Eat. Rest up." They knew what he meant; get as much rest as they could manage now, as they'd be riding to Bryan Station again soon.

The men stood, stretched, and were collected by their loved ones—wives or parents, siblings or cousins—and went off to snatch what normalcy they could for as long as they'd be able.

Those remaining in the crowd waited for Boone to speak. Most knew what was required when the militia was mustered—good horses had to be made ready, rifles cleaned, ammunition and food fit for travel prepared—but expected Boone to give official word and set them about the tasks. But Boone just stood, thinking to himself, as if he'd forgotten they were there. Finally, Rebecca clapped her hands together, waded into the crowd, and offered suggestions on how they could get started, more or less giving them the go-ahead.

As the crowd dispersed, Boone started making a list in his mind of the things that needed doing and the order they needed doing in. First, riders had to be sent to the other Fayette County stations, McGee and Strode, hitting any outpost or lone cabin along the way, as they needed every man they could scrounge. He'd send someone to Boonesborough to be sure they were aware of the situation, but the men there were part of the Lincoln County militia and would ride with Colonel Logan, if at all. It struck Boone as a bureaucratic distinction unhinged from reality, but he didn't make the rules, and he wasn't keen on facing court-martial a second time for breaking them.

Thomas Boone, Sam's youngest, guessed at what his uncle was thinking and sidled up to him. "You want me and some of the fellers to saddle up and send word?"

"No," Daniel said. The word came out sharper than he would have liked. He took a breath and put his hand on his nephew's shoulder. The boy took after his mother, which endeared him to Daniel; Sarah had taught Daniel to read and write as a boy, and he remained quite fond of her.

"No," Daniel repeated softly, smiling down at Thomas, a note of apology in his voice. Thomas was near enough the age Daniel's son James was when he and the Mendinall brothers were murdered by Indians while delivering a message through hostile territory—an errand Daniel had sent them on. He had no intention of repeating the mistake. Not now, not ever. It was a painful lesson, one he wouldn't make pointless by ignoring.

Sam Boone and William Scholl were talking when Sam overheard the exchange between his son and Daniel. He took a step toward his brother. "Scholl and I will head for the other stations. Wouldn't mind making ourselves useful, and we can still ride fast enough."

Although only a few years older than Daniel, both Scholl and Sam had aged out of militia service, being over fifty. Fact of it was, there were few people who were up in years in Kentucky; the journey to the frontier was arduous and mostly taken up by the young and ambitious, and, seeing as how it had been less than a decade since the first of the settlers arrived, there'd not been time enough for many to grow old, at least as measured by the calendar.

"Appreciate that, Sam," Daniel said.

Sam put his arm around Thomas and led him toward the stables. "Give me a hand gearing up, son." He figured on using the opportunity to explain to Thomas why his uncle had been curt.

Israel was watching, waiting for an opportunity to approach his father for a private word. He handed Jemima her apron and started toward him. William Scholl had the same idea and beat Israel to it; he'd noticed Daniel staring at the Hays cabin and figured the man had something that needed saying.

Israel stopped.

"Shame about Hays," Scholl said as he stepped beside Daniel and nodded toward the cabin.

Daniel grunted. "Most capable man in the settlement," he said after a moment. "I hate to have to ride out without him."

Daniel turned and slapped his friend on the back. "I'd best look in on him, and you'd best hurry to your saddle."

Scholl smiled, tipped his hat, and headed for the stables.

Daniel strode purposefully toward the Hays cabin, leaving Israel watching. Only Jemima noticed.

TWENTY

Saturday, August 17

Daniel had his horse in an all-out gallop right up to the gate of Boone Station, moving so fast the boys who'd been assigned gate duty barely had time to swing it open. Boone shot them a wave as he bolted past. The boys wiped their foreheads, then one smacked the other with his hat, blaming his friend that Boone had caught them not giving the task their full attention.

Once inside, Boone pulled up on the reins. It was early afternoon, and the fort was bustling with activity as his friends and relations hustled to prepare the militia for their ride out the next morning. The sense of urgency with which they went about the work gave Boone peace of mind; there was much to do and only so much he could see to himself.

He'd have preferred to start for Bryan's that evening, but the militiamen in the outlying stations needed time to prepare also, and, although it meant Bryan Station would have

140

to hold its own for another night, arriving in darkness with no cover and no knowledge of the enemy's position was foolishness. There was also the matter of Butler's Rangers.

Rangers were more akin to backwoodsmen than their redcoated comrades; they had good rapport with Indians and weren't prone to lining up on hilltops like apples on a fence rail waiting to be shot at, fighting instead while using the wilderness as cover.

Butler's lot was known for being especially cunning and ruthless. Boone didn't relish the idea of tussling with them, and he certainly didn't plan to do so in conditions that favored the Rangers and their allies. If any significant number of the Indians were Wyandot, as the information from Hay's men suggested, that was added trouble. Wyandot men were fierce grapplers and as deadly with knife and tomahawk as braves from any other tribe, but they also possessed a talent for strategy their fellows lacked.

As Daniel rode further into the station, he could hear Flanders' voice booming enthusiastically from the courtyard. He couldn't make out what his son-in-law was saying, but the tone of it was funny enough to make him chuckle.

Jesse and little Rebecca Boone had been on the lookout for their father and jumped from the porch of the family's cabin when they saw him. Daniel sprang from his horse, opened his arms wide, and hugged the children. They exchanged how dos and he handed them the reins.

"See that the horse gets watered and brushed," Daniel said before starting for the courtyard, "and I'll take some water myself, if you'd be so kind as to fetch it." The children didn't hesitate; Rebecca led the horse to the trough while Jesse darted into the Boone cabin.

Daniel spotted Flanders standing under the pitch pine that had been left in the station's center as a gathering place. Sitting on a stump beside Flanders was Thomas Boone, quill in hand, an empty whiskey barrel in front of him serving as a desk.

"Step this way, men," Flanders was saying, his voice just shy of a yell. "If you miss out on joining your friends in sticking it to the British, you'll have only yourself to blame and a lifetime of regret to comfort you at night while your wife lies with her back to you, ashamed and disappointed."

Folks were too busy to stop and listen at length, but everyone who passed laughed. Daniel shook his head. Flanders was certainly giving a good performance, but that's all it was—every man in the settlement of eligible age and good health would be riding with the militia, so long as they were assured their loved ones would be well-protected while they were away. Putting it to paper was just an exercise in bureaucracy and an imposition. Each man in turn would eventually pass through the courtyard, hurrying from one task to the next, huff, and grudgingly stroll over and scribble his name down.

That said, since it had to be done, it was just as well that Flanders was making it entertaining.

Flanders had protested when Daniel asked that he not sign up, but Boone needed a number of the men to stay behind; there was no way of knowing if the attack on Bryan's was an opening gambit designed to draw the frontiersmen away from their respective homes, leaving the other stations vulnerable. It made the most sense, then, to ask some of the family men to stay behind while the single men, who also happened to be younger in general and would have more stamina for the saddle, rode with Boone. For his part, despite the fact that he had a family himself and was twice the age the men he'd be riding with, Boone was the ranking officer in the area; staying behind wasn't an option. Not that he would have even had it been.

Flanders also had experience protecting a fort during a siege, having been with Daniel at Boonesborough when it was attacked by the Shawnee a few years prior. It helped Daniel knowing he was leaving the station in capable hands, and, with Will Hays down for the duration—he was clearly in worse shape than he let on—Flanders would have to do.

Daniel acknowledged to himself the possibility that he'd asked Flanders to stay because he didn't want to risk Jemima losing him. Jemima was far from fragile, but Daniel's memory of his daughter clinging to him in the days following her abduction had stuck with him. As her trauma eased with time, Jemima gravitated to Flanders. He became the ground upon which Jemima found footing; Daniel had shielded her, but Flanders observed something that Daniel, being her father, couldn't see; he noticed the more control Jemima had of her own life, the more secure she felt, and the more she thrived. Flanders was fine with Jemima taking the reins whenever it suited her, and as the years passed she became his bedrock as well.

A young man named Sam Shortridge passed through the courtyard, his arms loaded with firewood. He paused and shook his head. He then made a beeline for Flanders and shoved the firewood at him, which Flanders grabbed with a grunt. Shortridge reached over, took the quill from Thomas, dipped it in the small vial of black walnut ink that was sitting on the whiskey barrel, and scratched at the paper. Then he handed the quill back to the boy, snatched the wood from Flanders, and continued on his way. He nodded to Boone as they passed each other.

"You're a man of stout character, Shortridge," Flanders said as Sam walked away. Then he cupped his hands over his mouth and hollered into the courtyard, "Unlike some others I could name, them that ain't yet signed up to come to the aid of their neighbors that live down the road a piece!"

Thomas saw Daniel first. It was clear from the dust and sweat that covered him that his uncle had been long in the saddle. Thomas stood, got Daniel's attention, and pointed at the stump.

Daniel rubbed his backside. "Thank you, Thomas, but I reckon I'll stand for a bit." He smiled at the boy. "Perhaps a week or two." Thomas smiled back and reclaimed his seat.

Flanders grabbed the signup list from the barrel. "You must've rode like the devil to get to Bush's and back this quick," he said. "What word?"

"No sign of him," Daniel responded, taking off his hat and pushed back a few strands of hair that had fallen into his eyes.

He'd ridden out to the Bush settlement hoping to enlist the aid of his old friend William, the grizzled backwoodsman who'd been by his side in many a scrape, including Jemima's rescue. But the place was empty and looked as if it'd been that way for some time. Daniel didn't suspect trouble; it was likely as not William was traipsing through the Kentucky woods, the "jungle of luxuriance" as he called it, hunting game, or fortune, or both. Daniel figured it just as well; his motive for seeking his friend was mostly selfish, and William was certainly better off having not been found.

"I hit most of the outposts coming and going," Daniel continued. "Lot of them abandoned—folks having fled back east, I reckon. I suspect some of the remaining men will be joining us, though. I encouraged them to bring their families into the station, regardless."

"Here go, Grandpa," said a voice at Daniel's side. He looked down to see little Jemima, Susannah and Will's daughter. She was holding a tin cup about a quarter full of water and lifting it up to him. Daniel peered back in the direction the girl had come and saw on the ground a splattered trail that was quickly evaporating in the August sun. Jesse had delegated the chore of fetching the water to his four-year-old niece, apparently. Daniel smiled and patted the child on the head.

"Thank you, Jemima," he said. He drank the water down quickly and handed the cup back to her. "Would you take this back to the cabin and tell your Grandma I'll be up soon?"

"She told me to tell you to come on," the girl said.

Boone laughed. "Tell her I won't tarry, then." Jemima nodded and ran off.

Flanders waved the paper he was holding in front of Daniel's face; he was obviously proud of the number of men he'd badgered into signing it. Daniel looked at him, frowned, took the paper, and gave it a quick once-over.

"Respectable," Daniel said. He went to hand it back when something struck him; he paused and examined the page more closely.

"I'm just getting started," Flanders said. Then he thumbed to Thomas. "Although I may have to switch my helper out for a fresh one. Boy's been with me awhile and starting to get a mite antsy."

He patted Thomas on the back. "You're relieved now. Grab your fishing pole and send down your replacement before heading to the creek." The boy took off like a shot. Flanders chuckled. He turned back to Boone and was surprised to find him still engrossed in the list.

"Something wrong, Daniel?"

"Huh? No," Daniel replied. He placed the sheet back on the barrel. "Keep at it, Flanders." Then he turned and started for his cabin.

"Will do," Flanders replied, confused. Then he shrugged and resumed his peddling.

It was a fair assumption that the British and Indians were focused on Bryan's for the time being, so Jemima had taken one last opportunity to venture into the fields just beyond the fort's walls to dig potatoes and pick the few late summer vegetables that hadn't yet been eaten by bugs or deer. She was just passing through the station's gate when she spotted her father. Daniel was marching toward his cabin with a purposeful stride Jemima didn't like the looks of; there wasn't anger in it, exactly, but close enough to it she figured she'd best hustle. She set the vegetable basket on the ground and took off toward him.

His focus was so tunneled that he didn't see her approaching, which was another bad sign. "Pa," she yelled. He stopped then and waited. She reached him finally and played up that she was more out of breath than she actually was.

"Whew, Lord—now why would you make me run like that to greet my own father," she said as she went to give him a hug.

Daniel put up his hands. "I wouldn't do that if I were you," he said. "I'm hot enough to fry an egg on."

Jemima pointed to a tree beside the cabin, a short yellow-wood with a wide canopy, one of the few trees they'd left standing within the palisades for fear an enemy could set them ablaze with flaming arrows and burn the whole station down. "Let's sit in the shade for a bit, then," she said.

Daniel motioned to the door of the cabin with his hat. "I'd best get on in. Your mother—"

"Israel's asleep, Daddy," Jemima interrupted. "Couldn't get out of bed this morning."

Daniel's shoulders dropped and he sighed. "Fever return?"

"Seems so," she answered.

He walked to the porch and sat down on the steps. Jemima sat beside him.

"Whelp. Boy needs to get well, is all." Daniel said, spinning his hat in his hands by the brim. Then he laid the hat on the porch, put his arm around Jemima's shoulders, and squeezed her.

She laughed. "I thought you said you were too hot for touching?"

"Well," he began, "I've cooled a bit now."

TWENTY-ONE

Daniel shook his head. "Nope. That won't do."

"You've gone and lost your mind," said Sam Boone, crouched against the left haunch of a horse, holding up the hoof for Daniel's inspection. The horse's tail swished across Sam's face. He spit. "Looks near perfect to my eyes. You keep up this level of scrutiny, we'll be here till sunup replacing shoes."

"Best swap it out," Daniel said as if his brother hadn't spoken at all. He reached over to the stump where he'd placed his shoeing tools, grabbed the clinch cutter, hammer, and puller, then walked to Sam and tapped him on the shoulder. Sam rolled his eyes. Daniel stepped in, took hold of the hoof as Sam stepped out, and went to work.

Sam plopped down on the stump. He wiped his forehead and sighed. He heard giggling and whipped his head around. His son Thomas and nephew Daniel Morgan stood behind him, trying best they could to stifle their laughter.

"Don't encourage the man. Until he decides he's tortured us enough, you're stuck here same as me. Longer, since he'll be expecting you to pick all the spent nails and clinches out of the grass."

"Sorry, Pa," Thomas said through a chuckle.

It was getting on to four in the afternoon—the heat of the day—and the few small trees in the field didn't offer much in the way of shade. Making matters worse, the rising temperature seemed to be exacerbating Daniel's sour mood. Sam could see something was eating at his little brother—the weight of responsibility, certainly, but there was something else—and whatever it was, Daniel had been kneading it over and over in his mind, hour after hour, wearing his usual good humor threadbare.

Sam looked up at the horse pen across the way, saw there were still six horses grazing and waiting their turn, and sighed. Several of the men had lingered to give them a hand, either from a sense of obligation or a need to keep themselves occupied to avoid thinking about the coming morning. Others had gone to spend what time they could with their families. Sam was of a mind to do the latter; although not riding to Bryan Station himself, his sons Samuel and Squire would be. Yet here they all were, looking over work that had already been done at the insistence of Lieutenant Colonel Daniel Boone.

Making the exercise particularly absurd, all the men in the fort were above average farriers, as were a fair number of the women; it was more or less a requirement for living in Boone Station. Horses were key to survival on the frontier, and Daniel had made a point of prioritizing their breeding and training, making the settlement the best provisioned in Kentucky when it came to horses, relative to its population. Even still, not every horse was ideal to every situation, and an animal with the strength and endurance for farm work might not be the best for riding into a skirmish. Speed was important, certainly, but less so than steady nerves when surrounded by gunfire and the smell of blood, particularly the blood of other horses, which tended to send most into a frenzy.

Most of the men understood this, but Daniel saw now he'd have to cure a couple of their delusions regarding their own animals, seeing to it they traded or borrowed a more suitable mount from a neighbor. However it got done, no man riding from Boone Station would arrive at Bryan's on foot as he'd heard many of the Lexington men had on Friday.

"Isn't that Israel's horse?" Daniel heard an approaching voice ask. "You having to clean up your own son's shoddy handiwork?"

Daniel recognized the voice, so didn't bother looking up.

"Time for new ones, is all," said Daniel as he held up the shoe he'd just removed to examine it. He looked past it to see Peter Scholl walking toward him with his two brothers, Joseph and Abraham, from around the pen. The Scholl boys were peers of Israel's and looked every bit the product of their Dutch heritage, tall and fair-haired.

The rest of the men followed—Samuel Brannon, Charles Hunter, and John Morgan, along with Sam Boone's two other sons and his son-in-law, Tom Brooks—wiping the sweat from their faces and necks. It was clear they'd had enough of tending horses.

"Oh. Well, who's riding it, then?" Peter asked. He smiled and winked at Sam Boone as he said it. The elder Boone looked at Peter and shook his head a little, hoping the boy took his meaning; Daniel could take a needling as well as any man most days, but today wasn't like most.

Daniel chuckled. He tossed the old shoe to Thomas, who tossed him a new one. "Boy's ill, but on the mend. He'll be riding with us. Just letting him rest up. Get his strength back." This sort of teasing was typical of Peter, but Daniel liked him regardless.

"Israel's gonna be ill right up to the time we leave, I suspect," Peter said, "then he'll pop out of bed and run on down to Boonesborough to chase girls while we're chasing Indians."

The eyes of some of the men went wide. Joseph Scholl winced. He'd only recently worked up the nerve to let Levina Boone know his intention to court her, and the last thing he needed was for his brother to rile his would-be father-in-law.

Daniel paused.

"Israel's going," he said after a moment. "Best find someone else's horse to borrow, Peter, unless you're looking for an excuse not to go yourself." He extended a hand toward Daniel Morgan, who reached into the bucket he was holding, pulled out a collection of fresh nails, and dropped them into his father's palm, all while watching for Peter Scholl's reaction.

Peter swung his head from one side to the other, dumbfounded, looking for an answer in the faces of the men.

"Borrow a horse? I just shoed mine not two hours ago."

"Oh, I know you did," said Daniel as he started hammering. "And I could see the effort you put into it. Only you missed noticing that one of the hoofs is infected. Horse won't make it three miles before it's too aggravated to walk." Daniel pointed the hammer at his nephew. "Perhaps young Thomas there would be up for showing you how to spot such things in the future. He's right good at teaching his sisters."

Thomas and Daniel Morgan snorted. Brannon erupted into laughter, followed by Hunter, then the rest of the men.

Brooks, laughing so hard he had to hold his side, slapped Peter on the back with his massive hand. The man turned and glared at him. Peter's brothers were having a particular good time, cackling and holding one another by the shoulder, barely able to keep themselves upright.

Finishing with the shoe, Daniel eased the hoof to the ground, stood, and patted the horse. Daniel Morgan ran over and took the reins to lead the animal back to the stables.

"You fellers are right," Daniel said, tossing the tools to his brother. "We've done enough here. Let's head on up." The announcement made Sam Boone feel like a man reborn. Better still, Peter's ribbing, which Sam feared would lead to a row, had instead cut the tension, putting an end to Daniel's disagreeableness.

The men struggled to collect themselves, some with their hands on their knees trying to catch their breath. Peter stood in the midst of it all, smarting and embarrassed. Smiling, Daniel walked over and put out his hand; his victory had been decisive, and there was no point in continued pummeling.

"Come on," said Daniel, nodding toward the station. "Martha has a good horse, trained by my brother Ned. I'm sure she'll loan it to you."

Peter's brow relaxed. He shook his head, grinned, and shook Daniel's hand. Then they followed the others up the slight slope that led to the fort.

Flanders exhaled, annoyed. This formality struck him as particularly pointless and not particularly fun, likely because it was required. If he skipped it, who'd even know? And of those who knew, who'd care? Well, there was no harm in it, he figured. He cleared his throat.

"I'm supposed to read all these names aloud," Flanders said. There wasn't an audience to speak of, but a few folks were crossing through the courtyard. "If it so happens you've not signed and need to, or if you have and you want to scratch your name off, I'll be leaving the list here."

Those within earshot chuckled, including Daniel and his crew, who'd just returned to the fort; there were only eighteen or so men eligible for the militia in the settlement, so everyone knew more or less who'd signed, who hadn't, and why.

"Let's see," Flanders began. "Samuel Boone. The young one, that is." Flanders looked up at Daniel's brother and winked. Everyone laughed.

"Squire Boone," Flanders continued, then he looked up. "A confession, folks. Those boys signed first because they were sitting beside me at the kitchen table when I first started this sheet."

The crowd chuckled again. Flanders changed his mind; this wasn't so bad an exercise after all. "Daniel Boone, who didn't bother signing, but I put his name down anyway—hope you don't mind, Daniel."

Daniel picked up a stone and thew it at him. Again, everyone laughed. There was getting to be so much laughter that the crowd was growing, with folks coming out of their cabins to see what was causing the commotion.

"I'll take that as a thank you," Flanders said, bowing to Daniel. He went back to reading. "The Scholl boys, although somehow Samuel Brannon managed to squeeze his signature between Abraham and Joseph's, which I can't figure." Brannon started to explain, but Flanders cut him off.

"Sam Shortridge, John Morgan, Charles Hunter, Andrew McConnell . . ." Flanders looked up and over at McConnell.

"Figuring on one last ride there, Andrew? Well, I won't tell if you won't."

McConnell smiled from beneath the ridiculously wide brim of his hat, so wide it could barely support its own weight without flopping, made that way to protect his freckled face from the summer sun. It was true that he was just on the wrong side of militia age, but everyone knew why he was going; Indians had kidnapped his twin sons six years prior, killing an indentured servant of his in the process. McConnell paid a ransom for the boys and they were returned, but he couldn't let it go. He never courted trouble with the Indians, but he also never sidestepped it when it was right in front of him.

"John Searcy, Andrew Rule, and Thomas Brooks, who I practically had to force to sign."

"Some of us had work to do other than running our mouths all day, Calloway," Brooks yelled, his big hands cupped at his mouth to be heard over the laughter.

"That's fine, Thomas, that's fine—you did the right thing in the end," said Flanders. Then he walked to the big pitch pine and tacked the list to the tree with his knife.

He turned back to the crowd and dusted his hands. "Everyone have a good supper," he said. He nodded to Daniel and started toward his cabin to see how his own supper was coming.

The crowd dispersed, and most folks went back to what they'd been doing a few minutes earlier. Only the men who had been with Boone inspecting the horses thought anything of Israel's name not being read, and then only because they knew it was a sore spot for Daniel. None of them knew what to do; they just stood there, immobile and embarrassed;

they felt they couldn't simply wander off and leave Daniel thinking they thought less of Israel, which none of them did.

Sam struggled to think of something to say to his brother. It was plainly obvious that folks weren't expecting Israel to ride with the militia; everyone knew he was bedridden, same as they knew Will Hays was injured, same as they knew Flanders was staying behind because Daniel had insisted on it.

But Daniel didn't see it that way.

It was one thing that Israel hadn't come to find him to help with the horses—the boy truly had been sick, and Daniel didn't begrudge him a reasonable amount of time to recover—but he thought sure Israel would have heard the rumpus Flanders was making in the courtyard at some point in the afternoon and at least gotten out of bed to sign up.

Boone removed his hat. He held it at his side, gripping it firmly by the brim. Peter Scholl walked up beside him.

"I was just teasing before, Daniel," Peter said in a near whisper, a look of honest remorse in his eyes. "Israel's my friend. I wouldn't speak ill of him and mean it."

Daniel put his hat back on. Then he patted Peter on the shoulder and walked off toward the Boone cabin. Daniel Morgan followed after him.

TWENTY-TWO

Israel woke to the smell of fish frying. It didn't turn his stomach; a good sign. He could see the sky out the window from the bed and noticed the sun was low, which, along with the cooking, told him he'd slept the entire day away even though it seemed to him that he'd just closed his eyes. He sat up.

That accomplished, he swung his feet to the floor. He was a touch dizzy, but not nearly as much as he'd been when he'd tried getting up that morning and stumbled before making it to the doorway. He felt a chill but wasn't freezing; again, an improvement. A rush of excitement overtook him, which he did his best to tamp down.

Go easy, he thought to himself. *Even if you don't feel your best when you get to your feet, morning is a long ways off; plenty of time to get up to snuff before the ride to Bryan's."*

Making the tamping all the more difficult was the fact that it was Saturday, and for the last six Saturdays he'd had a standing sunset rendezvous with April beneath the large elm that stood outside of Boonesborough. He thought sure he'd have to skip it this week on account of his illness; now he felt he'd make it.

He placed his hands palms down on the bed to brace himself, then stood. He waited. Okay, so he was somewhat more dizzy than he initially figured and a little queasy, but not so much he couldn't hide it. His mother had a keen eye for such things, but he'd convince everyone she was just being overprotective, and his father would certainly take him at his word that he'd recovered. If he could keep down enough grub to make a decent show of having a meal, that would be proof enough to sway his ma—she wouldn't be happy he was riding with the militia, but she wouldn't make a fuss.

His heart raced again. He was finally going to get his adventure; fate couldn't cheat him out of it this time. The burst of adrenaline made him feel all the more healthy. He took a breath, opened the bedroom door, walked up the hallway, and sprang with measured enthusiasm into the main room.

Which was empty.

There was laughter coming from outside, followed by muted chattering. Israel had expected to see the family bustling about in the kitchen, preparing supper, but turned out they were already eating and doing so outdoors, which wasn't all that unusual in the summer; any opportunity to escape the stuffy cabin was worth taking, so long as the sun was down.

The cabin door had been propped open to let in what little breeze there was, so Israel stepped through it and onto the porch. He could hear plates clanking and people conversing at the far side of the cabin; sounded as if a good number of folks had come for dinner. He decided against wasting energy repeating his theatrical entrance; he'd need those reserves to convince everyone that he was fit for volunteering.

Israel rounded the corner and saw that the gathering of Boones was so large that two big tables had been shoved together to accommodate them all, plus a third consisting of an old cabin door laid across two sawhorses for the youngsters. In addition to the regular members of the household, Susannah and Jemima's families were there, along with Martha and her children, plus Sam and Sarah Boone and their lot. It was quite a crowd. The adults were passing bowls around and across the table as his mother walked over with a giant platter of fish and laid it at the center. The sight and sound of his family, combined with the beauty of the setting sun, made Israel feel nostalgic for something, although he didn't know what, since this life was all he ever knew.

His nieces and nephews were the first to notice him. "Hello, Uncle Israel," they yelled in unison. Israel threw them a smile and a wave.

The adults turned then and greeted him. Israel nodded. His father was seated at the head of the table, little Nathan balanced on his knee. Daniel didn't look up.

"Sleep all day and you still look a mess," observed Flanders as he shoved a piece of cornbread in his mouth.

Israel shook his head. Not the impression he'd wanted to make, but he knew Flanders was just making sport and would have said the same thing even if Israel had looked his best, which he assumed he did not.

Knowing his pa was about to tell him to do so anyway, Thomas Boone, the youngest of those sitting at the adult table, stood up, loaded plate in hand, and offered Israel his chair. The boy had to have been disappointed by the down-grade, but didn't show it.

Israel scratched the back of his head and took the seat. "Appreciate it, Thomas," he said as the boy shuffled away, eating as he walked to no doubt minimize the time he'd be relegated to sitting with the children.

Rebecca reached over Israel's shoulder and put a clean plate on the table in front of him. "How you feeling now, son?" she asked.

"Much better, Ma," he said, casual like, careful not to oversell it. He leaned toward the platter of fish then paused when he felt his mother's hand on his forehead. She held it there a moment.

"Well, you're less warm. That's a start." She smiled, patted him on the cheek, and took her seat. Israel picked out his fish.

He grabbed a piece of cornbread, took a bite before dropping it onto his plate, then looked over his shoulder. "Station's quiet this evening," he said as he chewed. It was so obvious a statement he felt stupid letting it leave his mouth, but he needed to steer the conversation toward the morning and couldn't think of anything better to say. It was true enough besides; neighbors could be seen in the near distance, many settling in for their own outdoor supper. There was a general sense of serenity, as if folks had prepared for the days ahead as best they could and were at peace with it, determined now to enjoy an evening with all their loved ones gathered in the same space, as it was the last such they'd have for at least a few days.

"It was bustling all day up to the moment the dinner bells rang," said Jemima. "I reckon those that've got a hard ride ahead of them in the morning are resting up while they can."

Jemima, you're good as gold, thought Israel. She'd placed the melon on the fencepost, now all Israel had to do was take aim and shoot. He waited a beat, not wanting to seem too anxious, then cleared his throat.

"Israel," Daniel said; there was such rawness in his voice that everyone turned to him. He was staring down at his plate, pushing his food around with his knife and fork. "I didn't hear your name read when Flanders was beating up for volunteers," he continued. "I'd expected to have heard it among the first."

He paused. He didn't look up.

"I am sorry to think I've raised a timid son."

He lifted a forkful of food to his mouth.

The table fell silent. Some kept their heads down, staring at their plates. Others cut their eyes toward Daniel, then Israel. No one moved otherwise.

Israel was stunned. Beating up for volunteers? What was the point of that? There were fewer than two dozen men of age in the station, and everyone of them that could ride with the militia would be doing so. It would've made more sense to have the ones *not* going put their names down.

The world Israel knew a second ago, the world he believed to be real all his life, ceased to exist. Everything he accepted as truth was now in question. Is this what everyone thought of him—that he'd been feigning illness to avoid joining up, when in reality he'd been worried all along that being sick would *keep him* from going? Did they think that little of him? He felt the blush of shame on his cheeks and bile rising in his stomach. He was shaking. Half his mind was encouraging him to explain to his father how absurd the words he'd just spoken were, how wrong he was, and once he understood . . . the other half was all anger and hurt, pushing him to lash out at this man he thought loved him who was calling his character into question with all the family as audience.

Frozen, trapped between the two extremes, Israel said nothing.

"Daniel," Israel heard his mother say, only the sound of her voice was so muted by the blood rushing in his ears he wasn't certain it was her. His vision began to tunnel. He stood, knocking his chair over. Everyone stared at him, even the children at the other table.

He ran into the cabin.

"God's sake, Daniel," Flanders said, standing. "The boy . . . it was written all over his face that he was about to . . . Christ almighty."

Daniel raised his head, looked toward the cabin, then looked down again and continued eating.

Jemima stood and took a step, but Flanders stopped her.

"Best let me go," he said.

By the time Flanders entered the cabin, though, Israel was gone.

Israel strode into the empty courtyard. It was the obvious spot for having men sign the list his father had alluded to, and he felt sure it was still there. It had to be.

Sure enough, he spotted it; pinned with a knife to the pitch pine. Israel grabbed the list and pulled it away, leaving the knife and a scrap of paper behind. He whipped his head from side to side, searching frantically, anger still pounding in

161

his ears; now that he had the damn thing in hand, how was he supposed to sign it? Flanders hadn't thought that through. Typical. Finally, he spotted the small vial of ink left sitting on a stump. The lid had been closed to prevent the contents from drying out and the quill was gone, but the ink was the thing—so long as there was ink, Israel would make it work. He reached up and snapped a low-hanging branch from the tree, then broke a smaller twig from that and plucked the leaves from it; there were any number of dried twigs on the ground at the base of the tree, but he needed a green piece that still had some spring. He pulled his hunting knife from its scabbard, sharpened the end of the twig to a decent point, replaced his knife, unfastened and flipped back the lid of the ink vial, plunged in the twig, slammed the paper onto the stump, and signed it big and bold and messy, making certain everyone who saw it knew the truth—Israel Boone was no coward.

TWENTY-THREE

He rode fast and arrived early. It was reckless behavior considering his general light-headedness and the encroaching darkness, but he did manage to cover the six miles between the station and Boonesborough in impressive time, driven at first by anger and humiliation, then by anticipation at seeing April. It was just as well in any case, as it would give him a few extra moments to collect himself before she arrived.

The rage that had fueled his ride from Boone Station was now watered down by a strange sense of loss; his perception of his father, the unspoken, unquestioned ideal of Daniel Boone, demigod, was gone, replaced by the sobering realization that his pa was just a man, as flawed as any other. Did other people know this? Was he the first to see it, or the last? He felt embarrassment for his father, seeing him brought to ground in such a way.

The night was warm Israel knew, but the chill brought on by his lingering fever kept him from feeling it, and the slight breeze made his waiting beneath the big elm outside the walls of Boonesborough significantly more pleasant than lying in bed in the stuffy cabin. He'd been trying to think of a good way to tell April he planned to ride with the militia in the morning, although he figured once she saw he'd recovered enough to make the ride here she'd come to that conclusion on her own. She'd be none too pleased, but he hoped when she arrived they could hash it out quickly and move on to the business of enjoying each other's company.

He leaned his head against the tree trunk, placed his hands palms down on the cool grass, and, looking up through the latticework of branches, watched clouds pass across the moon. He focused on the sound of the rustling leaves to distract himself from his headache.

"Israel?" He opened his eyes to see April standing over him, hands on her hips. "Israel Boone—did you fall asleep just waiting here for me?"

His heart skipped; every time he saw her fresh he was stunned by how lovely she was. Thinking how she'd risked sneaking out of her parents' cabin without knowing for certain if he'd be well enough to make their appointment made him feel quite impressed with himself. He stood, dusted off the seat of his pants, ran his fingers through his hair, and smiled at her. "I figured I'd best get some rest while I could, April—you have a tendency to exhaust me."

"Or you figured you'd sleep while you could, since you're riding to fight the Indians tomorrow?" April replied.

She gave him a little shove, then marched to the tree and began to climb it. She was barefoot, and Israel watched her lovely toes curl as they gripped the bark. In a flash she was sitting on a sturdy limb halfway up, swinging her legs and looking out into the distance. Israel's mouth went dry. His headache was forgotten. He kicked off his moccasins and started up the tree, but his lack of stamina became apparent right quick; he'd climbed the elm a thousand times living here in his teenage years, and had done so with April recently enough that repeating the task today shouldn't have been difficult, but it was. Waiting, April began to whistle, peeking down at him occasionally to note his progress.

"Whew," he said, letting out a breath as he finally plopped down beside her. "Seems I'm still getting my strength back."

April shook her head.

They took it as a given that the limb would support their weight, as children were known to hang, swing, and sit on it six at a time. The old elm had survived the hard winter of 1779 and no doubt a hundred other calamities over the course of its long life. It was a historic landmark of sorts for Kentuckians, inasmuch as the seven short years since the first of them arrived could be considered history. Representatives from the scattered settlements in the territory held their first conference beneath the big tree before the place they then called Fort Boone even had proper walls. Three years later, after the abduction of Jemima and the Calloway sisters had prodded the residents to properly fortify the place, the Shawnee sieged the fort, and the elm shaded a parlay between the tribe and settlers. Unfortunately, some among the Indians weren't of a mind for peace and began firing on the Boonesborough negotiators, two of whom were Richard Calloway and Daniel Boone. Through some miracle, all of the Boonesborough men made it back into the fort with their lives, although Daniel was later shot in the neck during the course of the eleven day siege. It still ached him on occasion, though not as much as the memory of the court-martial that followed.

Israel ached himself whenever his father spoke on the subject, because he'd not been there for any of it—he was in North Carolina with the rest of the family.

A year prior to the siege, a group of Boonesborough men, including Daniel, had been taken prisoner by the Shawnee while boiling salt at Blue Licks. As the months passed, everyone, Rebecca included, presumed Daniel and the others dead. Her only recourse, she felt, was to move the family back to North Carolina, as Boonesborough had become inhospitable to anyone named Boone; rumor was that Daniel had surrendered the men to the Shawnee without a fight. The Boone name, previously spoken of with admiration, was now being spit from the lips of many with scorn.

Israel hadn't wanted to leave Kentucky, but he was the oldest son and had a responsibility to his mother and siblings. Only Jemima and Flanders stayed behind, weathering abuses both subtle and overt, Jemima refusing to leave if there was the slightest chance her father was still alive.

Which he was. Daniel Boone had a knack for pulling off the improbable.

Thinking about it now, Israel supposed his father wasn't *just* a man after all.

April stared into Israel's eyes; he seemed to be looking past her, his mind adrift. She was giving serious consideration to slapping him when she saw sweat drop from his brow; she glanced up and in the moonlight noticed for the first time that his forehead was damp. Then, when he turned to look out at the horizon, she tilted her head and saw that the hair at the base of his skull was soaked.

She breathed in sharply then caught herself; she'd confided in her cousin Fanny her feelings for Israel, and Fanny advised her that men admired calm in a woman, that there was a fine line between caring for a man in a way he needed and fussing over him in a way he'd find annoying.

April reached up and removed her kerchief, exposing her neckline. Israel noticed and nearly fell out of the tree. Then April touched the cloth to his forehead and began dabbing his brow.

"Oh," Israel said, rolling his eyes up as far as he could to watch her hand. "That's just the fever breaking. It's a good sign."

"Does your father know you're still sick?" April asked. "Or better yet, your mother?"

Israel pondered on how best to respond for a second, settling finally on avoidance.

"You ever heard of a book called *Gulliver's Travels*?" he asked, staring out at the dark woods in the distance beyond the pasture. "My pa reads it over and over. Used to read it aloud to us children when we were little, making funny voices for the different characters. It was just me, Susannah, and James back then . . ."

His voice caught and he paused.

April reached for Israel's hand. She slowly rotated his wrist and placed her kerchief in his palm. He turned his head slightly away from her, quickly put the kerchief to both of his eyes, then turned back.

"Anyway, it's about this fellow, an explorer, who has these fantastic adventures and sees all manner of amazing things in far-off lands," he continued. "I like those sorts of stories. Do you, April?"

"Well, yes," she answered.

"That's good," Israel replied. "So, he's alone on these adventures, Gulliver. All the wonders he's beheld and no one to share the experience with. He has a wife, but she's left

167

behind." Israel turned to April, a sincerity in his eyes she'd not seen before.

"So what I figure is, you and I can work it so we have our adventures together."

April stared at him, stunned to silence.

Israel realized he meant what he was saying, surprising himself. He attributed it to the fever.

Embarrassed, he tied April's kerchief around his neck, placed his palms on the limb, and pushed off, dropping to the ground. He landed, bending his knees low to absorb the impact, then sprang to standing with only a minor wobble that he was quite certain April hadn't noticed. He pantomimed loading an imaginary rifle, aimed into the woods, then pretend fired.

He found that most young ladies were amused by his antics, egging him on with giggling approbation. April was different. She wasn't in the least impressed, and sometimes just up and walked away when he launched into foolishness, forcing Israel to chase after her. It didn't keep him from trying, though, and this time he glanced up and over his shoulder and saw April snickering.

Caught, April cleared her throat and painted her face with seriousness. "Your mother will never let you go if she finds out you're still ill," she yelled down.

"Not let me go?" Israel said, continuing to pretend fire but neglecting to pretend reload between shots. "And risk losing the whole war because of my absence?"

April laughed. "Your father said the British have already surrendered."

"Why, sure—but they'll change their minds, won't they, if they hear I've been yanked from the battlefield." Israel tossed the play rifle to the ground and began swinging an imaginary tomahawk. "We can't have that." He squared up to a nearby tree and flung the pretend tomahawk at it with an exaggerated flourish. "We can't have that at all."

"Israel, I've heard that your brother-in-law . . ." April began, then paused. "What happened when he and his men got to Bryan's didn't sound like a fight. It sounded like it was all they could do to escape with their lives."

Israel stared up at her; must everyone talk of Will Hays and his exploits?

"It won't be like that this time, though," he said. "We're ready for the Indians and those Rangers now we know what to expect. There'll be dozens of us—hundreds, maybe. Will was there with just a few men." Israel's head was starting to hurt again from the strain of craning to look at April on her perch.

The imagery of the two of them in that moment struck April suddenly, and she laughed. "We could be acting out *Romeo & Juliet* just now," she said. "Our families are even feuding. Isn't that something?"

Israel considered it and scratched his head.

"Well, I wouldn't know anything about that, but after I return as a victorious hero you can educate me, my head in your lap, sitting under this here tree some evening."

He lifted his arms toward her and wiggled his fingers. The moonlight made her blonde hair luminous, her skin smooth and angelic. His heart raced.

April looked back toward the fort to make certain no one was watching. Perched as she was she could see quite far, particularly with the moon so bright. Confident they were alone, she turned back toward Israel, smiled, and pushed herself from the limb. She wasn't entirely confident he could catch her without falling himself, and when he managed to she was somewhat disappointed that they hadn't ended up lying in the grass together instead. He eased her to the ground slowly and smoothly, the tips of their noses brushing as she descended. The moment felt fluid, the world around them muffled as if they were underwater.

April looked up at him. The speed with which Israel switched from behaving like a child to behaving like a man surprised and excited her.

"Now I think about it, you might be right," Israel said. "Fighting the Indians is likely to be all kinds of dangerous." He smiling at her. "You best go ahead and kiss me while you can."

She wrapped her arms around his neck and he kissed her, and suddenly the night was warm and the chill brought on by his fever faded. He nearly stumbled. April wondered if his loss of balance was a result of his illness or her kiss. Recounting the moment to her friends the next morning, she told them it was the latter.

TWENTY-FOUR

Sunday, August 18

The sunlight from the window told Israel he'd slept later than he'd intended. It'd been time well spent, though—he felt like a man renewed. He popped out of bed, stretched, and gave his condition an honest assessment. Aside from a slight crick in his neck—he must have slept funny—he felt wonderful; healthy and rested. He pulled on his hunting shirt, leggings, breechclout, and moccasins as quickly as he could manage, happy to be leaving the bedroom behind for good; he'd be back to sleeping on his pallet in the rafters once he returned from Bryan Station.

His mother was standing at the kitchen table, supervising a team of grandchildren as they wrapped bundles of jerky and hard biscuits and loaded them into packs. Rebecca looked up and smiled at Israel as he trotted into the room.

"Well, you're certainly in fine spirits this morning," she said.

He kissed her on the cheek. When he straightened, she put her hands on his face and looked him over.

"You look much better, son," she said. "How are you feeling?"

"Starving," Israel responded, smiling down at her. Then he nodded toward the table. "But not so hungry that I'll be eating any of this, as I expect I'm looking at my meals for the next few days."

Rebecca's stomach went cold and she stiffened. She was fearful of what lay ahead for her son and his father, but the time for expressing her concern had passed. She smiled at him instead. "Your father will be back soon. Best get yourself ready, as you know he'll want to give your gear a thorough going-over. I'll fix you some eggs."

Israel laughed. "My rifle's good and clean, but I suppose I can buff my moccasins."

"You might start with shaving," Rebecca said.

"Pa says you're to come to the house before you go, Uncle Israel," said Susannah's daughter Elizabeth from the table without taking a pause or even looking up from her task.

"That so?" Israel responded. He bent down and put his nose on Elizabeth's cheek. She giggled.

Rebecca pulled four eggs from the basket on the counter. "You go ahead and hurry back."

"Thanks, Ma," Israel said as he rushed through the open cabin door and bounded over the porch railing, ignoring the steps entirely.

Will Hays was standing on the porch of his cabin, watching the buzz of activity as his neighbors prepared to either ride with the militia or send their loved ones to do so. Men from McGee Station, Strode Station, and outposts between had arrived early that morning, each in turn greeted with coffee and biscuits and their horses taken to water; both man and animal had plenty more riding and who knew what all else ahead of them, and needed to be fresh.

Will couldn't shake the guilt that he wouldn't be joining them. He knew no one in the station thought less of him for it, although he was glad that the bandage around his neck served as a visual reminder of the reason.

He spotted Israel walking toward him. They nodded to each other, then Will turned and walked into the cabin. Israel was just bounding up the steps as Will reemerged, rifle in hand.

"Here," Will said. "Take this." He extended the rifle to Israel.

Israel raised an eyebrow, looked down at the weapon, then back up at Will.

"Yours is shite," Will said, by way of explanation.

Israel just stood there.

Will tossed him the rifle. "Go on—take it."

Israel caught it, examined it. The weapon had been freshly cleaned and oiled. He flipped it over and saw the engraving on the opposite side that confirmed what was obvious but he couldn't believe.

"It's yours," Israel said, as much a question as a statement.

Hays walked to the porch railing and stared out. "I won't be needing it," he said. "That is, assuming you boys send the bastards packing back across the Ohio. If you don't, and the Indians and Rangers make their way here . . . well, I can see then how I might regret lending it to you."

Israel paused.

"Thank you," he said after a time. It struck him then that the jealousy he felt toward Will all these years was built on a

173

foundation of admiration, and the wave of that understanding swept away the flimsy structure of his resentment.

He swallowed hard, then chuckled. "Can I borrow your horse, too?"

Will turned to him, eyes narrowed, then turned back toward the common area.

"I'm having second thoughts already," he said. Then he smiled. "Besides, your daddy asked to borrow Stoneheart an hour ago. He's likely saddling her right now."

"Don't that beat all," Israel said, laughing, surprised that Daniel Boone would ask to borrow anything from anyone, and more surprised that Will actually agreed to it.

"Don't dillydally," Will said as he made a shooing motion.

Israel nodded. "Thank you, Will."

He took off toward the Boone cabin, staring at the rifle all the while.

The wound on Will's neck was giving him so much pain that, as soon as his brother-in-law was out of sight and Will knew no one else was looking, he allowed himself to cry a little.

Daniel reached for the long rifle mounted above the fireplace in the heart of the cabin. He stopped, pondered a moment, then reached instead for the smooth bore fowling musket mounted above it.

The Kentucky long rifle was the preeminent tool of the frontier. They were thrice as accurate as a British Brown Bess at four times the range, and, although slower to load than a musket, a practiced backwoodsman (and they were most all of them well-practiced) could load a long rifle with a grease-patched ball so quickly that it made the difference negligible.

That being the case, Boone hardly used the smoothbore. However, it had a feature Boone considered advantageous for the current situation; it could be loaded with both ball and buckshot at the same time, creating a swath of mayhem with each firing. They'd be riding into Bryan's fast, fighting in close quarters, surrounded by the enemy. Better, then, to sacrifice accuracy and range for destructive power.

Besides, Israel's rifle had seen better days; Daniel figured it best to loan him his, especially since he intended to have the boy positioned outside the fray with a group of sharpshooters, laying down covering fire.

Because he's one of the best shots on the frontier, Daniel thought. *Not because he's my son and I'm trying to protect him.*

Daniel laid the gun on the kitchen table where his cleaning implements were spread and began taking it apart. It struck him odd to be in the room alone; the place was most always bustling, Rebecca cooking or knitting, children sweeping or running about, or everyone together at the table breaking beans and peeling potatoes. It unnerved him that the concerns of the moment had so disrupted the routine of his family. He couldn't remember ever having been in the cabin without at least one other person, and was quite sure he didn't like it.

Soon after deciding so, he heard someone running onto the porch and turned to see Israel walking into the cabin. Daniel could tell straight away that the rifle the boy was holding wasn't his own.

Israel gave the room a quick scan, realized he was alone in the cabin with his father, and became immediately uncomfortable. They'd not seen each other since the previous night when his father had embarrassed him in front of the family, and Israel had intended to put off speaking to the man as long as possible, which would have been significantly easier with other folks around. There was nothing to be done about it now though.

Daniel turned back to his work. "Will's rifle?"

"Lent it to me," Israel responded. He walked over and placed the rifle on the table, then pretended to inspect it despite knowing it had just been cleaned and was in perfect working order.

"Nice of him," Daniel said. He pulled the ramrod from the barrel of the fowler and examined the tow he'd wound around the end; looked to be pretty clean. "Your mother left you a plate of bacon and some boiled eggs."

Israel moved to the counter, happy for an excuse to leave the table, and spotted the plate, covered by a dishcloth. He peeled back the cloth and the smell of the food hit him, reminding him how hungry he was.

"You well?" Daniel asked, turning toward his son. Israel's back was to him, though, so he didn't notice.

"Yessir, much better," Israel answered as he tapped the eggs on the counter to crack the shells.

Then it was silent; Israel peeling his eggs, Daniel cleaning his gun. The silence dragged; Israel felt smothered by it. Finally, he heard someone walk onto the porch. Israel let out a breath he hadn't realized he'd been holding.

Jemima entered a moment later. She was carrying a bundle of folded clothing, her own and her children's. Israel supposed she was planning to stay to keep their mother company until he and their father returned.

Jemima spotted Israel, looked him up and down, then walked to the table.

"Ma was right," she said. "You nearly look yourself." She put down the clothes, patted her father on the back, then walked over and put her arm around Israel's shoulders.

"Nearly," she said, smiling. Israel laughed.

"Since I suspect I'm less concerned about you going than our mother but more concerned than our father, I hope you'll consider me a fair judge," she continued. "You seem rested, that's true, but not fully recovered. You should stay. Plenty that needs doing around here. Flanders could use help assigning duties, putting together a watch, and there'll be plenty of Indians to fight in the future."

Israel picked up his plate then ducked and slipped out from under Jemima's arm. He turned and shot her a wink. "That's true of the Indians, but not so the British. They've lost the war—some of them are just too pigheaded to admit it. They'll be packing up and turning tail sooner than later, and I intend to have a go at them beforehand."

He laid the plate on the table and took a seat, more comfortable now that his sister was around, figuring there was little chance of their father starting an argument knowing Jemima might take Israel's side.

"These are Rangers," Daniel said, running a fresh piece of tow down the barrel of the fowler to oil it. "Skilled, disciplined fighters. You'd do well not to be so anxious to square up to them."

Confusion, anger, and embarrassment sprouted up in Israel all over again. Last night his father humiliated him because he thought he *wasn't* going; now he was criticizing him for being enthusiastic that he *was*. What did the man want of him?

Jemima returned to the table and began fiddling with the bundle of clothes, placing herself between Israel and their

177

father. She glanced down and saw Israel's hand on the table, balled into a fist. He picked up his last egg with the other hand and took a bite, figuring he'd be less likely to say something he shouldn't with his mouth full. The dryness of it reminding him that he hadn't thought to get a cup of water before sitting. He chewed for a time, calmed himself, swallowed, and cleared his throat.

"You bringing the fowler figuring we'll be fighting in close quarters?" he asked his father.

Daniel was proud that the boy recognized the logic. "Some of us," he answered. "I intend for you to provide covering fire from a hill with that fine rifle of Will's there."

"The hell I will," Israel said.

Daniel rolled up his cleaning tools, grabbed the fowler, and walked through the door and down the porch steps.

Israel slammed his fist down on the table. He'd had his fill. He stood, walked his plate to the dish bucket, grabbed a cup from the shelf above it, then picked up the water jug. It felt light. He gave it a little shake, then poured most of what remained into the cup.

"I'll fill this before I go," he said, not exactly to Jemima, although she was the only one there to hear it.

"Don't mind him, Israel," Jemima said. "This business with the Indians . . ." she trailed off. "He's not himself, is all."

Israel drank down the water as Flanders walked into the cabin, daughter Sarah in one arm, son John in the other.

"Hoowee, what a commotion," he said as he set the children on the table and kissed Jemima. "How do, Israel?" Flanders said, turning to him. "Figure I'll make some coffee. Want a cup before you go?"

Israel snatched up the jug and marched toward the door. "How you figure on doing that without water?" he barked over his shoulder as he stormed out.

Perplexed, Flanders turned toward Jemima for an explanation. She shook her head and threw up her hands.

TWENTY-FIVE

The twenty mounted militiamen watched impatiently as Daniel fiddled with the straps of his saddle, checking for a third time that his gear was securely tied to Stoneheart. He felt sure he was forgetting something, but couldn't for the life of him figure what.

Then it struck him suddenly, and he turned on his heels and strode back down the line of family members that formed a path from his horse to his cabin.

His relations and neighbors watched with curiosity. Only Will Hays seemed beyond confusion, the one person among them who'd guessed what Daniel was retrieving.

Boone entered the home. There was silence for half a minute as everyone waited. Then he emerged, tying a scabbard to his waist on the side opposite his tomahawk as he walked, the shiny handle of a new-for-lack-of-use military sword protruding conspicuously from the top.

Each man turned to another, then back to Boone; the sight of any sort of formality on the man was completely foreign and somewhat unnerving.

Daniel stopped in front of Rebecca. She was holding Nathan in one arm. Daniel smiled down at the boy and gently touched the tip of the child's nose. Then he turned and caught his men staring at him. Embarrassed, they looked in all directions and began chatting amongst themselves. Daniel turned back to Rebecca and kissed her.

This brought the men back to the matter at hand, and each of the Boone Station riders reached down to their loved ones and began saying their goodbyes. Ephraim January turned to the other four men who'd arrived from outlying stations and waved them forward; they'd performed this ritual with their own families earlier that morning, and he felt it best to give these folks the courtesy of space.

"You've been a lucky man in this life, Daniel," Rebecca said, her free arm around her husband's waist. "Don't choose this as the occasion to push your luck."

"Rebecca, I love you, but luck's had little to nothing to do with it," Daniel replied. He smiled at her. "I'll be careful all the same."

She tugged the brim of his hat over his eyes. He laughed and hugged her. She closed her eyes, an ineffective dam for her tears. When she opened them she saw Israel standing a few feet away, holding the reins of his horse, looking down at the dirt. She released Daniel and offered Israel her hand. He took it and moved toward his parents.

"Look after your father, Israel," Rebecca said. "You know how little experience he has in dealing with Indians."

Daniel laughed and wrapped his arms around them both. Jemima and her family stepped forward, and Daniel kissed his daughter and each of the children while Flanders patted him on the back.

"Don't feel right not coming along, Daniel," Flanders said. Daniel heard in his voice that he meant it.

"Forget how it feels and accept the logic of it," Daniel replied as he shook his hand.

Rebecca pulled Israel aside. "Son, if you're still feeling ill there's no shame in—"

Israel cut her off. "I'm well, Mother." He smiled at her. "Truly." He looked down at Nathan and made a funny face. The child giggled. "But I am happy you're getting a break from fretting over me for a couple of days," Israel continued. "I don't know what you'll do with the extra time."

"I'll do plenty as you well know," Rebecca countered. She tapped him gently on his cheek, which was slightly warm to the touch. She watched him, concerned, as he walked to his horse. He put a foot in the stirrup, looked over, and smiled at her.

She could insist he stay, but this was no moment for causing a scene, and she knew the boy was determined to accompany his father, having waited every moment since that missed opportunity in the summer of 1776 to do so.

Susannah Hays held her two youngest children, William in one arm, Jemima in the other. Daniel kissed his daughter on the forehead, then tickled the children. They laughed. He turned and extended a hand to Will Hays. "It's a good thing I have another son-in-law to hold the fort, what with you injured and having lent out your good rifle," Daniel said.

"Never mind my horse," Hays responded, shaking Daniel's hand.

Daniel said goodbye to Levina, little Rebecca, Daniel Morgan, and Jesse, then swung himself into his saddle.

Israel patted his horse on the neck and glanced over the crowd. He knew April wasn't among them—she wouldn't have been allowed to make the trip to Boone Station by herself in peaceable times, let alone now—but that didn't keep him from hoping. He imagined her there, smiling at him, her lips silently forming the words *I love you* as a solitary tear slid down her cheek, then running for him, unable to hold herself back, yelling his name as he dismounted and she leapt into his arms and they kissed—

He felt a slap on his shoulder.

"Move along, son," Daniel said. His father had ridden right up beside him without his noticing. Daniel leaned in close.

"The sooner we get this over with, the sooner you can ride down and see her," he whispered.

Israel's cheeks went hot. Daniel nodded toward the gate, turned his horse, and was on his way. Israel and the rest of the Boone Station men followed. Relations and neighbors shouted goodbyes. The men yelled back as their horses galloped forward. Somehow, through all the noise, Israel managed to pick out the voice of Will Hays.

"Israel!" Will shouted. "I expect to get my rifle back in one piece!"

TWENTY-SIX

Boone had expected to find Colonel John Todd and his Lexington men waiting for them somewhere along the trail, as it seemed to him best to unite all the Fayette County militiamen for a coordinated offensive. Indeed, there were signs that Todd's group had ridden the trail not long before; but as Boone's men drew closer to Bryan Station with no sign of Todd, Boone began to suspect the worst—that the Lexington men had been ambushed, and he and his riders were arriving too late to prevent a slaughter.

They reached the rise just outside of Bryan's and paused, same as Will Hays and Levi Todd's group had done two days prior. It took all of Samuel Brannon's willpower not to turn tail; he wondered if the other men who'd been here that day felt the same, but the last thing he'd do was ask.

Tendrils of smoke rose in the distance, but all was silent. Boone and McConnell dismounted and crept to the top of the rise. They peered over. Then they turned to each other. McConnell shrugged.

The British and Indians were gone. There was no sign of the Lexington men either; only acre after acre of black, burnt fields, set ablaze hours before but still smoldering. They could see the station in the near distance, but couldn't make out through the smoke if its walls had been breached.

They walked back to their horses. As they mounted, Boone turned to the men.

"Nothing," he said.

He nudged his horse forward and the men followed, moving cautiously over the rise and down the trail. The air was thick with ash and the smell of burnt crops, but preferable to the stench that soon overpowered it—dozens of dead cattle, scattered as far as the eye could see through the smoke, interspersed with the carcasses of hogs and sheep, bloated from two days of exposure to the late summer sun. A number of the men shoved their noses into the crook of an elbow. One or two retched. The only distraction from the smell was the constant need to swat away the flies. Many of the men had seen similar—some when their own farms had been raided—but never at this scale.

They passed the burnt, indistinguishable foundations of what had once been outbuildings—a tannery, likely, a stable, perhaps a smithy—so little of the structures remained that it was difficult to tell. They'd have thought they were riding through Hell, but for one saving grace—they'd yet to see a dead settler.

Finally, they broke through the smoke and saw a dozen or so men and women clearing debris, working outward from the station's charred walls where the destruction was the lightest.

The fort, it seemed, had held.

A boy of around fourteen heard the horses and looked up; he spotted Boone, dropped his rake, and ran to meet him.

"Colonel Boone," the lad said. "My pa is inside with Colonel Todd. He told me to bring you when you got here."

The other settlers paused from their labor, leaning on shovels or setting down wheelbarrows, and waved or nodded to Boone's men. Several of the riders spotted people they knew, friends or relations, and dismounted to greet them.

Boone dismounted himself and shook the boy's hand.

"Henry Craig, ain't it? John Craig's boy?" asked Boone.

"Yessir," Henry responded.

"The men that rushed the gate on Friday as reinforcements—they make it?"

"Yessir."

Boone smiled. "That's good. Well, I reckon I can find your pa and Colonel Todd myself. But if you wouldn't mind seeing our horses are tended to . . ."

"No, sir. Don't mind at all."

"Appreciate it," said Boone. He waved his men forward. "Them that's interested, come with me."

The mood within the station was a defiant rebuke of the grim reality just beyond its walls; every person Boone and his men passed was in high spirits, thankful to be alive and rightfully proud of having fended off the siege. Their good cheer was contagious, and the men were right glad for it.

Boone spotted John Todd, his brother Levi, William Ellis, and John Craig standing in the station's courtyard, surrounded by a surprisingly large crowd—around three hundred people Boone figured, mostly men. After a moment he realized what he was seeing; the Lincoln County militia had arrived as well.

His eyes landed on Stephen Trigg, lieutenant colonel in Lincoln, which confirmed it. He also saw someone else.

Hugh McGary.

Boone wasn't surprised—he knew it was likely as not McGary would arrive with the Lincoln men—but he'd hoped Hugh would have been passed out drunk somewhere and missed the call to arms. But here the man stood, puff-chested and presumably sober, doing a fine impersonation of a man beyond reproach; Boone wondered if McGary felt even the smallest bit of shame over his behavior at the wedding festivities three evenings prior, or if it was simply that he'd been so far gone he didn't recall it. If the latter was the case, Boone was of a good mind to remind him.

John Todd spotted Boone, nodded, then walked to meet him. His brother followed.

John was the older of the brothers by a few years, which was exactly how he looked; difference in age aside, they could have been twins. They shared the same clear sense of morality, but John had a more relaxed manner than Levi and a more apparent sense of humor, which made him better liked. He'd been shot in the leg defending Boonesborough from the Shawnee five years ago and walked with a limp because of it, which he made great effort to hide, the hiding causing him more pain than the wound itself.

"John. Levi." Boone said as he approached. "You boys responsible for scaring off the Indians?"

"Gone by the time we arrived," John Todd answered upon reaching Boone. They shook hands and smiled at each other. Then Daniel turned to Levi and gave a slow nod as acknowledgement of the man's sound leadership two days prior, which Hays had spoken of highly. Levi nodded back.

"Happy to see you, Daniel," John continued. "How many men?"

"Twenty," said Boone.

"Good," Todd said, exhaling. "We'll need them."

Boone decided against asking Todd the same; an overwhelming number of the men he recognized in the crowd were from Lincoln County—well over a hundred of them, if he had to guess. Boone couldn't understand why there were so few from Lexington; had Todd exempted the men who'd fought beside Levi and Will Hays on Friday, or had they refused to return? They'd be within their rights in either case, but having a dozen or so fewer men than they would have otherwise posed a problem, at least to Boone's mind. As things stood, Colonel Todd was ranking officer, and his experience fighting both the Indians and the British was well-known. However, few of the Lincoln men knew him in a personal way, as a friend or neighbor, and convincing over a hundred backwoodsmen to acknowledge a man's leadership, particularly when difficult orders needed following, based on reputation alone could prove difficult.

"Come on," Todd said, pulling Boone back to the moment. "Craig and his people have much to tell, and we'd best get to the nut of it quickly."

TWENTY-SEVEN

Captain John Craig had a well-earned reputation as a stickler for tidiness. Indeed, Boone noted that Craig was the only Bryan Station man who'd taken the time to shave since the siege ended, making the connection between his personal hygiene and the order and discipline he'd maintained within the fort during the attack difficult to miss.

As the residents laid out the events of the siege for the militiamen, Craig acted as master of ceremonies, making certain tales were told without dillydallying and in the order in which they occurred. This made it necessary for Craig himself to do most of the telling, at least to his way of thinking. That was just fine with James Morgan, who was so consumed with concern over the fate of his wife that he was of no mind for talking.

Craig told the story of the raid on the Morgan cabin; how James, seeing no option other than to leave his wife behind for the sake of their baby, had stumbled through the dark forest, child strapped to his back, arriving at Bryan's just before dawn. The enemy was at his heels, so his warning gave the settlers time to secure the gates and post lookouts, but little else. Fresh water would be needed, and lots of it, if they had any hope of withstanding a prolonged siege.

A scheme was hatched; the women of the settlement would venture to the spring some three hundred feet from the station's east gate and collect as much water as they could carry. The hope was that the enemy—who'd already surrounded the fort, but didn't know the settlers were aware of them—would be reluctant to reveal themselves by attacking the women, knowing the station's men could fire upon them from the safety of the fort.

Every woman in the station—settler, slave, and indentured servant—grabbed any watertight vessel they could find. Many of the children were enlisted as well. They then walked in pairs to the stream, casually discussing the weather, crops, and clothing as they went. They calmly filled their buckets, pots, and bowls. Then they stood, turned, and walked back within the fort's walls. Not a one of them flinched.

The militiamen were captivated by the telling, and once it was done they whooped and applauded, bursting with pride and admiration for the women of Bryan Station. Any woman standing next to a man received a solid pat on the back.

Craig allowed the cheering for a moment before putting his hands up to quiet the men. He then urged William Ellis forward to tell of how he and his sixteen Lexington riders had, miraculously, galloped into the station unscathed.

But Ellis wasn't having it. He looked back at his men; if the story must be told, one of them should do the telling. To Ellis' mind, as the man who'd led them, doing so himself lacked humility. It didn't occur to him that the need for humility spoke well enough for the success of the endeavor.

In any case, the youngest of the men was more than happy to give a recounting.

The riders had rushed over the rise, beyond the sight of Hays, Levi Todd, and the rest. As it happened, the Indians were so busy butchering the settlers' livestock for supper that evening that they were caught unawares; by the time they managed to scoop up their rifles and run within firing range, the riders were past them. Lookouts within the station provided covering fire and opened the gate just wide enough for the horses to burst through. To the wonder of all, not a single rider or horse was so much as scratched.

In fact, only two settlers had been killed during the entire course of the siege; one a rifleman who'd been shot through the narrow slot he guarded along the wall, another who was hit by one of the many flaming arrows fired into the fort.

In addition to bolstering the spirits of the residents of Bryan's, the arrival of the riders also increased the number of riflemen within the station by a third.

Although useful details were being garnered from all the storytelling, Boone was struck by the absence of the nugget that was certainly most important. It'd become such a distraction to him that he couldn't listen any further not knowing.

"What's your best guess at the enemy's number?" Boone asked when the young rider had finished and before Craig had a chance to start up again.

"Couldn't say," Craig answered. "They mostly stayed hidden—we only ever saw a few dozen Indians at a time. Mix of tribes to be sure, but under two hundred would be my guess."

"And Rangers?" pressed Boone.

"Never saw a one," Craig said. He glanced back at the crowd. "The Girty brothers were among them, though. Of that we're certain."

Boone expected all eyes to shift to him; it was common knowledge that Simon Girty had befriended Daniel when he was a captive of the Shawnee, a fact that had been presented as evidence against Boone in his court-martial following the siege of Boonesborough. However, it was also true that just last year Simon Girty led a Wyandot attack on the settlement of Daniel's brother Squire, leaving several dead and Squire's right arm shattered by a rifle ball, an injury from which he would never fully recover. For that reason and more, Daniel had no affection for Simon Girty or his brothers, only a history mired in complexity. But such was often the nature of relationships on the frontier.

To Boone's surprise, though, the crowd began to laugh and turn their attention to a muscular young man sitting on a barrel behind them. Even Craig was chuckling. The crowd parted, and Craig waved the man forward.

"Well, come on," Craig said, "You best tell it yourself. I won't be able to do it justice."

The militiamen watched in unified confusion, save for the cavalry who'd ridden into the station with Ellis, who began to elbow their newly-arrived colleagues in the ribs to let them know they were in for a treat. The crowd pushed the young man through, buffeting him to-and-fro with firm pats on the back and head, hustling him front and center beside Craig.

Israel Boone recognized him—Aaron Reynolds. His sandy blonde hair was wild and undone, and he was wearing heavy, intricately stitched buckskin trousers despite the summer heat. Israel smiled and shook his head. The residents were right; this was bound to be good.

Captain Craig put his arm around Reynolds' shoulders, then turned to Todd, Boone, and the other officers. "By last night, it was as clear to the Indians as it was to us that they had no chance of breaching the fort without artillery," he began, "and we would certainly be able to hold out until you men arrived.

"So Simon Girty crawls up on a stump and signals he's got something to say, which we agreed to allow without shooting him. As everyone knows, the man takes great pride in his speechifying, and we were in desperate need of entertainment. He starts his yapping, mentions that many of us know him personally—as if that would help his case—claims they have artillery on the way and we'd best surrender while the surrendering was good, as he couldn't guarantee that he could control the Indians and prevent them from killing us once the walls were shot through with cannonballs.

"He says his piece, crosses his arms—quite proud of himself, thinking his talk has us stumbling over each other to surrender and trust to his mercy—when Reynolds here, having spent the time stacking barrels in a chimney that he could climb so as to pop his head through the top, yells back to Girty . . ." Craig smacked Reynolds gently on the arm. "Go ahead now, son. Just keep it clean where you're able."

The crowd laughed. Reynolds was the most prolific and creative swearer in Kentucky, and he'd apparently made an exhibition of the skill when responding to Girty. He looked at the ground, embarrassed, set his feet shoulder width apart, and cleared his throat.

"Well, anyways," Aaron began. "I says, 'Girty, is it? I have a pair of good-for-nothing dogs, one I've named Simon, the other Girty, because their, uh, backsides remind me so much of you.'" Reynolds looked directly at Boone. "You should have seen him after I said it, sir. He looked as if he'd been smacked straight across the face by his mother."

Boone chuckled. Aaron beamed.

"Then I says, 'We have God's own supply of ammunition and powder, plenty to beat such a sonabitch as Girty . . .'" Reynolds winced for letting that one slip through. But when he glanced at the crowd, no one was looking at him as if they were scandalized—indeed, they seemed quite captivated—so he pushed on. "'But if you or any of your, uh, naked rascals get into this place, we won't even bother using it—we'll thrash you out with switches we've gathered for that very purpose, for you ain't worth wasting good powder on.'"

Cheering and clapping erupted from the crowd. Aaron, his confidence buoyed, began to strut from one side of the audience to the other.

"'We've got reinforcements coming ourselves,'" Reynolds continued, his voice booming now, "'and if you and your gang of murderers stay here another day we will have your scalps drying in the sun on the roofs of these cabins.'"

The crowd roared. Hearing of Simon Girty being thrashed in a duel of oratory was a tale in which every settler could find satisfaction.

Israel turned and saw Captain Robert Patterson shaking his head with disapproval yet smiling despite himself. Many of the Fayette County men had served under Patterson in one excursion or another; Israel and Reynolds had met during one such jaunt earlier that year. Reynolds cussed and cut up throughout, and Patterson, despite being famous for his patience, tired of the behavior a few days in. But rather than censure Reynolds, Patterson made him a bargain; if he quit swearing for the duration of the expedition, Patterson would gift him a quart of liquor. They shook on it. When the conditions were met, Reynolds received his payment.

As the laughter continued and folks circled around to pat Reynolds on the back, something caught Boone's ear. He turned. In the distance, one of the boys who'd been guarding the main gate was yelling out and rushing toward them. Colonel Todd heard him too, as did Israel, but they couldn't make out what the boy was saying. As he drew closer and the crowd quieted down, they understood.

"Rider!" the boy was yelling. "Rider approaching!"

TWENTY-EIGHT

The settlers rushed to the gate. Some men broke off and headed for rifle positions along the wall on the chance the single rider became many and turned out to be hostile.

It was well-known that Boone could distinguish a white man from an Indian—could even distinguish Indians by tribe—at a great distance, so when the crowd pooled at the threshold, Boone was ushered to the front.

He squinted. The corn and hemp fields still smoked, but he spotted the rider through the haze. The first thing he noticed was the man's horse—an Arabian. He recognized the breed, having seen them brought in from Europe while in Richmond. Impressive animals, swift and powerfully built. He'd never known of one in Kentucky, although he'd heard tell . . .

The rider was dressed in black. He wore a short cloak which billowed as he sped down the trail, revealing a deep red lining. The fellow didn't fit at all with the backdrop of the wilderness; he didn't seem out of place so much as unintegrated, existing solely unto himself. The thing of it was, Boone couldn't figure where the man would fit any better.

He smiled.

Never let it be said the man was bashful about being conspicuous, Boone thought.

Boone turned and worked his way through the crowd back into the fort. Everyone watched him, perplexed. Israel stood in the rear, equally confused. Daniel nodded for him to follow as he passed.

Colonel Todd surmised that Boone had identified the rider and assessed him as friendly. Todd was curious as to the man's identity, but not so curious as to ask Boone outright and make his curiosity plainly known. So he kept looking, trying his best to suss it out for himself. Hugh McGary was too frustrated to give the matter as much consideration.

"Well, who in hell is it?" McGary asked as Boone walked past him. But Boone kept right on going, and McGary and everyone else turned back toward the rider and squinted.

A few stragglers running for the gate passed Boone and Israel as the two walked into the courtyard. Daniel plopped down on a log, reached into his rifle bag, and grabbed the well-worn river rock he kept for sharpening his hunting knife. He looked up at Israel and patted the log, directing his son to sit. Israel did so as Daniel went to work sharpening the blade.

Moments passed. Finally, Israel heard relieved chuckling and how dos from the gate. Folks began to file back into the fort, smiling. The rider appeared, flanked by the Todd brothers, who were laughing and patting the man on the back.

Boone stood, dropped the rock back into his bag, sheathed his knife, and walked toward them. Israel recognized the rider an instant later and jumped up to follow. The man, speaking to Colonel Todd, stopped mid-sentence when he sensed the Boones approaching.

"John," Boone said, looking up at the man and offering him his hand.

"Daniel," John Floyd said in return, giving Boone's hand a firm shake. Colonel Todd thought they looked a pair; Floyd had a good six inches on Boone in height, Boone about the same on Floyd in build. "Been a while," Floyd continued. "What news?"

"Let's see . . ." Boone began, placing his hands on his sides and straightening his back. "Jemima and Flanders married. I was taken prisoner by the Shawnee a few years back, adopted into the tribe as Chief Blackfish's son, replacing the very son I killed that day we rescued Jemima and the Calloway girls. Lived with the tribe for a time before escaping to warn Boonesborough that the Shawnee planned to attack. Helped defend the fort, after which Richard Calloway accused me of conspiring with the Indians. Faced court-martial, found innocent, for innocent I was, and was promoted to major as evidence of the fact, now lieutenant colonel. Oh, and Rebecca had a baby a year back. We named him Nathan." Boone figured that last bit of information would throw Floyd, but the man didn't flinch. "Yourself?" Boone asked.

Floyd took off his hat and began to brush the dust from it. "Became a privateer," he began. "Taken prisoner at sea by the British, then dragged across the ocean and thrown in an English jail. Escaped to France after a time, gained passage back to Virginia. Returned to Kentucky to pick up life where I left it, only this damn war refuses to end, making that difficult." He put his hat back on. "Oh, and acquired a wife and child along the way."

Boone raised an eyebrow. "That all?" he asked.

Both men laughed. They hugged, patting each other on the back. Then Floyd turned and extended a hand to Israel.

"How are you, Israel?" he asked.

"Just fine," Israel responded, shaking Floyd's hand. He felt immediately that he should say more, but couldn't for the life of him think what.

TWENTY-NINE

"Gentlemen. Each minute we debate is a gift to the British," Colonel Todd announced. "Let's settle this quickly."

The militia had gathered by the spring on the station's north side, the officers in conference at the end nearest the fort's rear gate, the rest of the men a short distance downstream watering and readying their horses. The trees along the bank provided some shade, and the location was blissfully upwind of the slaughtered livestock on the opposite side of the station.

Boone knew the militia was top-heavy, but seeing the officers now, segregated from the rank and file, made the absurdity of the imbalance plain; twenty-seven officers to one hundred fifty-five regular militiamen.

No good could come of it.

"Colonel Logan is on the way," said Lieutenant Colonel Trigg as he soaked his cravat in the cool spring, wrung it, and wiped the back of his neck. Trigg was blonde and trim and, at thirty-eight, slightly older than the other officers (aside from Boone), though no one would guess it by looking at him.

"He was well to the south last I heard, but he'd already gathered a good number of men to respond to the attack at Hoy Station."

"Folks say your friend the Raven was spotted near Hoy's around the time of the attack," Captain Allison said, turning to Boone. Allison was a tall, narrow-faced man with close-set eyes who served under McGary. He stared at Boone as if challenging him to dispute the statement.

Boone put his foot on a stump and rested his forearm on his thigh. "Folks are mistaken. Savanukah was at Boone Station round about then, a guest of my family." He turned his head and spit. He'd have to talk to his men; they'd back up his story, but they needed to know what that story was.

Allison cocked his head to the side and opened his mouth to speak, but Trigg beat him to it.

"Anyway," Trigg began, anxious to finish the point he'd been midway through making, "as soon as my courier reached the colonel to tell him of the situation here, Logan needed only to shift his destination. I suspect he and his men will be here by morning."

"Too late to stop the Indians from crossing the Ohio," Major Todd responded, more sting in his voice than Boone would have expected from Levi when addressing a friend.

Sure enough, Trigg was taken aback. "Could be," he said after a moment. "But our forces would be doubled. Tripled, perhaps."

"Logan's men would have quite a few miles under them by then, though, and would likely be quite exhausted," Levi said, some sympathy for Trigg slipping into his voice.

Ah, now Boone understood Levi's game; as second in command in Lincoln County under Logan, Trigg was in a mental tug-of-war, caught between his loyalty to the chain of command and his friendship with the Todds. Levi needed to pull Trigg toward their way of thinking, and had to start with that first firm tug to uproot the man's feet.

"Difficult to do arithmetic when you don't have the figures," Major Bulger said. Boone had hunted with Bulger and found him skillful and competent. Like Trigg, Bulger was in his late thirties, smack between the ages of the other officers and Boone. He had a large nose and big ears, not so sizable as to be humorous, but big enough to speak of.

"I'd assess the enemy's number inconsiderable," responded Captain Craig, pulling his shoulders back as he said it. "Sure, they hooted and hollered to make it seem there were a good many of them, but there's little chance we could have held out as we did—or that they'd be running now—if there were more than a couple hundred."

"Assuming escape is their aim," Major Harlan interjected. "Might be they're hoping we pursue. Might be they're meeting up with a war party somewhere up the trail, the plan all along being to draw as many of us as possible into an ambush, just as they did at Hoy's."

Boone didn't know Silas Harlan personally but decided then and there that he liked the man. Harlan wasn't quite thirty but had an innate gruffness that gave his words a ripeness they hadn't had time to come by naturally, although they did have the weight of his reputation behind them; it was said that George Rogers Clark, brigadier general in Kentucky, under whom Silas had served during the Illinois campaigns, considered Harlan one of the best soldiers to ever fight at his side.

"The more the merrier, if that's the case," Colonel Todd said.

The comment struck Boone like a bolt. His eyes darted to Floyd, who was standing alone at the edge of the stream. Floyd returned the look. Todd had a tendency for recklessness that he sometimes confused with bravery, and Boone sensed that impulse on the rise within the man.

"Colonel, there's more here to consider than numbers, as your own brother can testify," Major Bulger said, thumbing toward Major Todd. "The British in discussion here are Butler's Rangers. A single one of them is more trouble than a dozen redcoats. Let's not forget what they did to Colonel Crawford and his men."

This was no trivial detail, and Boone inwardly commended Bulger for mentioning it, as it brought down the temperature of the conversation.

"All the more reason to pursue," Major Todd said a moment later. "It's likely William Caldwell is with them; the very man responsible for Crawford's torture. Would we allow so brutal a murderer, a band of murderers, to escape when it's within us to prevent it?" He pounded his fist into the palm of his other hand. "Do we suppose that would encourage such men to be less brutal in the future?"

Boone considered Levi's perspective invaluable. Craig and the residents of Bryan's had survived the enemy, but without direct confrontation; Levi Todd was the only man present who'd engaged them outright. But that same experience seemed to have unsettled Levi, which had to be taken into account.

"There's also Anne Morgan to consider," Captain Craig said, pointing downstream toward John Morgan, who was packing borrowed gear onto a borrowed horse. "We put her in further jeopardy every moment we delay."

No one argued against the point.

"Well, Floyd?" McGary said. "You're the big man here. Anything to contribute, or you just come to watch?"

Floyd was crouched by the stream, filling his canteen. He stood, took a swig, then turned and stared at McGary, saying nothing.

Moments passed. Finally, not knowing what to make of Floyd's seeming indifference, McGary huffed, waved his arm toward Floyd, and turned away.

Boone, though, had to admit that he had wonderings similar to McGary's. Not concerning Floyd's silence; the reason for that was plain enough—although both Floyd and Todd were colonels, Floyd, for all practical purposes, ranked just below General George Rogers Clark where Kentucky was concerned. Anything he said, even if spoken in agreement, would undercut Todd's authority.

But why was Floyd here, alone, far from Jefferson County? Floyd said he'd learned that a war party was gathering across the Ohio—from Catawba spies, most likely—but hadn't been told when or where the force would strike. He then rode to Lexington to warn Todd, but was told upon arriving that the attack he feared was coming had already occurred here, at Bryan Station. So on he came. The fact that he'd done so alone spoke volumes; it meant that General Clark didn't give Floyd's information much credence, and that Floyd was here in an unofficial capacity, acting less as a military colonel and more as a friend.

As for silence, Boone had decided it best to keep his own mouth shut. It was widely known that he cared little for Logan, as the colonel had joined Richard Calloway in calling for Boone to be tried for treason following the Boonesborough siege. That in mind, the other officers would likely not give much credence to Boone's opinion that Logan was an arrogant simpleton.

John Todd, on the other hand, was a man Boone trusted. The two had fought and bled together. True, Todd could be brash, but that worked in his favor as often as not. Adding Logan's men to their number would no doubt add to their strength, but what good were a hundred or even a thousand more men when led by an incompetent fool, or if there were no enemy to fight by the time those men arrived? No, Boone decided; he'd keep his thoughts to himself unless opinion began to swing in the wrong direction.

"Logan is a twit of low character and even lower judgment, and his arrival would offer nothing more than to serve up his men as additional targets for the Indians and British," Boone heard himself say aloud.

Bulger, who'd been in the process of making some point or another, put a period on it and turned to Boone. The other officers did the same.

Colonel Todd nodded. This had been his concern, although he'd been reluctant to express it himself, not wanting to come across as self-serving. Once Colonel Logan arrived, the man would sure as sunrise make an argument for taking command based on numbers alone, as the vast majority of the militiamen were from Lincoln County. If Logan were the superior leader, that would be one thing; but self-serving or not, Todd didn't see it that way.

As debate continued among the officers, Colonel Todd turned toward the men gathered downstream. Not a one of them cared a whit about soldiering, despite many of them having that experience. They were expert hunters and woodsmen, courageous and industrious. They were also, almost to a man, the best marksmen in the country.

But what they weren't was patient and disciplined. Authority, to the extent they conceded to any, was gifted and done so tenuously, and could be withdrawn on a whim at the slightest perceived infraction. Rugged independence was their nature. It had to be.

Todd calculated that if he agreed to wait for the arrival of Logan it was likely half the men would throw up their hands and return to their families and responsibilities, and the other half would ignore the order and rush ahead to engage the Indians anyway. Better to begin the pursuit now, gaining knowledge of the enemy along the way, adjusting strategy as necessary. They could always pause for Logan further up the trail.

Todd was about to present his decision when McGary kicked at the dirt.

"By Godly, if Trigg won't say it, I will!" McGary yelled. "We Lincoln men trust Logan's leadership. And numbers is numbers! The more men we got, the easier the victory. That this is even in debate is stupidity!"

And just like that, any rational argument for waiting was lost. McGary was speaking to the group, but his wild, bloodshot eyes were fixed solidly on Daniel. All present now understood McGary's desire to wait for Logan was largely based on their mutual dislike of Boone—his hatred of the man was as palpable in that moment as the humid summer air.

Boone held his temper as everyone else held their breath.

"I'm surprised at you, Major," Colonel Todd said. He knew that if he didn't assert his leadership now, he'd never again have opportunity. "You're the last man I'd consider for giving wise council, but also one of the last from whom I'd've expected timidity."

A chill descended on the group, passing through each man from head to foot in an instant. McGary's head snapped toward Colonel Todd. He was hunched like a madman, both fists balled. Todd stood stock-still and straight, his eyes fixed on some point just above McGary's head. McGary's eyes grew wet, and this taut, animal posture slowly morphed into a shamed slump. His fists relaxed.

All save Colonel Todd turned away slightly, embarrassed. Hugh had been cowed, and all the officers, in that moment, pitied him. Even Boone.

McGary shot upright, sniffed the snot back up his nose, and released a primal growl. Then he turned and stomped off toward the militiamen downstream.

"Ready your men," Colonel Todd said to the other officers as they watched McGary recede into the distance. "Pursuit begins immediately."

Todd turned and started for the fort. Boone thought sure the man's limp was more pronounced now than it had been previously.

THIRTY

"I can muster some men to join you," Craig said. He was standing with Colonel Todd at the head of the militia in the field by the spring as the men with their horses divided into companies under their respective captains.

Todd examined his saddle straps. "That won't be necessary. You and your people are exhausted," he responded, which Craig understood to mean that Todd considered the Bryan Station men too worn out to be of much use. "You've quite enough work on your hands here besides."

Craig rubbed his chin; the man wasn't wrong. Just thinking about the destruction on the other side of the fort and the effort it was going to take to make things right tired him.

"James Morgan will insist on joining you on account of his wife," Craig said after thinking on it. "And Aaron Reynolds . . ."

"I wouldn't deny Morgan," Todd said. "He and I have discussed the matter. And Reynolds I'll take—he seems to have energy and spirit enough."

Craig snickered then walked off to tell Reynolds he'd be going and to assure the other Bryan Station men that they would not.

Todd turned to give his horse a final once-over—a tall, white Quarter Horse, nearly seventeen hands high—and caught Boone approaching out of the corner of his eye.

Up until this morning, he hadn't seen Boone in quite some time. Much had changed, and much hadn't, which was Todd's concern. Both men had been captains in the days they'd lived and fought together in Boonesborough, with Boone the fort's ranking officer. But as the years unspooled, Todd surpassed Boone in rank, whether from Daniel's lack of concern for such things or lack of political connections, Todd didn't know. Both, likely. Whatever the reason, Todd was now the commanding officer of a frontier legend. He found it disquieting.

"Colonel," said Boone once he was close. "A moment?"

"Daniel," Todd said. "Concerns?"

"None newly arisen, no," Boone said. "I just figured you should have this." He held out his sword, secure in its scabbard, for Todd to take. "I noticed you were without. Figured if there's just the one among us, it should be worn by the man doing the leading."

Todd hesitated, then reached out slowly and took the weapon. He grabbed the handle, unsheathed the sword partway, and inspected it.

"Thank you, Colonel," Todd said as he tied the scabbard to his waist and nodded. "I'll return it soon as this is done."

"I'm counting on it," Boone replied with a smile. Then he turned and walked back to Stoneheart.

The transaction struck a curious chord with the men who happened to witness it, triggering an emotion in them they couldn't put a finger on; they had little affection for military ceremony, but seeing Daniel Boone participating in it lended legitimacy and heft to the concept.

Israel Boone was gobsmacked. He knew the sword held importance for his father, although it struck him suddenly that he didn't actually know how he'd come to acquire it; the man hadn't offered up the information, and Israel had never thought to ask. A vague recollection from his childhood struck him. He seemed to remember overhearing a guest, he couldn't remember which, sitting with his parents at the kitchen table after dinner, telling of how Daniel had won the sword in a shooting contest as a young man in North Carolina. But tales of Daniel winning shooting matches were plentiful, and was it the sword he'd won this particular time, or a hunting knife? Israel couldn't recall.

Lost in thought as he was, Israel didn't notice Aaron Reynolds sidling up beside him, holding a stick of jerky and tearing off a bite with his back teeth.

"Heard an Indian called out your pappy while each stood on opposite ends of a rope bridge spanning a ravine," Reynolds said out of the side of his mouth. "Each shed his gear, then they charged each other, and your pap threw the Indian over the side to his death. When he collected the Indian's belongings he discovered the sword, the Indian having taken it from a British officer he'd kilt previous."

Israel squinted. He watched as his father swung up onto Stoneheart at the head of the company.

"Nah," Israel responded without bothering to look at Reynolds. "That ain't how it happened."

Only he wasn't so sure.

THIRTY-ONE

Caldwell rode, posture straight and tense, seething silently in the saddle. He'd only lost five men in the failed siege, all Indians, but would have sacrificed ten times that number for a successful outcome. Hell, he would have sacrificed the entire lot of them.

They'd seeded fear in the minds of the Kentuckians, certainly, and his superiors might consider that success enough, but Caldwell couldn't care less for half measures that gained only psychological currency; he craved decisive victory in the here and now. Anything less, for a Ranger, was disgrace.

Worse, attacking that pitiful station had been a concession, an eleventh-hour pivot after Caldwell's plan to march on Wheeling had crumbled.

Caldwell had invested years as an officer in the British Indian Department, establishing lines of communication with the tribes, gaining their trust by making bargains that tilted in their favor and embedding himself in their culture. But the eleven hundred Indians he'd spent the last several months priming for war lost all enthusiasm when their scouts

211

arrived at Chillicothe reporting that General Clark was preparing to lead an invasion force from Louisville to the Indian towns on the other side of the Ohio. The information proved erroneous, but the damage had been done; two-thirds of the braves Girty had roused for world conquering just days before simply walked away, returning to protect their homes from a phantom threat. Left with just over three hundred Indians, six—or five, rather—redcoats, and his fifty Rangers, Caldwell was forced to select a smaller target.

And yet, even the backwoods churls of Bryan Station had managed to hold his men at bay. Caldwell's superiors had refused him artillery, likely because they doubted even Girty, for all his bravado, could talk the Indians into dragging the equipment for miles through the thick wilderness. Indians made for stealthy soldiers, moving more like deer than men, but that speed came largely from carrying few provisions. Time and attention were wasted gathering, hunting, and preparing food, as was apparent when the rebel reinforcements slipped past the Indians and galloped, unscathed, straight into the fort.

Now that the engagement was over and an unknown number of Kentuckians were on their tail, the Indians were impatient to return to their homes, content with the horses they'd pillaged, the leather they'd stolen from tanning vats, and the good meals they'd managed from the settlers' crops and livestock. So impatient, in fact, that several dozen had slunk away from camp the night before, deserters, leaving under the cover of darkness to avoid Caldwell's fury.

Caldwell both despised and admired the braves for having no embarrassment for their lack of ambition, no shame in retreating from failure.

But was it a retreat? Since leaving Bryan's, Caldwell had been pondering a strategy for making the campaign a success— as he defined success. It was why he'd decided not to follow the same route out of Kentucky that they'd taken into it, much to the dismay of his subordinates.

Caldwell raised his arm and waved a finger, signaling Captain Elliot to ride forward.

Sir?" Elliot asked. Caldwell thought Elliot a good officer, although he found that the genuine affection Elliot held for the natives clouded his judgment.

"Bring Girty forward," Caldwell said without looking back.

"Which of them, sir?" Elliot asked.

Caldwell sighed. "The one that matters."

Caldwell made a clicking sound with his mouth and his horse trotted ahead, making it clear to Elliot that he had no further interest in answering stupid questions.

"Yes, sir," said Elliot, mostly to himself.

Caldwell heard the heavy hoof falls of a horse racing up behind him and the voice of Simon Girty barking at anyone he perceived as being in his way. Girty had been in a foul mood since being verbally bested by the young man at Bryan's two nights ago, which was the one crumb of satisfaction Caldwell had extracted from the debacle.

Girty's horse galloped forward, destined for a collision with Caldwell in a matter of seconds. Caldwell knew it was a power play, that Girty was hoping he'd be frightened into clearing the path. But Caldwell didn't flinch, and his battle-tested horse continued on, unfazed.

Disappointed, Girty pulled back on the reins; his horse slowed abruptly, kicking up dirt and rocks, then jerked right and slid up beside Caldwell's horse, matching its pace. Caldwell shot Girty a glance. The white Indian was staring at him, a wide, mirthless grin on his face. Caldwell turned away, disgusted that he had to deal with such a foul creature. He despised Girty more with each passing day; the man was coarse, undisciplined, and unpredictable. Unfortunately, he was also necessary.

"Enjoying the ride, Captain?" Girty asked, making a show of straightening himself and staring forward to mimic Caldwell.

Caldwell took a breath to calm himself. "You know these woods well, Girty?" he asked after a moment.

Girty placed his hand over his heart. "Your king pays me to know them. Pays me well, in both coin and fine clothing." He tugged the lapels of his bloodstained red coat, the coat he'd stripped from Private Becker's body. "So, yes," he continued, his smile fading, his eyes narrowing. "I know these woods."

A horse approached behind them. Neither man turned to look—they just stared at each other. When the rider was close, he slowed the horse and pulled up on Girty's right. It was Elliot, finally catching up after Girty had sped off and left him down trail.

"The Kentuckians are surely in pursuit by now," Caldwell said to Girty, paying Elliot no mind.

"Of course," said Girty.

"How many would you assume?" Caldwell asked, clinching his jaw.

Girty scratched his chin. "No way to know just yet. There aren't as many white men in Kentucky to fill out a militia as there used to be, thanks to the work of these fellers and their like," Girty thumbed over his shoulder in the general direction of the Indians following behind them, most of whom were hidden in the surrounding woods, "largely encouraged by you and your like." He winked at Caldwell.

"Those boys have been either running the settlers off, or . . ." Girty stuck out his tongue and pantomimed scalping himself. Then he faced forward and stuck his nose in the air. "There will also be fewer than otherwise because of that little distraction I arranged to the south . . ."

Caldwell's head whipped to Girty. Simon smiled. Caldwell cursed himself for giving the man the satisfaction of a reaction.

"Oh. You didn't realize Hoy Station was my idea?" Girty said, feigning injury. "Whew. That explains why you hadn't thanked me. I was beginning to feel hurt." He examined his fingernails. "That little production sent the majority of the Lincoln County militia scurrying in the wrong direction. They'll be at least a day behind however few ruffians the local leaders managed to scrounge up."

Elliot cleared his throat, then leaned forward in his saddle to look past Girty for a clear view of Caldwell. "I ordered our rear scouts to hang back a mile or so, Captain," Elliot said. "They'll know how many Kentuckians are following us on the chance they ever get that close."

Girty leaned forward, filling Elliot's field of vision. He stared at him and smiled. "And I ordered my scouts to conceal themselves just outside Bryan Station. One of them will ride like his life depends on it to catch up and let us know how many militiamen there are and how far behind."

Elliot sat up straight again. Girty matched the movement, never taking his eyes off of him, smiling all the while. "Another will ride just ahead of the Kentuckians to keep

215

track of their movements, sending word to me—that is, to us—regularly."

Caldwell grunted. He was impressed, but there was no reason to let Girty know it. "Well, assuming the militia can follow our trail up till now—"

Girty laughed. Hard. It went on for some time.

"They want to follow us, they won't have trouble doing so. There are white men hereabouts who can track as well as any Indian. If Boone is among them . . ." Girty wiped tears from his eyes. "You asked if I knew these woods? Boone knows them as well as he knows the faces of his own children. Better, likely. Yep, they'll be on our trail certain, which I assume is your aim, Captain. That's why you started us down a different path when we left camp—the landscape upriver's not particularly well-suited for ambush."

A smirk crawled across Caldwell's lips. "And how do you find this route for such a spot?"

"Why, I find it ideal," Girty responded. "Cuts right near a place Boone himself is very familiar with, which will add to the fun."

Caldwell's smile vanished. "We fight to win, Girty. Not for your amusement."

Girty brought his horse to a full stop. Surprised, Caldwell instinctively turned to face him. Girty stared at Caldwell, blinking, concern painting his face.

"Well, who in hell is amused by losing, Captain?"

Girty turned his horse and galloped back down the trail, forcing the Rangers in his path to pull to one side or the other to allow him to pass. Caldwell now understood why Girty rode in the rear—it allowed him to get information from his scouts without anyone overhearing.

Damn the man, Caldwell thought.

He cracked his neck, trying to calm himself. Then he turned and looked to his left.

"And you, madame?" Caldwell began. "Would you rather we pause and greet your men, or hasten on to Chillicothe and whatever fate awaits you there?"

Anne Morgan looked up. Her hands were bound together with rope, the other end of which was tied to Caldwell's saddle. He hadn't decided what to do with her, whether to take her to Detroit to be held as a chit for the British, or give her to the Indians to be ransomed or adopted into one tribe or another. Adoption was the least likely prospect, as women were in greater supply than men, braves having been lost in battle or through some form of male recklessness—a malady common to all tribes and races.

Anne was dirty and exhausted, her eyes empty; she was beyond feeling frightened now, beyond feeling much of anything. She hung her head again, staring at the ground as she walked.

"Yes, think it over," Caldwell said. "You've plenty of time."

THIRTY-TWO

The militiamen rode out of Bryan Station in late morning, the day already blazing hot. They passed again the slaughtered livestock, the burnt and uprooted crops, the smoldering ashes of fences and outbuildings. Several in the militia had been involved in campaigns led by General Clark where similar tactics had been employed against Indian villages, and many of them felt a wave of shame now, fully understanding the destructive consequences of their actions for the first time. Others understood it as a strategy of war like as any other, dirty but effective, the revenge they sought now part of the same cycle. Those who had never been on the receiving end or involved in the commission of such actions simply felt despair which they repurposed as a thirst for retribution, as that was of more use to the task at hand.

Most all the residents of Bryan's were outside the fort as the militia left, doing what they could to clear debris and set things right. A team of men, their mouthes and noses covered with rags to cut the stench, struggled to load the cattle carcasses into carts for disposal further from the fort. Up a hill in the near distance, the riders saw men shoveling in what they figured to be the station's cemetery, digging graves for the two men who had been killed in the assault.

Instead of improving as the morning progressed, the crick in Israel's neck had gotten worse. It was throbbing and constant now, and the relentless beating the sun was delivering wasn't helping none. It seemed to take forever to cross the wide clearing that spread out from the fort, and Israel was never more thankful for shade than when they finally entered the lush canopy of the forest on the other side.

The British and Indians had left the area by way of an oft-used hunters' trail that ran along Elkhorn Creek. Figuring that was easy enough—scouts from Bryan's had found evidence of it the day before, and any child could track an army of several hundred, particularly when so many were on horseback.

What troubled Boone was that the trail was just as easily followed the further they traveled. He'd have expected that from British regulars untrained in wilderness warfare—but Butler's Rangers, let alone Indians? Never. Common practice would dictate that they divide into ever-smaller groups, allowing the trails to become many and the markings less obvious.

He also felt certain they were being watched.

The high ranking officers—colonels, lieutenant colonels, and majors—rode together at the head, leaving the captains to manage their respective companies. There were so few Fayette County men that Colonel Todd placed Captain Patterson in command of the lot of them. This suited most of the men just fine, as many had served with Patterson previously and liked him.

Patterson was a painfully thin man with a bad lung, an Indian having shot him through the chest on the trail to

Pittsburgh six years earlier. He weathered his infirmity with good humor, though, and, despite being a by-the-book sort of fellow, had earned the respect of the men through his dedication to fair play.

Although not a well-worn trail, the ride was steady, and they'd quickly put several miles between themselves and Bryan Station. Still, a palpable uneasiness descended on the group when it became obvious to all but the newcomers to Kentucky where they were headed and where the Indians had likely camped the night before.

Trigg ducked to avoid a low-hanging pine branch as his horse emerged into a clearing. He looked up; not far in the distance were the charred, jagged remnants of stockade walls and, behind them, the hollowed-out, roofless cabins of what used to be a fort. Daniel Boone and the trail scouts were waiting there, standing in the center of the ruins while their horses grazed freely.

"What is this place?" Trigg asked.

Major Harlan leaned to the side in his saddle as close to Trigg as he could manage. "Ruddle Station," he answered, his voice uncharacteristically soft. He leaned to his opposite side, spit, then righted himself. "You're looking at what happens when the British have the presence of mind to carry along artillery," Harlan continued. "Folks at Bryan's should thank the good Lord for whatever tangle of bureaucracy keeps those bastards ignorant."

Trigg waited, hoping Harlan would provide more details without him having to ask, but none were forthcoming.

"Two shots was all it took, Colonel," said Major Bulger, who was riding just behind Trigg.

Surprised, Trigg looked back at him.

"The settlers here raised the white flag," Bulger continued. "Only fort in the territory to ever surrender."

"Damn cowards," McGary muttered. It was the first time he'd spoken since leaving Bryan Station. He'd been riding beside Bulger, silent and sullen, stewing over Colonel Todd having insulted him.

Seeing opportunity in McGary's pouting, Harlan had nudged his horse forward and claimed Hugh's usual spot beside Trigg. McGary noticed, which added to his anger, but Harlan calculated the play was worth the tradeoff. He disliked McGary, sure, but what motivated him now was concern over McGary's influence on Trigg. Anything he could do to tamp that down would surely be of benefit.

"Don't see as they had much choice," Bulger continued. "Not that it mattered. The Indians accompanying the British immediately set to killing and scalping, and those that weren't kilt were stripped naked and force-marched all the way to the Indian towns across the Ohio. Least that's the way the few settlers who managed to escape tell it."

Trigg faced forward, having now heard all he cared to.

As his horse passed through the ineffectual remnants of the fort's wall, Israel saw the officers—including his father, but absent Floyd—circled up in the courtyard. He took in his surroundings; nature had been busy in the two years since the attack on Ruddle's, embracing the station back into its fold, making use of the debris and decay to enrich the soil and fuel the reclamation. The speed at which the forest was erasing the work of human hands felt supernatural, the sight of it somberly mesmerizing.

As Israel turned a corner, however, the spell was broken; he saw grass trodden flat by the hooves of dozens of horses, the cold ashes of multiple cook fires, and bones strewn about from the feast the Indians and Rangers had made of the beef they'd plundered from Bryan's. This and more made it abundantly clear that the raiders had camped here the previous night.

Something in the distance caught Israel's eye. He gave the reins a gentle tug and peeled off from the other Boone Station men to investigate. The men assumed he needed to relieve himself or some such and didn't give his leaving much thought. Aaron Reynolds, who'd been talking more or less nonstop since they'd left Bryan's, half the time asking Israel questions about his father, kept right on yapping.

Squatting to examine something on the ground, Daniel glanced up and saw Israel cut away from the others. Then he turned and caught sight of McGary, whom he'd been making a point to keep an eye on, standing with a group of his own men, laughing and elbowing one another in the ribs. Boone suspected a flask or two among them, but saw none.

For his part, Colonel Todd wasn't in the least concerned that McGary didn't seem inclined to join him and the other officers on account of his bruised ego. Todd paced in front of his horse as the animal grazed, waiting impatiently for the captains to file in so Boone could give his assessment of the situation without having to waste time repeating himself.

"Well?" Todd asked Boone once they'd all arrived.

Boone stood and gestured to the multiple burnt patches that dotted the surrounding ground, campfires from the night before.

"I'd guess five hundred," Boone replied.

The officers exchanged looks. Todd's eyes went wide.

Boone suspected the combined number of Indians and Rangers was closer to four hundred, but he saw no harm in inflating the tally a mite to encourage caution in Todd. As time passed and the tactics Caldwell and Girty were practicing became more obvious, Boone began to look more favorably on the idea of waiting, despite his dislike of Logan.

"Sounds preposterous," said Captain Allison, his close-set eyes narrowed. "Doesn't fit with what Captain Craig saw at Bryan's. If it were anywhere near that number," he flung his thumb over his shoulder toward Major Todd, "the Major and his men would surely have been overwhelmed when they retreated from the cornfield."

Levi Todd's shoulders stiffened.

"They've been trying to conceal their numbers up to this point," Boone continued, unfazed, although he noted that Allison served under McGary, "and doing a right good job of it. Meaning they know we're following, but don't want us knowing what's in store if we catch them."

"They're taking the same risk, not knowing our number." Colonel Todd said.

"They know, or will soon," responded Boone. "They've been watching us since we left the station. Watching us right now, likely."

Floyd, who'd split from the group just before arriving at Ruddle's, rode into the courtyard.

"They wouldn't have scouts this far back, surely," blurted Captain John Bulger, Major Bulger's brother. The siblings had the oversized ears in common, but nature had spared the captain the big nose.

"They surely do," said Floyd as he dismounted. "There's sign of them a mile or so back."

"I'll take some men to hunt for them, then," Major Todd said.

"Save your energy," Boone responded. "You'll never see them, let alone capture them."

Colonel Todd scanned the forest. The idea that they were being observed but could do nothing about it galled him. "In that case, we press forward. I'll send the scouts northward to the fork of the Licking—"

"They ain't headed that way, Colonel," Boone said. "They're headed to Blue Licks."

Todd paused and considered it. "They intend to make a stand there?" he asked after a moment.

"It's a better place than most," Boone answered.

"I were you, Colonel, I'd listen to the hunter," Floyd said. "I once knew a man who doubted him, a headstrong fellow who was made to look a fool soon thereafter."

Boone glanced at Floyd and grinned. Floyd shot him a wink. Daniel looked quickly to where Israel had ridden; he was proud the boy had seen what he had, but was nervous that someone else might notice Israel's inspecting and become curious.

John Todd removed his hat and rubbed his shirtsleeve across his forehead; it came away sopped with sweat. Then he looked across the courtyard at the crumbling remains of Ruddle Station.

"Boone and I have been through enough together that I trust his insight when it comes to Indians," Colonel Todd said. Then he turned to Boone, smiled, and patted his lame leg. "Haven't we, Daniel?"

Daniel laughed, bent his left leg at the knee, and tapped his ankle, which had been shattered in the same battle. "We have."

"It's settled, then," said Todd. "We continue towards Blue Licks until nightfall, make a fresh account of the situation in the morning. If we don't like how it feels, well, we can sit around and talk about our old injuries until Logan and his men arrive."

Todd looked at the officers and recorded a nod of agreement from each in turn, Levi holding out a beat longer than the others.

"Our change in route should be plain enough for Logan to follow," Todd continued, satisfied. "Have the men mount up. There's a small creek three miles or so ahead—"

"Three and a half," Boone interrupted, smiling at Todd.

Todd laughed. "Three and a half. We'll give the horses a good watering there and press on till evening."

The officers split off to inform their men. Trigg walked toward McGary and his cohorts. Boone's eyes followed.

He found Trigg generally competent, but his lack of leash on McGary was concerning, if not understandable; McGary had a reputation for threatening violence, which extended even to his superiors. Five years earlier, hearing his stepson William had been set upon by Indians, McGary sought permission from the local militia leader, Captain James Harrod, to lead a rescue attempt. The captain refused, assessing the situation as too dangerous. McGary insisted at the point of a rifle. The captain relented, but it made no difference; William was already dead, and McGary had to settle for revenge. He caught the Shawnee who'd done it, shot him, and chopped the body into pieces to feed to his dogs.

As Boone turned to collect Stoneheart he caught McGary staring back at him, a fire behind his eyes that Boone knew couldn't be contained forever.

THIRTY-THREE

The creek was serene, idyllic, and its vibrant beauty reminded many of the men why they'd uprooted their families and made the difficult journey to Kentucky in the first place.

The opportunity to splash cool water on their faces and eat while not being bounced in the saddle had softened the mood of the frontiersmen, and knowing it was likely they would wait for Logan's forces to join them before engaging the enemy cut the general anxiety.

Israel drank his fill of water, then gave his horse a once-over. Happy to see nothing of concern, he removed the saddle to let her cool, patted her side, and left her to her grazing.

The area was crowded with the men's horses, so Israel was mindful of where he stepped as he carried the saddle to a nearby tree. He bent to place the saddle against the trunk, only the bending sent a shooting pain up his neck through the base of his skull. He dropped the saddle. Slowly, he lowered himself and sat beside it. The sharp pain dissipated, leaving only the constant throbbing he'd come to reluctant terms with.

He took off his hat and laid it on the saddle. He began inspecting his gear, although he knew it was fine; the reality was, he needed to talk with his father and was putting it off. They'd hardly spoken since leaving Boone Station; natural enough, Israel figured, considering Daniel rode with the other officers. It didn't bother Israel to be treated like any other enlisted man—he preferred it, in fact—but he was sore that his father hadn't volunteered him for scouting duty, as everyone knew he was one of the best scouts in Kentucky, let alone in this small band.

Israel looked over the crowd; he spotted his father, standing apart from the group at the edge of the woods, brushing Stoneheart. Israel stood, walked over to him, swallowed hard, and cleared his throat.

"I've been trying to figure why you didn't tell Colonel Todd about the Indians that split off," Israel said, his voice low to be certain no one else heard.

Daniel turned toward Israel, a touch of pride etched on his face. The boy was a mighty fine tracker. He turned back to the horse and continued brushing.

"Couple of reasons," Daniel began. "No way to know how many took that trail, but it was certainly a smaller bunch. They were all on foot, so no British were among them, meaning Caldwell, and likely Girty, are still with the larger force."

Israel scratched the top of his head. "So, Colonel Todd would want us to follow the larger group, and if he knew there were fewer of them than there had been, he might be more reckless."

"Less cautious," Daniel corrected. He turned and smiled at his son.

Israel considered pressing his father on why he hadn't volunteered him for scouting, but the conversation as it stood had been positive, and he had no desire to risk turning it sour. He returned the smile, nodded, and started back to the tree and his saddle.

"How you feeling?" his father yelled after him.

Israel turned to face him, extended his arms wide, and began walking backwards. "Never better," he said.

"Well, you don't look it," Daniel responded. Then he pointed to the ground. "And watch where you're stepping."

Israel pivoted, saw the hazard he was about to step into, and jumped clear of it, nearly stumbling. Daniel laughed and shook his head.

Israel laid under the tree, his head on his saddle. He tried to doze, but the hurt in his neck made it impossible. He opened his eyes and saw John Floyd sitting not too far off on a large rock that hung out over the creek beneath the canopy of a good-sized tree. He was holding and inspecting something, though what it was Israel couldn't tell. Israel squinted for a better look, but as he did Floyd tucked the object back into the folds of his cloak. When his hand reemerged, he was holding an apple.

"You ask your pa about the Indians that took that second trail?" Floyd asked without turning to Israel. He took a bite.

Israel raised his eyebrows, then glanced left to right to be sure no one else was within listening range. He scrambled closer to Floyd and crouched a few feet from him.

"Yeah," Israel said, as much a question as a statement.

"He say it was to keep Colonel Todd from thinking our odds were better than they are?"

"Yeah," Israel said again. He moved a bit closer. "How'd you know about that?"

"I reckon I learned a lesson or two from your old man myself," Floyd said. He stood, walked to his horse, and gave the Arabian the rest of the apple.

"Best saddle up," he said.

Israel turned and saw the officers heading toward their own horses. Floyd was right; it was time to move on.

Now that it had been determined that the raiders were pushing on to Blue Licks—meaning ambush wasn't waiting for the militia behind every cluster of trees or behind every hill—the men settled into a fair approximation of normalcy, laughing and conversing amongst themselves. Boone rode a half mile or so ahead of the other officers to look for sign, riding back periodically to report what he'd found. After a time, Floyd took to joining him.

"Any news of your friend Reid?" Boone asked Floyd.

"Left for the war. Hasn't been heard from since," Floyd responded, a note of sorrow in his voice.

Boone let it sit a moment.

"Baily Smith left Boonesborough for Green River a few years back," Boone said finally. "Sam Henderson took Betsy back to North Carolina not long after you left. I think the tension between her father and me had something to do with it."

"There's been a lot of that," Floyd said. "Folks in this part of the territory leaving Kentucky, I mean. I've written Governor Harrison more than once to tell him we'd have a similar situation in Jefferson County if it weren't that the Ohio River only runs the one way."

Boone laughed. "Yet, somehow you found it advisable to drag your new wife from refined living in coastal Virginia to this untamed wilderness."

Floyd chuckled. "Didn't require any dragging. She knew going in that I planned to come back." He smiled, and, for the first time he could remember, Daniel saw a twinkle in Floyd's cold, dark eyes. "Jane's exceptional—she'll do fine."

"I'm happy for you, John," Boone said, reaching over and clasping the man's shoulder. "I look forward to meeting her and your boy one day."

"How's Rebecca?" Floyd asked.

Boone reflected on all he and his wife had been through since the night Floyd left Boonesborough; how Rebecca, thinking him dead after he and the party he was with were taken prisoner by the Shawnee, took the children back to her family in North Carolina; how, after a year in Shawnee captivity followed by the siege on the fort, he had gone after her to bring her home. It was difficult to convince her to return to Kentucky, and the decision put a strain on their relationship, but return they did, establishing Boone Station. There'd been many a tough time between then and now, but their marriage seemed the stronger for it.

"She's good," Boone said.

"I'm glad. She's fine woman, Daniel."

"You're right there," Boone responded with a smile.

"And the children?" Floyd asked. "Israel seems a good man, and I suspect he does right well with the young ladies, although he looks sicker than a rabid dog today."

"The children are thriving," Boone said. Then his face turned grim. "You're right to mention Israel's illness. I should have left him home."

Floyd shook his head. "Ah, I doubt you could have stopped him from coming, Daniel. Seems to me Israel's looking for something he's not going to find sitting at Boone Station, if he finds it anywhere. He's got a thirst that'll likely never be quenched." Floyd turned and looked at the trail ahead. "I should know," he said.

Boone thought on it a moment.

"Well," Boone began, "I reckon the boy could always sign up to be a pirate like you did."

Floyd laughed. "Privateer, Daniel. Privateer."

The hours dragged on. Late in the afternoon the scouts rode back to report that the stream crossing their path a couple of miles ahead was still running—there'd been concern it might have dried up on account of the summer heat. Colonel Todd sent word down the line, letting the men know that they'd be stopping briefly to water the horses. The promise of relief from the tedium of the saddle rallied the men's spirits, at least temporarily.

It took until just before sunset to reach the stream, though, and by that time the men were tired and growing irritable. Boone was equally spent but better tempered, as Colonel Todd seemed more firmly set than previous on the idea of waiting for Logan. For Boone, this meant the end of telling Todd half-truths and exaggerations to steer him from what Boone felt certain was ruination and death. He preferred to deal with folks straight, but men's lives were at stake here, and he'd done what he felt was necessary considering the politics of the situation.

Most all the officers seemed to have warmed to the idea of waiting as well, the passage of time and their general weariness having tamped down the impulse to act in haste. Standing by the stream as the horses rested, they found themselves discussing life unrelated to the chase; family, farming, the anticipation of fall hunting. Boone, John Todd, and Floyd were recollecting on the shenanigans of a mutual friend who'd recently passed when Israel and another fellow, whom Boone had seen among Trigg's men but didn't know personally, rode slowly past them.

"Israel? Where you headed?" Daniel asked.

"Scouting," Israel answered. "I reckon it's my time."

Colonel Todd stopped the conversation he was having with Floyd and turned to Boone.

"Fresh scouts to guide us to good camping ground, Daniel," Todd said. "Needed men skilled in scouting at night. I sent for Israel specific and asked Trigg to volunteer his best man."

Boone looked to Israel then back to Todd.

"He ain't going."

Israel turned his horse. A good number of the men had overheard and were watching now, both regular militia and officers. Israel leaned forward in his saddle, closer to his father, his eyes shifting left to right.

"Pa," he pleaded in a whisper.

Colonel Todd realized then that Boone was serious, though he couldn't see why, at least not in that moment.

"Daniel," Todd began with a nervous chuckle, "you said yourself that the Indian scouts were just keeping an eye on us, not engaging. There's little danger."

"He's ill," Daniel said.

Israel could see in his father's eyes that there was no arguing with the man. He couldn't believe it; he'd been working all day to hide his illness from the others, and now his father was stating it outright? Israel felt everyone staring at him. Sweat rolled down his back. His ears buzzed. There were only two options he could see; acquiesce to his father's will and tuck tail, or make a show of rebelling by galloping off like a recalcitrant child. Either choice would be accompanied by further embarrassment.

"I figured on taking this turn myself," said Floyd, stepping forward. He turned toward Todd. "I'm not nearly the scout Israel is, but I did some surveying in this area several years ago, so I expect I'm well enough suited, Colonel." He looked up at Israel. "You wouldn't mind, would you, Israel?" He asked it as genuinely as any question ever had been.

"No," Israel said after a moment. He nodded at Floyd, grateful for the man's assistance, turned his horse, and rode back down the line to join the other Boone Station men. Everyone went back to their business, or at least made a show of pretending to.

Boone wondered if he'd ever handled a situation worse. Not that it mattered—it had to be done.

Floyd checked the saddle of the Arabian and swung himself up. He glanced over his shoulder to Boone and gave a subtle nod. Then he galloped off to catch up to Trigg's man, Ensign John McMurtry, who'd found the whole affair so uncomfortable that he'd ridden ahead.

Only Floyd understood at the time—although some of the men, including Colonel Todd, grasped it later—that the root of Boone's strong reaction was the memory of the murder of his son James.

Israel understood of course, which only made things worse.

THIRTY-FOUR

Caldwell found these nightly campfire chats tiresome. He relished any opportunity to discuss strategy, whether academically in drawing rooms or in practice on the battlefield, but there was too much coddling involved in these sessions with the Indians, too much pretending that he cared in the least about their concerns. He preferred a clear chain of command where opinions could be offered—when requested—but his opinion was understood to be the one that mattered. That was still the case here, despite what Girty and these chiefs may have thought, but much time was wasted in the charade of massaging egos. Still, it was impossible to conduct a war without soldiers, and this was the price of keeping the three hundred Indians presently under his command in check.

Caldwell admired the Indians as fighters; indeed, he had learned much from them, lessons he tried to push upstream to his superiors for implementation in the ranks of the British regulars, lessons they clearly disregarded. Otherwise, he wouldn't be in this godforsaken wilderness, continuing to wage a war in which his side had already surrendered.

He ordered two redcoats to pull a large log close to the fire —he refused to have himself or his officers sit on the ground crosslegged as the natives did. The fact that McKee and Elliot may have preferred to do so was the very reason he didn't allow it; both men had Shawnee wives and were deeply embedded in the culture. McKee, despite having been raised by the Shawnee—the circumstances of which Caldwell neither knew nor cared about—could be badgered to reality on occasion; Elliot, however, was a lost cause. It was one thing to be cordial with the Indians; in fact, it could be quite productive—Caldwell himself had a relationship with a Mohawk woman that had netted him a son—but the Indian cause was a lost one, and it was best to view them as a resource in decline, too inflexible to bend with the inevitable winds of time, too brittle to stand against it.

Simon Girty sat across the fire from them, moving his head with the unpredictable rhythm of the flames. He was happy to sit on a blanket on the ground like an Indian; part of his act, to Caldwell's mind. Girty's brothers stood behind him, beyond the firelight, mute and invisible enforcers.

One representative from each of the six tribes completed the circle, three to each side—Wyandot, Mingo, and Delaware, Miami, Shawnee, and Cherokee. The chiefs' faces were painted in the manner of their individual tribes—even their war paint had been purchased by the British Indian Department—and had become more faded, patchy, and cracked with each passing day. The writhing shadows created by the fire made their features difficult to make out, so Caldwell wasn't certain, but the Wyandot representative seemed to be a different man than he'd dealt with previously. Perhaps the former chief's authority had been challenged and he'd lost the position, or perhaps Girty had replaced him with someone he could more easily manipulate. Caldwell didn't care either way; he just wanted this done with. He moved comfortably among the Indians in the daytime, felt superior to them, but at night, by the fire, they appeared wraithlike and supernatural, which set Caldwell ill at ease.

He despised that weakness in himself.

"Three miles," Girty said, unbidden.

Caldwell tilted his head slightly. Girty stared at him, blinking; it was clear he had no intention of elaborating without being asked.

Caldwell sighed. "Three miles until where?"

"Until nothing," Girty responded, poking the fire with a stick as if suddenly indifferent to the matter. "From us. Three miles is how far behind the Kentuckians are now."

Caldwell's back straightened. "Your scouts," he said. He was frustrated; he'd sent out his own spies, competent, reliable men, so as not to have to rely on Girty for information, but they were late in returning. Perhaps they were never to return.

Girty smiled, staring into the fire, working it with the stick.

Elliot turned his head toward Caldwell. When the captain didn't acknowledge him or speak, he leaned forward, agitated, and looked at Girty through the flames. "Well, are we planning to welcome them into camp for a smoke around this fire?"

Caldwell raised a hand in Elliot's face. Elliot sat back.

"They'll bed down well before fording the Licking," Girty responded without looking up. "That's as close as they'll want get before morning. They know we're here." Girty pulled the stick from the flame. He put it close to his face and examined the embers. "Boone knows."

The Shawnee representative leaned toward Girty and spoke to him softly.

Caldwell understood some Indian talk, but little Shawnee. He turned to McKee, impatient for a translation.

"He doesn't want Boone killed," McKee said.

"Says Boone's his cousin," Girty elaborated. He waved the stick—now smoking, its light dying—from McKee to Caldwell. "Go ahead and explain it to him."

McKee had a history with the Girty brothers and held some sway with them, although it was clear Simon held the reins of the relationship.

McKee's mouth tightened. "When Boone was captured by the Shawnee a few years back he was adopted into the tribe—"

"I know that," Caldwell interrupted. He rolled his hand at the wrist in a circle several times to encourage McKee to get on with it. "Adopted by Blackfish as a replacement for the son Boone himself had killed . . ."

"Yessir," McKee continued. He nodded toward the Shawnee chief. "This man is the son of Blackfish's brother." McKee turned and spoke a few words to the Indian. The chief responded. McKee turned back to Caldwell.

"He wants to bring Boone back to the family."

Caldwell raised an eyebrow and stared at McKee. Then he laughed loudly, just for a moment, before remembering where he was. He cleared his throat.

"Doesn't he imagine that if Boone had wanted to remain part of the family he wouldn't have run off? Or, for that matter, that they wouldn't have had to keep him there by force in the first place?"

"That's not how it works, Sir," McKee responded, his voice and manner completely earnest.

"Don't expend too much energy thinking on it, Captain," interjected Girty. He pointed the stick at the Shawnee. "Cheeseekau here has a brother who's also part of our group," he waved the stick out into the night, "who'd just as soon see Boone dead. So there ain't what you'd call a consensus on the subject." Girty sat back and tossed the stick over his shoulder. It flew between his two brothers, then disappeared into the darkness. Neither man flinched.

"Anyways," Girty continued, "you have bigger things to concern yourself with, such as how best to greet Boone and the Kentuckians when they arrive."

"Here." Caldwell said. It was a question, but he'd grown sick of asking questions of Girty, so it came out as a statement.

"Up over the ridge," Girty said. "I'll help you with the details. Your problem, at the moment, is that these fellers object to fighting here."

Caldwell was losing patience; he gave real thought to pulling his sword and cutting off Girty's head. In the light of day, with the Indians and Girty's silent brothers at a distance, he might have done so; but this wasn't the light of day. Much as he hated Girty, he valued his own life enough to swallow much of his anger—much, but not all.

"And why is that?" Caldwell spit.

Girty smiled. "The area near here is a salt lick," he explained. "Attracts all manner of game."

Caldwell narrowed his eyes; he knew what a salt lick was.

"They're concerned a battle here will defile the hunting grounds," Girty continued.

Caldwell sat back. "That hardly seems likely," he said. *Fools*, he thought. "If the area is rich in minerals, nothing will keep the animals away."

"It ain't that so much, Captain—it's the principle of the thing," said Girty, his arms outstretched, palms up. His head turned from one side to the other as he looked at the each of the tribal leaders.

"And what are we to do about it?" Caldwell asked, his voice ladened with condescension.

"Don't you worry none, Captain," Girty said, springing to his feet. "We've already worked it out, haven't we, friends?"

Girty stepped out of the circle and began to walk its perimeter. He touched one chief on the shoulder, patted the next on the back, grasped the uplifted hand of the third, speaking a word or two to each in their native tongue as he passed. None turned to look at him or reacted with any surprise. He reached Elliot and patted him twice on the head. Then he was behind Caldwell. Girty leaned forward and whispered in his ear.

"See, Captain—you still need me. You'll always need me."

Girty straightened and slapped Caldwell twice on the shoulders. He then tugged McKee's earlobe and continued around the circle to greet the remaining three chiefs.

Anne Morgan, lying behind the log on which Caldwell and his officers sat, listened. She wasn't tied; Caldwell knew she understood there was no hope of escape. If she ran, she'd never make it the three miles to the Kentuckians before being recaptured. She couldn't even trust that Girty was telling the truth; they could just as easily be ten miles away, or twenty.

She didn't know if her husband had gotten their child safely to Bryan Station; didn't know if he was out there now, riding with the militia, to rescue her.

She hoped not.

THIRTY-FIVE

Riding out from the little stream, the militia had followed a disused, overgrown buffalo path well into the night. By the time they made camp, they'd covered thirty-eight miles since leaving Bryan Station.

Floyd and McMurtry selected the site on the bank of Stony Creek, just over three miles from the ford of the Licking River. They'd had little trouble following the trail of the raiders, even in darkness, which in itself gave credence to Boone's theory that Caldwell wanted to be followed. It was clear from the freshness of the tracks and other sign that the militiamen were gaining on the raiders—little surprise, as the Kentuckians were all on horseback—not that it mattered much; Boone had predicted where the Indians and British were headed, and, sure enough, here they were, just shy of the Blue Licks.

The hour was later than Colonel Todd would have liked—much later—but there'd been no choice other than to press forward, at least the way he figured it. If he didn't close the gap between themselves and the raiders as much as possible, and the enemy decided to continue on rather than make a stand, it wouldn't matter if he waited for Logan or not—the militia would never catch the raiders before they crossed the Ohio and could be easily reinforced.

As the first of the men rode in, Todd informed them they'd be making a cold camp; the hour being what it was, there was no point wasting time cooking, not that any of the men had the energy to do so anyway. Still, the lack of a hot meal at the end of a taxing day didn't do much for the general mood, and when Lieutenant Lindsay, the commissary, led his two packhorses through the camp to make certain each man had at least a hard biscuit and jerky, he was more often greeted with grunts than thanks.

Israel couldn't have cared less for food, hot or otherwise; the pain in his neck and head had become overwhelming as the day went on, each bounce in the saddle making it worse. At Captain Patterson's suggestion, the Boone Station men had ridden in back, covering the rear position for the final stretch. Israel suspected Patterson had made that decision on his account, wanting to spare him as many stares and whispers as possible after the scene with his father.

Still, Israel was thankful for it; he made a point to be the last man, falling ever further behind, torn between letting his companions know how truly sick he was—which would paint him as frail but at least partially explain why his father had kept him from scouting (although, hell, some might think he was feigning illness to avoid fighting)—or continue to pretend he was fine and have it thought his father had done what he did to keep his incompetent son out of harm's way.

Thing of it was, Israel hadn't been fooling anyone in the first place; everyone could tell just by looking that he was sicker than a dog.

Word made it back to the Boone Station men that the front of the line had reached camp. Israel slowed his horse, hoping Squire, Samuel, and the Scholl boys wouldn't notice. They pulled further ahead and vanished around a bend. Israel dismounted. He walked his horse just off the trail, dropped her reins across a crooked sapling, then collapsed beneath the nearest tree. He knew he should remove the horse's saddle and hobble her proper, but there was plenty of grass for her to munch on, and he needed to rest. Just for a moment.

Then someone was jostling him. Groggy, Israel opened his eyes, saw leaves rustling on branches and, beyond them, bright stars in a clear night sky. For a moment he thought he was back in Boonesborough beneath the big elm, April waking him.

Then he felt the kick at his leg again, slightly more power behind it this time. He raised his head and saw John Floyd standing beside him, staring down.

Israel sat up and looked around; no one else was about. He rubbed his eyes. When he opened them again, Floyd's outstretched hand was in front of his face. He took it, and Floyd helped him to standing.

"Why're you this far back?" Israel asked.

"Reconnoitering," Floyd said. "Pointless I reckon, but I couldn't help myself." He craned his neck and made a show of looking up and down the trail. "You, uh, bringing up the rear, I take it?"

"Tired, is all," Israel said. He walked to his horse and patted her on the neck, then felt something unusual underfoot and looked down—he was standing on his hat. It'd fallen off at some point and he hadn't noticed. He picked it up, put his left foot in the stirrup, and, with some effort, hoisted himself up.

Floyd raised an eyebrow, then swung into the saddle of the Arabian and followed Israel up the dark trail. They rode in silence for a spell.

"Why'd you leave back when?" Israel asked after a time.

Floyd, having asked himself the same question and being gifted plenty of time to ponder the answer in the six weeks he'd spent in irons in the belly of a British ship intent on delivering him to the gallows in England, had a ready answer.

"When that rider arrived at Boonesborough carrying word that we'd declared independence," Floyd began, "I knew no matter how far west we pushed, how far beyond the colonies proper, war was going to find us, and the longer we put off facing it at the head, the worse it would be facing it at the tail. So, I figured it only made sense to take the war straight to the British." He removed his hat and looked up at the stars for a moment. Then he hung his head and stared down into the hat.

"A man doesn't always find freedom by pushing forward and away from things, Israel. Sometimes he has to turn and fight for it."

Israel stared at him. "You came back though."

Floyd laughed and put his hat back on. "Well, I went and got myself captured, so my strategy of singlehandedly defeating the British didn't work out as well as I'd imagined. The war found its way to Kentucky anyway—it may very well end here—so I followed after it."

Israel looked back up the trail, at least as far as his eyes could manage in the darkness. "I hope I can meet your wife someday," he said.

"I'm not so sure that's a good idea," Floyd responded. "I hear you've got a way with the ladies, and I wouldn't want you stealing her away."

They laughed and rode on.

They soon caught up with the rest of the militia. Israel had only dozed for a moment, apparently, as his cousins and friends had just started to wonder where he'd wandered off. Floyd continued on to join the officers.

Riding in the back as they'd been, the Boone Station men, Aaron Reynolds accompanying them, were the last group to lead their horses into the common area, a small, flat clearing with plenty of grass where the horses could be hobbled and belled, safe and satisfied, for what remained of the night. Israel struggled to get his horse's hooves cinched—any amount of bending made his head throb—and at one point nearly blacked out. Samuel and Squire saw him struggling and took over. Israel thanked them.

"Not even worth mentioning," Samuel said. He put his arm over Israel's shoulder. "Come on—you best bunk down proper before you end up underfoot of these horses."

Aaron Reynolds and Joseph Scholl, having finished tending their horses, were waiting for the Boones at the edge of the clearing. The five headed back to their spot in camp. They passed several companies along the way, spread out in clusters of five to eight men, twelve feet or so between clusters. Most of the men had undone their bedrolls and were lying down, but few were sleeping; tired as they were, the events of the day and speculation over tomorrow made it difficult to tamp down their anxiety.

Reynolds told a particularly bawdy joke, and his companions laughed despite themselves; even Israel, despite every chuckle sending a painful shockwave through the base of his skull.

"It ain't right," Israel and his fellows heard a man say from one of the clusters. "Most every man here is from Lincoln County. Ain't no doubt in my mind that Todd had us hightail out of Bryan's so quick to keep Logan from taking charge once he showed." The man was speaking loudly, as if wanting to be overheard outside of his own group.

The Boones, Scholl, and Reynolds glanced over; there were half a dozen men, sitting or reclining on the grass in a rough circle ringing a good-sized rock. Despite the darkness, Israel recognized them as Captain Allison's men.

Meaning Hugh McGary's men.

Israel's group kept walking.

"Yeah—and Daniel Boone's carrying Todd around by the scruff," another of Allison's men said as they passed. There was no doubt now that the men were trying to rowel them. "He's likely marching us right to the bastards to hand us over."

"Wouldn't be the first time Boone's betrayed settlers to the Indians," said another.

Aaron Reynolds stopped.

"What's that you say?" Reynolds asked over his shoulder, pushing a few loose strands of his blonde hair from his eyes.

"Speak up, Reynolds," the man yelled back. "You had backbone enough to run your mouth at Simon Girty from the safety of a stone chimney; surely you can say your piece to me with the same degree of courage."

Reynolds and the Boone Station men turned. The man who was speaking stood—he was big. The biggest of the group, or as least that's what they hoped. Then the other five stood.

So much for hoping.

Others were now aware that a situation was brewing and began to gather around. Reynolds started walking toward Allison's men, rolling his sleeves as he went.

"Aaron . . ." Israel whispered after him. He was wasting his breath but had to try; he knew Reynolds, knew there was no chance of holding the man back now that he'd been challenged, and knew what was coming.

The man with the big mouth, the first who'd stood, craned his neck, pretending to look around Aaron. "Letting Reynolds fight your battles for you, little Boone?" Bigmouth said. "Protecting you same as your daddy did?"

Allison's men laughed.

Bigmouth's eyes narrowed. "Your daddy is a traitor, boy. An Indian lover. I heard he went so Indian that he took one for a wife when he lived with them. I wonder what your momma thought about that?"

A twig snapped behind Allison's men and they turned.

"Just passing through," the man said from the shadows, raising a hand apologetically as he stepped off to the side.

Bigmouth turned back and saw Reynolds rushing toward him. Then Israel, emerging from the darkness, passed Reynolds in a flash and tackled Bigmouth. They hit the ground; Israel took immediately to pummeling the man's face. Reynolds stopped, shrugged, then, figuring one victim was as good as the next, turned to make a selection when he was tackled by two of the men, driving him hard to the ground. Two more of Bigmouth's friends jumped over and grabbed Israel, struggling to pull him off of Bigmouth, but Israel moved so wildly they may as well have been trying to wrangle a rabid badger. One of the pair took a punch to the nose on Israel's upswing, and the crunch of the impact could be heard even over the whooping and hollering of the crowd. Samuel and Squire came up behind the men and pulled them from their cousin. Israel stood, his fists bloody, Bigmouth unconscious on the ground beneath him. He turned, saw the sixth man rushing toward him, then saw the man's jaw thrown out of alignment with the rest of his head by a punch from Joseph Scholl. They turned and saw Reynolds on the ground being pummeled, laughing and cussing as the two men whaled on him, then one of the men reared up, screaming, his hand at the side of his head, blood rushing down his neck and shoulder. Israel picked up a tree branched and clubbed the second man with it as Reynolds, his face bloody, turned his head to spit out a tooth and the piece of the man's ear he'd bitten off. He laughed. Israel turned to help Joseph help his cousins, but the crowd decided the fight had gone far enough and closed in to break it up.

Then Patterson and Allison were there, along with Joseph Scholl's two brothers, pushing their way through the crowd. More men followed, word of the scrape having spread. Allison went to talk, but Patterson stepped in front of him.

"I ain't asking and you ain't going to tell me," Patterson yelled, standing between his men and the two of Allison's men who were still standing. "In normal conditions the lot of you would be reprimanded official, but we need every man and don't have that luxury." His voice calmed. "Tend to your wounds and rest up. Lieutenant Lindsay has supplies if you need them, but I suggest you don't, as he'll have to make a record of what's been used and why." Then Patterson turned to the crowd. "Well—go on now."

The crowd slowly dispersed. Some helped Bigmouth and the man Israel had whacked on the head with the branch to stand. The man Joseph punched sat on the big rock, holding his jaw. The man who was now missing an earlobe was in the worst shape, and a few were doing what they could to help him clean and wrap it.

Patterson looked his men up and down; Israel with his bloody fists, Aaron with his bloody face and one eye already swelling, Samuel and Squire battered and scuffed. Joseph was the least scathed, but held his black-and-blue swollen fist behind his back to hide it.

They tucked their heads, all except Reynolds, who smiled at Patterson, a black gap where his front tooth had once been. Patterson shook his head and walked off.

When the captain was out of sight, Peter and Abraham Scholl ran up to their brother and the others.

"I can't believe we missed it," Abraham said, pounding his fist into the palm of his hand.

"Yeah, why didn't you tell us?" Peter asked. He slapped Joseph on the arm.

"We didn't plan it," Joseph responded, his voice tinged with exasperation as he examined his fist.

Israel spotted the man who'd stepped on the twig. He was walking alone, away from the crowd.

"Hey," Israel yelled as he hustled after the man. The running made his head ring. "Sorry, I don't know your name."

The man turned. "Netherland," he said.

Israel had heard the name bandied about during the day's riding. He knew Netherland was a new arrival to Kentucky, but that was about it, other than the men always said his name with another word in front of it.

Yellow.

"Well, I appreciate your help back there, Netherland," Israel said.

"Oh," Netherland began as he turned to walk away. "Like I told the man . . . I was just passing through."

THIRTY-SIX

Israel's head throbbed, the pain so bad it brought tears to his eyes. He could feel his heartbeat in his temples, each pulse a hammer pounding an anvil.

He and the others had joined the rest of the Boone Station men in their section of camp and were met with back slaps and congratulations. As soon as Israel could, though, he grabbed his bedroll and headed into the woods; he'd reached the limit of his endurance and needed to be alone, away from the bustle of the camp. He walked up a rise and found himself on a low ridge looking over a small branch of the creek. He made his way down, crouching low and moving slowly, had a long drink, washed his hands and face, and climbed back up the ridge, using exposed roots as foot and handholds. If he'd known going into it the effort involved, he might have kept both his thirst and the dried blood on his hands. But he'd done it now and, having gotten through it, sat at the edge of the ridge, closed his eyes, and did his best to focus on the sound of the flowing water.

"I hear you put on quite a show."

Israel quickly wiped his eyes and tried to look over his shoulder, but the pain shot through his neck and put a stop to it. It didn't matter, though, as he knew the voice belonged to his father.

"Patterson tell you?" Israel asked, squaring himself up with the creek again.

"Nope. Your friend Reynolds passed right by the officers on his way to clean the blood from his face and told us everything at the first asking. We couldn't get him to stop telling, actually."

Daniel eased himself down beside Israel, grunting just a little, his joints and muscles sore from the day's riding. They sat in awkward silence awhile, looking out over the landscape.

"You know, we named you after my oldest brother," Daniel said suddenly, still staring at the trees on the other side of the creek. "Boy, how I looked up to him. He was eight years older and seemed to me more a mythological hero than a man, completely unconfined by earthly limitations." He looked down and brushed a blade of grass from his knee. "Hard to believe he's more than twenty-five years gone."

Daniel leaned back on his arms and let out a sigh. "I was about the age you are now when he passed," he continued. "Even so, there were two brothers between him and me, so I was spared the sudden responsibility you inherited when James was killed."

Israel turned his head toward his father slightly. A sharp pain grabbed hold of the nerves just behind his right eye socket as he did so, but he said nothing. His father looked young; wrinkles that marked not only the passage of time but a hard life fully lived were blurred by the soft light of the moon. His eyes, despite all they'd seen, were still bright and clear; even the sadness of recalling James' murder didn't dull them, although the faint quiver of his lip told the tale.

Daniel sat forward. He turned from Israel, pried a small stone from the dirt, and began examining it.

"Your mother and I were so sick with grief, and I was filled with so much hatred for myself for having failed to protect him . . ." Daniel tried to swallow the lump in his throat, but it wouldn't go down. "I never considered that you'd lost your hero same as I'd lost mine."

Israel was embarrassed, for his father as well as himself. He'd never heard the man speak this way and decided he didn't like it. He tried to say something, to change the subject to get his father to stop talking despite wanting for years to hear him say exactly what he was saying now but figured he never would, but his body was frozen, his mind disembodied.

"You were still a boy," Daniel continued, "and had the burden of now being the oldest son without benefit of me putting my grief aside to allow you to do it proper." Daniel put the stone back where he'd found it. "Well, you've done a damn fine job of it despite me," he said.

He placed his arm around the boy's shoulders. Israel stiffened a bit, moving for the first time since his father began speaking, jolted back to reality.

"Jemima asked me to paddle the canoe for her and the Calloway sisters that day," Israel said. "Only my friends asked me to go hunting and I forgot that I told her I would."

His father shot him a quizzical look. "That been bothering you all these years?" he asked.

"I'd've been there with my rifle," Israel said.

"And the Indians likely would have killed you and taken the girls anyway," Daniel responded. "There were five of them, Israel."

Israel stared at the little creek as tears filled his eyes.

"Jemima sore at you over it?" Daniel asked.

"No," Israel responded. "I told her how sorry I was after you brought her home, and she forgave me."

"Then let it go, son. Life's too short to have guilt over things that don't warrant it."

Daniel stood and brushed himself off. "Reckon I'll turn in," he said casually, as if the last few minutes had never happened. "A man ought to grab sleep every chance he can in these situations." He turned and started back the way he came.

"Sleep well, Israel," he said, disappearing into the trees, into his element.

Israel sat for a time. He found reflecting on his father's words unnerving, so he steered his thoughts toward April, which was none too difficult. He decided he'd ask her to marry the moment he returned. He'd already eyeballed the perfect plot of land, and if he started right away, with a little luck and help, he could build a right decent cabin before winter set in, where he and his new bride could ensconce alone for a few weeks, perhaps emerging for Christmas Day and New Year's Eve, then hole up again through February before hosting both their families for a picnic in the spring.

Yes, he figured setting up house with April would suit him just fine.

The pain in his neck never let him drift too far from reality, but he figured that, with a little sleep, it'd be gone by morning. He didn't feel like being alone all of a sudden. He picked up his bedroll and turned to make his way back to camp. He came to the gap in the trees that marked the thin path his father had taken down but passed it, figuring on finding his own way, even if it took a bit longer.

He knew he was close, but the silence perplexed him. A moment later he stepped into the clearing where the Fayette County men were camped and was surprised to see all of them staring up at a good-sized fire blazing on a hilltop in the distance.

Surely the Indians aren't so brazen as to light a bonfire in plain view of a militia intent on fighting them, Israel thought.

"It's the Indians," said Reynolds, suddenly at Israel's shoulder, looking up at the fire while chewing on a stick of jerky.

"Huh," said Israel. "What's my father got to say about it?"

"Ain't seen him," Reynolds responded. Then he shrugged, walked to his spot on the ground, and plopped down on his blanket. Israel lingered, trying his best to suss out the purpose of the bonfire. He gave up after a time and walked to his own spot, nodding and saying how dos to the other men as he went. He dropped his bedroll in front of his saddle, which had been placed between Samuel Brannon and Joseph Scholl. He nodded to Brannon, but the man was so mesmerized by the fire on the hill that he didn't notice.

Israel glanced down at Joseph. Scholl smiled and pointed at his own right hand, swollen to half again its size as a consequence of punching the Lincoln County man in the jaw. Israel chuckled. Then he looked over at Reynolds and got a better look at the man than he'd managed a moment ago. Aaron was looking up at the fire and munching his jerky, his face bruised and one eye swollen completely shut.

"Can you even see?" Israel asked.

"Out of the one eye, yeah," Reynolds responded without turning to him.

Israel unrolled his blanket and dropped onto it. Feeling hungry suddenly, he pulled a biscuit from his saddlebag. It brought to mind his mother, his nieces, and Jemima. He smiled. He unwrapped and ate it while looking up at the fire. Squinting, he noticed now a single figure sitting stock-still beside the blaze.

Most of the militiamen lost interest in the spectacle after a time; even the bizarre becomes commonplace if it continues long enough. Some of the men cleaned their rifles and glanced up at the fire only occasionally. Most, including Israel, had drifted off. The only man to attempt a constant vigil was Brannon; the fewer of the men he noticed watching, the more he felt duty bound to do so himself. Even so, exhaustion caught up to him eventually. His eyes got heavy and his head bobbed, jerking him awake. The process repeated itself a few times. On the fourth, Brannon saw something that kept him awake.

The figure by the fire was now standing.

The silhouetted man raised both arms high over his head, then swung one down in a violent arc. The fire sparked wildly and the flames rose, and when they settled again the figure was gone.

Brannon turned and saw that Joseph and Aaron were sitting up and had seen what he had. The three looked at each other. Then Aaron waved a hand in the direction of the fire and laid back down.

Boone had left the officers to camp near his own men, but not too near, and found a nice, isolated spot close by in a cluster of good-smelling pines. He'd just dozed off when Joseph Scholl, Aaron Reynolds, and Samuel Brannon pushed through the trees into his little clearing, nearly stumbled over each other in the process, half out of breath.

Boone opened an eye.

"Fellers . . ." he said, annoyed.

"They cast a spell or something up yonder," Brannon blurted. He pointed to the fire on the hilltop, barely perceptible through the tall pines.

"I tried telling him not to be ignorant, Colonel," Reynolds explained, wanting to make certain Daniel Boone didn't associate him with Brannon's histrionics. "Tried telling him it's just a man who snuck off from the rest of the Indians to enjoy a jug of whiskey, is all." He paused. "That's likely right, ain't it, Colonel?"

Boone sighed. He glanced up at the fire. Then he the settled his head back on his saddle, closed his eyes, and turned on his side away from the men.

"Get some sleep, boys," he said.

He was asleep himself before they left.

THIRTY-SEVEN

Monday, August 19

Morning came same as most others. The fire on the hill had burned itself out over the course of the night without leaving behind so much as a single tendril of smoke as evidence it had ever even existed. All the men who'd been rattled by the spectacle in those dark hours, even those who'd been most rattled—especially those—felt silly now in the light of day.

The men were given time to make fires and breakfast, Lieutenant Lindsay making certain each had coffee, which did much for the militia's collective spirit and largely negated the fact that they'd only had a few hours sleep. So positive was the general mood that the chase of the previous day and the potential danger ahead seemed very much like the Indian ritual they observed in the night; distant and dreamlike.

Daniel Boone was nowhere to be found, although that, too, was perfectly normal, at least as far as the Boone Station men were concerned. It baffled Major Todd, however, who'd been sent by his brother into their ranks to collect Boone.

"Rode on ahead is what I'd guess," Squire Boone told Levi while pouring himself a fresh cup of coffee.

Levi glanced at the rest of the Fayette County men; none of them, Israel included, seemed inclined to speculate on Boone's likely whereabouts. Frustrated, Levi turned and walked back up the line to report to John.

Thirty minutes later, right around seven o'clock, the militia broke camp and continued up the trace out of the Stoney Creek valley. They rode for nearly three miles until the trail opened up near the southern bank of the Licking River, the brush having been trodden down over the decades by buffalo making their way to the mineral deposits at Blue Licks.

Two scouts that Colonel Todd had sent ahead were there to meet them, shaking their heads and smiling. They pointed to the foot of an adjacent hill—there stood Stoneheart, grazing leisurely. She was saddled, but minus Boone. Todd and the officers ranking above captain dismounted and started up the hill.

Boone heard them coming. He said a silent, halfhearted prayer asking that McGary, by some miracle, not be among them, then figured the prayer unreasonable and felt guilty for asking. He swallowed his disappointment when the officers crested the rise and he spotted McGary at the back of the bunch. He took a breath, then nodded the men over to a clearing that offered the best view of the valley below and the hill that rose on the other side.

The men walked to the edge of the ridge. They saw the Licking where it appeared from around the bend of the western side of the hill across from them, running southeast to the narrow ford at Blue Licks, then continuing, eventually curving around itself before turning north and up the other side of the hill and beyond.

Boone didn't bother pointing out the obvious—there were two Indians casually milling about at the top of the bare hill above the Blue Licks, passing a pipe between them, framed perfectly by the morning sun.

"Colonel, they aim to fight us," said Boone.

McGary snorted. Boone ignored him; there were no margins to be gained in losing his temper now.

Colonel Todd looked at Boone, then back at the two braves in the distance. "Look like stragglers to me, Daniel," Todd said, "or possibly scouts, told to hang back and track our movements, but being a mite casual about it now their leaders have ridden ahead. May mean we've lost our chance entirely."

Boone took a breath, extended an arm, and pointed. "The other side of that hill is thick with trees. I suspect the Rangers and most of the Indians are there, well-hidden and well-covered, ready to pick off anyone who comes within range." He swung his arm east. "Now, likely part of their forces are behind that ridge there, cozy and secure, waiting for us to stroll past before swinging down and cutting us off."

"And we'll have the river behind us blocking our retreat," Todd said. He stared out, taking in the landscape, the variables churning in his mind. He suspected Boone was right, that Caldwell's plan had been to stand and fight at Blue Licks. But had it remained so? Caldwell surely had no way of knowing how close Logan's men were, no way of knowing if he'd be facing just shy of two hundred Kentuckians when the sun rose, or a thousand. Perhaps he'd reconsidered at some point in the night and chosen retreat instead.

Boone caught a subtle change in Todd's posture and knew his argument had come up short. "Don't you see, Colonel?" Boone asked. "This is just like what they tried at Boonesborough—to draw us into the open where they have the advantage. We didn't fall for it then. Let's not do so now."

It was Boone's final salvo; if Todd was still unconvinced, then so be it.

Floyd took a step forward. "John, if Daniel's right and you push ahead, I doubt you'll have to live long with the embarrassment of ignoring his counsel."

Todd turned to him, then turned again toward the Blue Licks. The officers looked at each other nervously, but remained silent.

"We should wait."

Everyone turned to the man who'd spoken—Levi Todd.

Boone knew that had sealed it. If Levi, who'd been anxious for a rematch with the Indians, saw the wisdom of waiting, John would also.

Colonel Todd sighed; he'd had about all the advice he could stomach on this trip. "Could be you're wrong and the Indians are already on the march," Todd said. "Could be you're right and the Indians are there, but they eventually grow impatient, attack, and catch us twiddling our thumbs waiting here for Logan."

"I'm not suggesting we just sit here," Boone said. "Send out a pair of scouts; let's see what they find." He thumbed at the two Indians across the way. "Just advise them to ride wide of those decoys."

McGary let out a low growl. "Again with the scouts. By Godly, let's make a decision and have done with it. I feel like I'm watching a finch build two nests at the same time, neither of them worth a damn for want of the finch's full attention."

Todd ignored McGary, turned, and brushed past him, heading back down the hill. The officers followed, Boone with them, but had to slow their pace slightly so as not to overtake Todd on account of his limp, which had been aggravated by the climbing.

McGary followed, sullenly, at a distance.

Colonel Todd walked—with difficulty but purpose—back to where the militia waited. He began speaking when he was barely within earshot.

"I need two volunteers for scouting," he announced. Most of the men were still mounted, but a handful had left their saddles and were leaning against the trees that lined the clearing, searching for shade. The heat of the day had come early.

"Soon to be on the move again, Colonel?" asked Captain Allison. He craned his neck, searching for McGary among the officers standing behind Todd. There was no sign of him.

"Not yet," Todd answered. "I need men to cross the river and scout the next rise. The Indians and Rangers could be holed up there, hoping to catch us in an ambush."

The men passed the message to those too far back to hear it directly. Todd waited. It occurred to him after a moment that his request held little appeal the way he'd phrased it.

"Or could be we scared them off and they've already crossed the Ohio," he added. "We just need to know."

Boone couldn't volunteer himself; the need for scouting had been his idea, and any result he returned with would be suspect in the eyes of some. He was surprised, though—and relieved—that Israel hadn't spoken up. Could be the boy was hoping Daniel would recommend him for the job by way of an apology. If so, he was hoping in vain—Daniel couldn't send Israel or any of the Boone Station men for the same reason he couldn't go himself.

But where was the boy? Daniel searched the crowd. Finally, he spotted Israel standing just at the edge of the woods behind the rest of the men from Fayette County. It was the first time he'd seen his son that morning, and what he saw shocked him. Israel was sallow and dripping with sweat; he'd backslid and looked as sick now as he had four days ago. It was clear to Daniel that the boy could barely stand, much less ride a horse into dangerous territory where he'd need his wits about him.

Israel met his father's gaze, rubbed the back of his neck, and shook his head. Then he looked down at the ground. Daniel ached for him. He knew his son wanted nothing more than to prove himself, and the fact that he wasn't fighting for the opportunity meant he felt like absolute hell.

"Pitman, Coburn—saddle up, "Trigg said from behind Boone. "Get as close as you can without getting yourselves killed, then hurry back." Boone had no way of knowing if Trigg had witnessed his exchange with Israel, but it was the first time the lieutenant colonel had shown authority since all this began, and Daniel was thankful for it.

Pitman and Coburn looked at each other.

"Well get," Trigg said, "We ain't got time to wait is the reason I'm asking."

The men hurried to their horses. Boone watched Israel step backwards a few paces into the woods and collapse against a tree.

THIRTY-EIGHT

"I'm sending you home," Daniel said.

Israel looked up at his father.

Daniel sat on the ground beside him and took off his hat. "I spoke with Abraham Scholl. Soon as you're rested, the two of you are heading to Boone Station. Unlikely to be any hostile Indians between here and there. Any there were would have joined up with Girty's group by now."

"I ain't going," said Israel.

Daniel turned his hat in his hand and looked up into the trees.

"I figured you'd say that," he said after moment, "but everyone can see you're ill and in no condition for a tussle." He turned to Israel. "No one will begrudge you."

He put an arm around Israel's shoulders and placed his other palm against his son's forehead. *God, the boy's burning up,* Daniel thought. He pulled Israel in close. Israel rested his head on Daniel's chest.

"I'd be a poor excuse for a father if I let you stay, son."

Israel considered fighting the tears, but let them come.

There was a sudden commotion from the trail. Israel raised his head. He and his father listened for a moment, neither believing what they were hearing; the scouts had already returned.

Daniel jumped to his feet. "Stay here," he said, pointing down at Israel. Then he took off running.

He broke through the trees and was on the trail just as the scouts were slowing their horses to dismount. John and Levi Todd stood in front of them. A crowd was quickly gathering, including Trigg and a handful of his officers.

"Ain't nothing there, Colonel," Pitman said.

"Yeah, even those two stragglers took off when they saw us coming," said Coburn as he took off his hat. He and Pitman looked at each other and nodded.

Boone pushed his way into the circle and stood beside John Todd.

"How close did you get?" Colonel Todd asked. "What did you see—and don't say 'nothing' this time. Had the Indians lingered there or hadn't they?"

"Oh, they'd been there all right," said Coburn. He wiped his brow with the back of his hand. "There's evidence of it, trampled grass and the like, but ain't no sign of them now."

A murmur rose among the men who were in hearing distance. The two scouts again looked at each other and nodded. Boone noticed they'd skipped right over the question of how close they'd gotten.

Colonel Todd turned to Boone, who couldn't conjure a response and didn't return Todd's gaze. He knew the Indians and British were there, they had to be, but how could he argue the point? He couldn't rightly tell Todd the scouts had seen something they'd obviously made every effort to not.

"How close?" Boone asked the scouts. "Did you ride behind the east ridge? God knows you didn't dawdle if you did." He was getting agitated, which he knew was unlikely to coax the pair into being more forthcoming.

"We split up," Pitman said. He turned, putting his back to Boone to face Lieutenant Colonel Trigg. "You told us not to get too close out of concern of our lives—which we appreciated, Colonel—but when we didn't see indication that the Indians were still there we pushed further even than we'd intended. Nothing still."

Boone leaned toward Todd and thumbed at the scouts. "Colonel, these men are clearly scared, and while I'm sure they did their best considering, them seeing nothing isn't the same as nothing being there."

Todd considered the point. Being reprimanded for bad scouting by Daniel Boone was enough to make any man jumpy and defensive, but Boone was right about the scouts being too scared to have done a proper job of it.

Most of the militia had now circled up. Not all were in hearing distance, but word of what was transpiring was passed to the men further back.

Boone caught sight of Floyd and Levi. Their faces were painted with concern, but neither interjected; if Daniel Boone couldn't convince Colonel Todd on a matter related to scouting, what chance did they have?

Boone turned suddenly and began walking toward Stoneheart. "I'll do the scouting myself like I should've done in the first place."

"There's no time for that now, Daniel," John Todd yelled after him.

The murmuring from the crowd swelled. Boone stopped.

"I believe you're right," Todd said.

Boone took a breath.

"But if they are there," Todd continued, "and they decide to make a break for the Ohio before Logan arrives—"

"We can cut them off, Colonel," Boone interrupted, relieved that he now had firm footing. "They're expecting us to cross here where we'll be easy targets and the river makes it difficult to retreat, but there's a better ford two miles downstream—"

"In all the years I've know you, Boone, I never figured you for a coward," Hugh McGary barked. His voice was gnawed to gravel by pent-up rage as he pushed into the circle, rifle in hand, leading his horse.

Boone was shaken. He was a patient man as a rule but also plain spoken, not one for measuring his words for the sake of diplomacy. He'd pushed what little skill he had in that regard to the limit the past few days, chewed down all he could in the cause of statesmanship, but he wouldn't chew down being called a coward. He couldn't. Especially not by McGary.

No; he was no statesman.

In a flash Boone was nose-to-nose with McGary. "I reckon I can go as far in an Indian fight as any man," he yelled, his voice and body shaking with anger.

"Then why all this talk," McGary spit back, "all this watching and following and waiting? By Godly, what did we come here for?"

McGary turned in a mad circle, his wild eyes scanning the the crowd that surrounded him. "What have we come here for!" he shouted.

"To fight the Indians!" one of Allison's men answered from the back. "To fight the Indians!" yelled another man from a different company. Then another, then several, then dozens.

"By Godly, then why not fight them?" McGary shouted, thrusting his rifle over his head.

A cheer erupted from the men; not all of them, but many. Those who didn't join in, mainly the Fayette County company, turned to each other in stunned confusion; a fervor had swept through the ranks in an instant—or so it seemed. It dawned on them suddenly that McGary had likely been building its foundation, stone by stone, since before they'd left Bryan Station.

McGary swung up onto his horse and held his rifle high again. The horse reared. "All who aren't damn cowards follow me, then, and I'll show you the Indians!"

He broke for the river at a full gallop, men and horses parting to let him through. Other men, whooping and hollering, mounted their own horses to follow.

The sight of it snapped Boone from his anger; this was no good. He exchanged glances with Colonel Todd and Floyd. The pot had boiled over and was now too hot to pull from the flame, they knew. Men rode off by the dozens, including many of Trigg's majors and captains. It was difficult to know how many, like Allison, had been turned by McGary, how many were caught up in the frenzy of the moment, or how many were simply trying to catch up with their men to bring some order to the situation.

Boone saw Trigg and could tell by the man's face that he'd finally realized, too late, that he'd failed; McGary had been his dog to leash, and he'd done a poor job of it.

Harlan cursed. He and Trigg exchanged looks. He cursed again, turned, ran to his own horse, and took off after McGary.

It was clear to Boone that Harlan had been tasked with keeping tabs on the drunkard, although whether Trigg had assigned him the job or Harlan had given it to himself Boone couldn't say.

Levi Todd was already on his horse. He was a cavalry man, and he'd be damned if he'd allow the men in his charge to ride into battle without the benefit of his leadership.

The remaining officers knew Levi was right and ran for their own horses. The only option they had now, other than turning tail and saving their own skins—an idea not a one of them entertained—was to do their best to wrangle the men and form something resembling a plan.

"Sir?" someone asked from behind Boone. He turned.

It was Israel; he was on his horse, the rest of the Boone Station men on theirs behind him, the animals dancing nervously, agitated by the surrounding excitement. Israel still looked pale and fevered but was forcing it down; his willpower had gained the upper hand, at least for the time being. Daniel knew it was impossible to keep his son out of the fight now that all the men, himself included, had been roused or shamed into making conflict inevitable. It was pointless to try.

The men stared down at Daniel, waiting for his orders.

"Come on, then, boys," Boone said. He turned and ran toward Stoneheart; the horse was waiting nearby, calm as could be. Daniel swung into the saddle. "Though I fear we are all slaughtered men," he said under his breath.

Stoneheart galloped ahead, and the men in Boone's charge followed.

THIRTY-NINE

Boone and his men were at the river within moments of the others, most of whom were still struggling to cross the ford; it was narrow, the surrounding water less shallow than they had reckoned, and difficult to cross as Boone had warned them. Only McGary and a handful of his men had made it to the other side and were riding ahead.

Levi Todd, not content to wait in line for shallow water, eyeballed his own spot for crossing and turned his horse toward it. The animal hit the water at a full run and was across in a flash; the sight and speed of it reminded Boone of alligators he'd seen on his expedition to Florida.

Levi's mount bounded up the riverbank. The major turned to face the men whose horses were either working to cross the river or waiting their turn to try. The effort of it tamped down a small measure of the frenzy that had gripped the men just moments earlier, and when Levi ordered each to halt as they emerged from the water, every man obeyed. McGary glanced over his shoulder, saw no one else was following, and led his men back to the river.

Still on the opposite bank, Boone, John Todd, Floyd, Trigg, and Harlan pushed ahead of as many of the militiamen as they could and rushed the ford. Once across, they shouted and pointed and made a good enough show of authority to wrangle the men into haphazard approximations of their respective companies. Boone was thankful Harlan seemed to have the allegiance of at least as many of the Lincoln men as McGary did, and Trigg appeared to have won the respect of a few himself now that he'd found his spirit.

The chaos McGary had enflamed was far from squelched, however, and before the last of the companies could form up the first of them were galloping across the thousand or so feet of flatland that sprawled between the river and the foot of the hill. Boone, Patterson, and the Fayette men exploded after them. Their horses climbed the slope, careful to stick to the well-trodden buffalo trail to avoid the hazard of the long ravine on the western side of the rise.

They arrived in moments where the others had stopped— near the top of the hill, just shy of the tree line. Colonel Todd pointed and waved, directing Major Bulger's men to form a line at the eastern edge, keeping well in from the steep slope that led down to the curving river.

Todd spotted Boone. "Daniel!" he yelled. "Take the west!"

Boone didn't argue. He cut his horse to the left; his men followed. He stopped a fair distance from the trees that hid the drop-off to the Licking on the western side, leapt from his horse, and lashed the reins to the saddle. He then turned toward the wooded hilltop where he suspected, hidden in its shadows, the enemy waited to pounce.

"Leave the horses," Boone said to the men. Some of them looked at each other.

"You heard him," shouted Patterson, noticeably out of breath. He was already half spent on account of his bad lung, and Boone was concerned he wouldn't make it through.

The men dismounted. Boone looked east down the rest of the line; Harlan's company abutted his, followed by McGary's, then Bulger's, Trigg with him. Boone was shocked to see many of the men still on horseback, including the officers; indeed, Harlan had pulled two dozen men forward and looked to be forming a cavalry. Was it Colonel Todd's plan to have those men rush the enemy as an advance force? There was little chance of that working to Boone's way of thinking; any man on horseback would be an easy target for the Indians and British positioned and protected behind the trees.

As quickly as the question had entered Boone's mind Harlan and his company were off, galloping up what remained of the rise and into the tree line. McGary and his riders followed a second later. Instinctively, Boone burst forward on foot. It didn't occur to him to announce the charge, but the Fayette men followed anyway. Boone was uncommonly fit for a man of his years and felt he was moving at a good clip until younger men, which most of them were, began passing him.

A volley of rifle shots rang out an instant later. A riderless horse appeared from the trees and ran frantically down the rise directly toward Boone. He leapt, hit the ground, then spun to see the horse still running down the slope. Harlan's horse. Boone stood, turned, and saw three men from Harlan's company—likely the only survivors—retreating. McGary's men got the message; they dismounted, each ducking behind one of the small trees at the edge of the woods, and leveled their rifles. Their horses, confused, ran back down the hill.

Then the war cry went out. Braves, dozens of them, exploded from the trees, firing their muskets as they ran.

Through the noise Boone heard a second war whoop, further away and from the east. He turned and in the distance saw Trigg shot from his horse as a second company of Indians swarmed, flanking Bulger's men.

The Kentuckians knew they'd been pursuing a coalition force carved and cobbled from tribes they'd traded, squabbled, hunted, or fought with in times past, depending on the mood and politics of the day. But now that the battle was upon them, the enormity of what they were up against dawned on the militiamen for the first time.

Boone rushed headlong into the onslaught, shots zooming all around him. His bad ankle screamed, but he pushed through it; better to live with the pain than die from a lead ball to the head because he slowed to indulge it. He glanced to his right as he ran and saw Colonel Todd, easy to spot on his white horse, riding hard to help Bulger's men; saw Todd fire his rifle then watched as the colonel was hit by a shot to the chest and thrown from the saddle. Todd landed on his back; his rifle flew from his hands, but he managed to keep hold of the reins. He struggled to his knees and clutched his chest. The Quarter Horse was well-trained and circled to allow the man who'd done the training to remount. Todd gripped at the saddle, but his hands, covered with blood, slipped on the first attempt. He tried again and succeeded this time, pitching forward in the saddle as he settled; then, in a single motion he straightened his back and drew the sword from its scabbard—Boone's sword. The horse charged. Todd was shot a second time. Boone knew this shot had killed his friend, as Todd showed no instinct to protect himself from impact as he fell. His body hit the ground, doll-like, bouncing and rolling limply before coming to a sudden and permanent stop.

The Fayette County men pressed forward, scattering, shooting, and crouching behind any cover they could find to reload as they went. A Wyandot charged Boone from his periphery. Boone raised the butt end of the fowler and thrust it forward, creasing the Indian on the temple. The man went down, but Boone couldn't take the time to ensure he stayed that way. He heard a shot behind him, very close, and assumed one of his men had finished the job.

A good-sized boulder lay ahead, just a few feet from the tree line. Boone pondered whether to leap it or use it as cover for shooting; he'd yet to fire the fowler, saving his shot for a clear target. A Mingo popped up from the blind side of the boulder and leveled his musket at Boone, but before he could pull the trigger Daniel had fired the fowler in a running shot from his hip.

"You be there," Boone heard himself yell out, as if demanding the shot to find its mark. Then he remembered he'd loaded the fowler with four balls and eighteen buckshot. The Indian was in close range. The demand wasn't necessary.

The Mingo was thrown backward and his head cracked against the boulder that had protected him seconds earlier, spraying deep red across its surface. Boone dove, rolled to the rock, swept the dead man's body aside, and reloaded the fowler using the boulder as cover. Several of his men ran up beside and around him, crouching or flattening themselves in the grass to take aim.

It was their turn now.

FORTY

The Fayette men pushed their advance, forcing the Indians nearly a hundred yards back into the woods. Once they had trees to use for cover, the frontiersmen would fire from behind one, rush ahead to the next, reload, and fire again.

A shot hit the side of the narrow dogwood Boone was pressed against, kicking debris into his eyes. He cursed, spun around the tree and returned fire, forcing the Delaware who'd shot at him to take cover himself until he could reload. Absorbed in the moment, Boone barely heard the voice calling out behind him.

"Boone!" McGary repeated a third time. Daniel turned. McGary was a few yards away and, through some miracle, still on his horse. A shot tore through McGary's shirt at the shoulder but somehow missed flesh. McGary raised his rifle, returned fire, then turned back to Boone.

"For God's sake, man—retreat!" McGary said. "Todd and Trigg's line has given way! The Indians are all about you!" Working to reload, McGary then turned his horse and galloped back the way he'd come, allowing the animal to find its own path.

Boone looked past McGary and beyond the trees toward the battlefield. His blood ran cold.

There were no Kentuckians advancing behind him—only Indians.

McGary rode toward a line of a half dozen braves; he fired, one man dropped, and the rest scattered to avoid being trampled.

Boone pressed his back against a tree and tried to force down his adrenaline to clear his mind and think. He looked back into the woods. He and his men would soon be surrounded. A victory that seemed within reach a moment ago now seemed a fool's dream, although a dream he considered embracing; surviving even in retreat was questionable now, and he'd rather die pushing forward than back. Then he remembered his men. The Scholl brothers. His nephews.

Israel.

"Retreat!" Boone shouted at the top of his lungs, hoping someone from his company would hear over the din of battle and pass the command through the line.

He breathed in to repeat the command just as the crook of an elbow closed around his throat, pinning the back of his neck to the tree and cutting off his airflow. The Delaware shifted to tighten his hold. Boone dropped the fowler, pulled his hunting knife, and thrust it around the tree and into the Indian's side. The man screamed and stumbled away.

Boone saw a number of his men running out of the woods; they'd heard him. He rushed to join them. As he broke through the tree line a Cherokee grabbed him, pulling him backwards, keeping him off balance. Boone knew if he allowed himself to be taken to the ground he was a dead man. A second Indian, Miami, rushed him from the front, whooping, knife drawn. Boone threw himself back, catching the Cherokee by surprise and causing him to stumble. They hit the ground. Boone thrust his elbow into the man's stomach, then raised his legs and caught the advancing Miami with his feet, using the attacker's momentum to throw him up and over. Boone spun, lifted his torso, then slammed his elbow into the Cherokee's larynx.

Caldwell watched, Girty beside him. Caldwell and his Rangers had fired the opening salvo that cut down Harlan's men before advancing through the woods at a diagonal as the Indians he ordered to flank the militia closed in from the east. Without having to ask Girty, Caldwell knew that the Kentuckian grappling with the two Indians was Daniel Boone, the myth that so fascinated both the Indians and his superiors. Seeing him now, in the flesh, Caldwell understood why. The man fought like nothing he'd ever seen; similar to an Indian in many respects, but with an underpinning of something Caldwell couldn't identify, a quality his worldview didn't allow for—some remnant of Boone's Quaker upbringing, perhaps. *Pride* was the best Caldwell could manage at an interpretation because his mind simply refused to concede what his eyes saw clearly; it was *nobility*. Not the type inherited by chance of birth like that of the king Caldwell served, but a valiant, inherent nobility that was the birthright of all people, yet only men like Daniel Boone managed to reach inside themselves to seize.

The damndest Quaker I've ever seen, thought Caldwell.

Boone stood and pulled his tomahawk. The Miami charged again. Boone kicked him in the gut, and the man dropped to the ground, his wind gone. A Shawnee leapt from Boone's side; Boone whirled and swung the tomahawk, smashing the flat of it against the man's head. The brave twisted mid-air before landing face-first and unconscious.

Breathing heavily, Boone looked up to make a quick assessment of his surroundings. The battlefield behind him was thick with smoke, but what he could make out was chaos; their line was broken, the militiamen in complete disarray. Then he turned toward the woods and spotted him; a Ranger, an officer, standing in plain view, rifle at his side, flanked by shadowed forms crouched in the brush and peeking from behind trees. Boone and the man locked eyes. It didn't take much guessing on Boone's part to figure the man for who and what he was.

A Wyandot sprang from the brush behind Caldwell. He notched an arrow on his bow as he rose and leveled the weapon at Boone. A shot rang out on Boone's left and the Indian fell, the lead ball striking him in the forehead. Boone whirled. About twenty-five yards behind him he saw smoke rising from the muzzle of the prettiest rifle he'd every laid eyes on. Will Hays' rifle.

Israel knelt to reload. It occurred to Daniel that the entire time they'd advanced up the hill, he'd never once seen Israel fire the weapon; the boy had saved his shot for a sure target.

Hell of a lot of nerve, Daniel thought.

Eight of the Fayette men ran to flank Israel, including Squire, Samuel, and Joseph Scholl. Each dropped to a knee and took aim. Boone turned back to Caldwell. He knew the captain was in a bind; if his men fired, they'd likely hit a number of the Indians advancing behind the Kentuckians. That consideration might hold their trigger fingers for a moment, but Boone could see in Caldwell's eyes that it wouldn't do so long. Boone let loose a guttural yell, sounding more bear than man, and flung the tomahawk. His men fired.

McKee read the throw in Boone's posture an instant before it happened. He reached up, grabbed Caldwell by the jacket sleeve, and pulled him down just as Boone's tomahawk whirled past and buried itself into a tree behind where Caldwell's head had been a second prior. But rather than thank McKee for saving his life, Caldwell tore his arm from the man's grip and glared at him. Then Caldwell whipped his head toward Girty, expecting to see the white Indian's smug grin. But Girty and his brothers were gone. Simon found slaughter neither entertaining nor challenging; his had been a game of wills, and it was Caldwell, not the Kentuckians, who'd been his opponent. He'd won. The game was over, and there was no point in lingering.

The instant the tomahawk left his hand Boone turned and ran toward his men, figuring his life worth more than the indulgence of waiting to see if the weapon found its mark. The Rangers hesitated only for a moment before opening fire themselves; Boone felt like thanking them when two Indians that had gotten between him and his men dropped, victims of the Ranger's rifles. Witnessing this, the line of Indians behind Israel and his comrades fell back to avoid getting shot themselves. Boone passed through the smoke caused by the rifles of his men as the Rangers hurried to reload. A dozen more Fayette men were with Israel and the others now. Each man got off a final shot, then jumped up and ran down the slope.

The speediest of the Rangers fired again. A shot hit Squire in the thigh, shattering bone and spinning him; he fell to his knees, took the opportunity to reload, pivoted, and fired toward the Rangers. He struggled to stand but the leg couldn't support his weight and he stumbled, rolled down the slope, and was swallowed up by the chaos. In the confusion of the moment, none of his friends noticed.

Boone's men were quickly out of range of the Rangers' muskets. It didn't take much; as skilled at soldiering as the Rangers were, the Brown Bess was an infamously inaccurate weapon. Within seconds the Fayette men had dropped below the horizon entirely; if the Rangers wanted to keep shooting at them, they'd have to pursue. This realization caused Boone to notice that few of the Indians on the battlefield were taking the time to reload; most had abandoned their rifles altogether for the thrill of close combat.

"Group together!" Boone yelled.

The men passed the order around and within moments had formed a tightly packed cell. They moved down the hill as a unit, angling west, the men on the perimeter facing out, firing their rifles, rotating inside the circle to reload as the men behind them stepped forward, fired, and repeated the cycle, always keeping the injured at the center of the pack. Someone, Boone didn't see whom, shoved a long rifle into his hands. Boone began to load it—miraculously, he'd not lost his rifle bag in his scuffle with the Indians—and noticed the weapon was splattered with blood.

The men weren't surprised to see that the horses had long since fled; without a rider to steady it, even the best-trained animal could be spooked by the sounds and smells of the battlefield, and if one horse lost its calm and took off running, those around it were certain to follow.

Boone's group resigned themselves to making the long trip down the hillside on foot, watching their step to avoid stumbling over bodies—sometimes an Indian, but more often one of their own. Every yard of ground they gained reduced the number of attackers; the majority of Indians were behind them now, some in pursuit but most choosing easier, more isolated prey, pouncing upon the scattered militiamen of the other companies as they retreated or struggled to reload, two, sometimes three Indians to each white man, killing then scalping them, or just as often scalping then killing. Caldwell's Rangers held back, allowing the Indians to practice that at which they excelled; brutal, unrelenting hand-to-hand combat.

Boone's men pushed the scene from their minds; turning back to try to save a poor soul already lost would surely mean the death of them all. Any Kentuckian in their path, however, was brought into the circle; they slowed several times to scoop up wounded men, once attempting to drag a man to his feet only to discover he was already dead. They lowered the body to the ground as gently as time allowed and continued down the slope.

FORTY-ONE

The Wyandot Israel Boone shot through the forehead landed inches from her, arrows from the quiver on his back spilling across her feet. Tied to a tree and facing away from the battlefield as she was, Anne Morgan had no way of knowing who'd pulled the trigger, but she did know immediately upon seeing the blank stare in the Wyandot's cold, unblinking eyes that the Indian was dead. The hole in his head only confirmed the fact.

That morning, Caldwell decided he was no longer amused by having Anne underfoot, so he grabbed the first Indian he spotted and saddled him with the responsibility of her. This presented the Wyandot with a dilemma; how was he supposed to join his fellows in battle while keeping watch over a prisoner? Frustrated, the best he could think to do was tie a rope from the woman's bonds to his waist and have her sit a few feet behind him while he waited with Caldwell's men for the militia to get within rifle range. The woman's spirit had been so trampled that she offered no resistance, allowing the Indian to pay her little mind.

The Indians and Rangers fired, reloaded, and fired again; then, they were on the move, Anne struggling to keep pace with the Wyandot as branches whipped her face and brush cut her legs. Finally, Caldwell put up a hand and they stopped. Through the trees, in the distance, she caught a brief glimpse of a Kentuckian—Daniel Boone?—struggling with a pair of Indians before the Wyandot shoved her to the ground, undid the rope that connected them, and tied her hands behind her back around a small tree. It struck her as oddly courteous that he'd positioned her behind the tree, shielded from potential rifle fire.

Moments later, she heard the shot and the Wyandot fell. She craned her head as far around the tree as she was able and saw Caldwell, from behind, standing in the open, along with the backs of several Rangers and Indians crouching in the brush behind trees and fallen timber, aiming their rifles ahead. Most importantly, they were paying her no attention whatsoever.

She grasped one of the arrows between her feet and bent her knees to bring it closer in, then released it. Then she dug her heels into the ground, flattened her back against the tree, and struggled to stand, shifting left to right against the bark to gain traction. When she was partially upright, she worked herself around the tree a step at a time, eventually facing her captors. She held her breath. None turned to face her. Slowly, she slid back to the ground. Then the firing started, first toward her, then away as the Rangers and Indians returned fire.

She reached out blindly as far as the ties would allow, patting the ground in search of the arrow. Finally, her pinky hit upon it and she exhaled, realizing that she'd been holding her breath the whole time. She flicked at the arrow, pulled it closer, then wrapped her fingers around it and worked it forward until she grasped the base of the arrowhead. Then she got to sawing.

The arrowhead was far from razor sharp, the momentum of being launched from a bow not requiring such to pierce flesh, but several moments of sawing added to the pressure of pulling her wrists apart did the job; the tie snapped, and she was free.

She didn't move. She hadn't allowed herself to hope to get this far and hadn't thought past the moment. She knew the Indians and Rangers had left their horses on the other side of the hill, but the animals were a ways back and she remembered Caldwell ordering the redcoats to stay behind to tend to them. She couldn't go forward without getting caught in the crossfire any more than she could run east and into the path of the advancing Indians. So that was that.

She was up and running before finishing the thought, surprising herself. No point in overthinking it; the longer she delayed, the worse her odds of escaping. She burst west, keeping low at first, rising gradually as if rediscovering her humanity the more distance she put between herself and her captors. The woods grew thicker; her feet squished down on damp leaves and underbrush perpetually shielded from the sun. The shaft of a broken sapling stabbed her bare foot but she knew better than to cry out and kept running, full-out, her arms up to protect her face, until the ground vanished beneath her.

FORTY-TWO

It was Israel's turn on the perimeter; he rotated out, sighted a Delaware, fired, and saw the man fall before spotting John Floyd on his periphery. A Cherokee, tomahawk drawn, leapt at Floyd from behind.

"John!" Israel shouted, but he was too far away for the man to hear.

Floyd turned at the last moment and avoided the swing of the tomahawk, but the Cherokee's shoulder plowed into his abdomen, forcing the air from his body. The two men grappled, rolling down the slope until they collided with the body of Major Bulger.

The Cherokee was astride Floyd and had somehow managed to keep hold of his tomahawk despite the tumbling. He raised it high, the dull blade directly over Floyd's face. Israel saw it happen just as he was swept back into the circle. He pulled a cartridge from his bag, worked to reload Hays' rifle, and wondered at Floyd's fate.

The tomahawk swung down, but Floyd reached up and grabbed the man's wrist, bringing the weapon to an abrupt

stop. Floyd still couldn't breathe. His vision tunneled. The
Cherokee put his other hand on top of the first, pressing the
Tomahawk slowly down as Floyd struggled to keep it at bay.
His opponent's strength was waning, the Cherokee knew. The
blade inched closer. The Cherokee wondered at the reason the
white man wasn't using his other arm but barely had time to
consider the question before it appeared from the fold of
Floyd's cloak clutching a Dragon—a single shot blunderbuss,
a pistol of the sort pirates use on the high seas, a remnant of
Floyd's time as privateer. The Indian's eyes went wide and he
jerked backward, but Floyd still held the man's tomahawk
arm, preventing escape—the white man wasn't as weak as the
Indian had thought. Floyd put the barrel of the pistol under
the Indian's chin and pulled the trigger. The Dragon roared
and the Cherokee's head vanished. Floyd released the brave's
arm and the man fell off of him without contest. Floyd
stashed the pistol securely back into its hidden holster; it was
too valuable to leave on the battlefield, and he had every
intention of living to use it another day.

Boone watched as a figure, about two hundred feet to his
east, emerged from the smoke, heading up the hill rather
than down. Boone squinted and blinked; it was John Floyd.

A Mingo charged Floyd. John aimed and fired the rifle he
was holding and the Indian fell. The discharge of the weapon
created a waft of smoke and Floyd passed through it, his gait
steady. He tossed the rifle aside, bent down, still walking, and
picked up another that had once belonged to some poor
soul who no longer had need of it. Floyd leveled the weapon
at a Shawnee who was rushing toward him and pulled the
trigger—empty. The Indian closed in; Floyd flipped the rifle

and swung it, shattering the stock on the brave's head and sending him flying. Floyd tossed the weapon, picked up the next one in his path, and fired it at a Wyandot who was a moment away from scalping a struggling militiaman. The shot threw the Indian backward and the militia man stood, confused, but not so much so that he hesitated for more than a second before exploding into a full run down the hillside.

Floyd repeated the process over and over; picking up a rifle—sometimes the Brown Bess of a dead Indian but more often a long rifle that once belonged to a comrade and perhaps friend—and pulling the trigger, his advance constant whether the weapon fired or not.

Boone witnessed this repetition a couple of times, turned to tend to his own troubles, then turned back to Floyd to see the pattern unchanged. Something had possessed the man. Finally, when his friend was close enough to hear him over the sounds of battle, Boone called to him.

"John! Go!"

Floyd seemed to not hear; he was in a trance.

"Go!" Boone yelled again.

Floyd heard a distant echo that sounded like Boone's voice. He turned, took in his surroundings, and quickly grasped his situation; as Boone and his men had done earlier, Floyd was advancing in the cause of a fight already lost. Death, perhaps preceded by torture, were the only spoils that lay ahead. Floyd turned, picked up a rifle, and began his retreat.

Less than ten minutes had passed since the first shot of the battle had been fired.

FORTY-THREE

A number of the militia's horses were congregated at the edge of the ravine that cut across the hill, apparently not yet so spooked by the battle that they considered it worth the effort to cross.

"Move, move, move!" Daniel shouted. The unit split, and each man who was able raced for the first horse he could snag, helping those too wounded to manage on their own into a saddle.

Boone spotted a horse at the western edge. He grabbed Israel by the sleeve, and they sprinted toward it. The animal remained calm as they approached, allowing Daniel to take hold of its bridle. Boone turned to his son.

"Go!" he said, nodding for Israel to get in the saddle. Daniel knew the horse could carry them both, but the added weight would cost them in speed.

Israel looked over his shoulder and watched as Andrew McConnell was overtaken and dragged to the ground by a pair of Cherokee. One of the Indians reached down and yanked the wide-brimmed hat from McConnell's head.

Israel turned back to his father.

"I won't leave you."

Daniel gathered up the horse's reins and pushed them into Israel's hands. "Dammit, I'll get the next one. Go."

Israel stared at him and didn't move.

Daniel saw a stubbornness in the boy's eyes that was powerfully familiar; he'd seen it in Rebecca's many a time and suspected she'd say the same of him. There was no use arguing and no time to. A second horse was close by; he turned and started for it. He'd barely taken a step when he heard the shot.

He looked back. Israel was slumped against the horse, his hands at his throat. Blood sprayed from between his fingers. Daniel rushed to his side, pulling off his hunting shirt as he went. The horse stood calmly as Israel slid down its shoulder and leg to a sitting position on the ground. His hands fell to his sides. Daniel was kneeling beside him in a flash. He started to rip his shirt into strips to wrap the wound, to stop the bleeding, but saw instantly it would make no difference. He placed the shirt whole over Israel's throat and applied gentle pressure, hoping it would somehow lessen the boy's pain. He put his hand behind Israel's head. Israel stared at him, choking on his own blood.

"Go," said Daniel. "It's okay. Go now, Israel. I'll be fine."

He prayed God would come for his son soon, would end his suffering. Israel turned from his father and closed his eyes.

He was gone.

Daniel sat on his knees, unmoving, his hand on his son's chest. The sounds of the retreat echoed all around him, but that world seemed distant, spectral, and he wanted to keep it that way; rejoining it would be too painful. He wanted to sink into his sorrow and vanish. But he realized he couldn't.

He'd promised Israel he'd be fine, and he had no intention of making his last words to his boy a lie.

He looked up and took in his surroundings. The horses had run off without his noticing and there were now no others. He could hear shooting, screaming, and whooping just up the hill, but the smoke on the battlefield was so thick that he could only make out vague shadows. The shot that struck Israel had come from that direction, but it occurred to Boone he'd never know who killed his son or if the Indian or Ranger who pulled the trigger even knew himself.

The lack of visibility also worked in his favor, however; he was at the edge of the battlefield and had yet to be noticed. That wouldn't last long, he knew. He picked up Israel, gently but hurriedly, and carried him into the trees by the western slope. He knew this land better than any man alive; he'd hunted here, camped here, drank here, sang here without audience other than his hunting dogs, rescued Jemima and the Calloway girls near here, and was captured himself along with a number of his neighbors while boiling salt at the Blue Licks, just below where he now stood. He'd be damned if he'd let the Indians make a trophy of Israel's scalp the way they had with James, and knew where his son's body would be safe in death, at least for a time.

He reached the bluff that dropped toward the river he knew was below but couldn't see on account of the thickly packed trees that rose up from the water's edge. The bluff was too steep to climb, but there was a small cave beneath the lip of it where he'd waited out more than one downpour. He laid Israel's body at the bluff's edge, then climbed down into the brambles; if a man were surefooted, the brush could support his weight for a moment, which was all the time he'd need.

He pushed aside the roots and vines that concealed the cave's mouth, then reached up, put one hand beneath Israel's shoulders, the other beneath his knees and pulled his son forward and into his arms. The brambles beneath Boone shifted. He steadied himself. Then he slid Israel into the shallow cave. Daniel pushed the curtain of vines closed again and crawled back to the top of the bluff.

Boone made his way back to the clearing. He spotted his blood-soaked hunting shirt hanging from a branch. The shirt had snagged on it, apparently, and been pulled from Israel's body as Daniel carried the boy through. Boone grabbed the garment and pulled it on. As he neared the edge of the woods he could still hear fighting, not as cacophonous as before but close by, most of his fellows either dead or having retreated further down the hill and, he hoped, across the ford.

The first thing Boone saw when he emerged from the trees was a horse; Martha's horse, the animal Peter Scholl had borrowed and ridden here—the horse his brother, Edward, had trained. The animal looked up, anticipation in his eyes as if he'd been waiting for Daniel's arrival. Boone sprinted toward it. He spotted Will Hays' rifle on the ground, snatched it up as he ran, then he swung into the saddle. The Horse bolted with no prompting.

FORTY-FOUR

Benjamin Netherland ran down the hill at such a pace that his feet came out from under him and he rolled head over heels the remaining thirty yards, bouncing over rocks and roots before the earth flattened enough that he could get to his feet. Falling as he did likely saved his life, as rifle shots whizzed by where his head would have been otherwise.

He looked around to get his bearings; all about him was chaos as his fellows desperately grabbed whatever horse they could find, some successfully speeding away, others dragged from their mounts by pursuing Indians and tomahawked before they could get their feet securely into the stirrups.

Something caught Netherland's eye to his left; he turned and saw an Andalusian with a dappled gray coat standing calmly within the calamity, Daniel Boone's horse he was almost certain, not twenty yards away. He bolted for it. A Wyandot stepped in his path and Netherland plowed through him and didn't look back, his eyes fixed on the Andalusian. He grabbed the horse's bridle and started it running, then swung into the saddle just before the filly's speed outstripped his own. The horse, calm as could be a moment earlier, now ran like lightning straight for the ford; Netherland wasn't even conscious of guiding her. There was no doubting it now—it was, indeed, the horse Boone had been riding. She leapt into the river with no hesitation and pushed through the water with all her might, slowing gradually but less than expected as the depth of the water steadily rose to halfway up her neck at the river's midpoint.

Netherland saw four other riders crossing the river ahead of him and many men running into the river horseless. Rifle fire kicked up water all around him; two men were shot as they swam, spasming with the impact before dropping forward into the water and sinking beneath it.

Stoneheart closed in on the opposite bank, picking up speed as she rose from the water. When she hit the shallows she was out like a shot, hooves digging into silt, then dirt, as she bounded over the bank and darted for the tree line. Tears came to Netherland's eyes; he thought certain he was a dead man a moment ago and now he was alive, thanks to what was surely the finest horse on the frontier. He intended to give Boone whatever he wanted for the Andalusian, or to make the same offer to Boone's widow if the man didn't survive.

The thought made him pull back on the reins. Stoneheart stopped immediately. Netherland turned and got the full picture of the scene that being on the bank opposite the battle allowed; at least two dozen militiamen were retreating down the hill, same as he had done, some lucky enough to get past the Indians and into the water, most not so. The majority of the horses had now been claimed by Indians who were crossing the ford themselves, tomahawking or shooting militiamen who were swimming for their lives. There was no resistance;

the Indians reloaded casually and shot down one man after the next.

Netherland gave a tug to one rein and made a clicking sound with his mouth. Stoneheart responded and turned smoothly as if they were out on a casual ride through a placid meadow, then rushed back toward the river.

Netherland spotted the body of a frontiersman lying on the bank, rifle beside it. He leapt from the filly and snatched up the weapon. Militiamen were pulling themselves from the water, drenched and exhausted. Netherland raised the rifle over his head.

"Let's halt, boys, and give them a fire," Netherland's voice boomed. It was so loud, clear, and commanding that at first he thought it had come from someone else.

It took some of the men longer than others to tamp down their fear and adrenaline, but each man stopped. Those that still had their rifles, dry powder horns, and lead got to work loading. Those that didn't searched the ground around them and borrowed from the dead whatever components they were missing.

The Indians fording the river saw what was happening and stopped. Those who hadn't yet crossed the midpoint turned back; two on horseback who were nearest the white men encouraged their horses forward, tomahawks raised, attack their only option, hoping to set upon the settlers before they could load their weapons. These were seasoned frontiersmen, however, many of whom had been rushed by angry bears, wild boars, and, in some cases, antagonistic Indians in the past—they were more than experienced in loading rifles under stress. Netherland had already loaded his and had his sights on the first of the two Indians, a Delaware. He breathed in, taking his time to find his mark; if he shot and missed it was all over, so there was no point rushing things. The Delaware, realizing he was fighting against time as much as anything now, leaned forward and to his side, riding at a near right angle to his horse. He extended his tomahawk arm, intent on decapitating Netherland before the man could get off his shot. It wasn't to be. Netherland fired. The ball hit the Delaware in his left eye and the brave hit the shallow water, still clutching the tomahawk which drove itself on impact into the wet silt.

A man to Netherland's right took out the second rider. Four other mounted Indians had turned back the way they'd come but not yet cleared the water; the frontiersmen fired and all four fell from their horse and into the river.

Having let loose their first volley, a few of the frontiersmen scurried up the bank for higher ground. They flattened themselves on the grass and took aim at Indians on the opposite bank who were too busy killing and scalping white men to notice. At long last the frontiersmen were able to utilize their primary advantage—the range of the Kentucky long rifle. The shooters fired and five Indians fell. The militiamen those Indians had been attacking ran for the river with all their remaining strength, some so badly wounded that they died while crossing, sinking peacefully beneath the water to be slowly carried downstream. The remaining Indians scattered, desperate to get out of rifle range or find cover, which was none too easy; they were on the barren field of the Blue Licks, all vegetation gnawed away by animals of every kind that were drawn here by instinct for the minerals provided by the rich soil. The Indians, particularly the Shawnee and Cherokee, had taken advantage of this for centuries, and the area had become an important hunting ground.

Now they were the hunted.

The Kentuckians fired again; more Indians, quite far up the hill now, fell. The few who managed to escape would return soon and bring others with them, likely in numbers too great for the handful of frontiersmen to pick off before running out of ammunition and being overtaken. Still, every Kentuckian that now crawled exhausted from the river was a life saved that wouldn't have been otherwise.

The shooters helped their fellows from the water and hoisted the wounded onto what horses could be wrangled. Each man thanked the shooters for what they'd done.

"It was Netherland's doing," said James McCullough, one of the shooters. The others nodding in agreement. "He was the one brought us to our senses so we'd start loading rifles."

Yellow Ben Netherland? the survivors thought, although none said it. Only later would they learn, in bits and pieces, that Yellow Ben had volunteered to help defend Fort Moultrie in Charleston in the early days of the war; that he'd fought with General Nathanael Greene at the Battle of Guilford Courthouse in North Carolina in March of 1781, and, having had enough of war, had just recently traveled to Kentucky to start a new life, only for the fighting to find him here.

The thankful men scanned the area for Netherland and spotted him patting the neck of Will Hays' Andalusian, talking to the animal affectionately after having helped a wounded man into the saddle. They caught Netherland's attention and nodded.

Yellow Ben nodded back.

FORTY-FIVE

Squire stumbled, and the bone protruding from his thigh pushed a half inch more from his flesh. He yelled; one more shout added to the din of the battlefield wasn't likely to draw much attention, so he saw no reason to hold it in. He shoved the muzzle of his rifle into the dirt, put his weight on it, and hoisted himself back to standing.

Hopping on his good leg, he continued down the remaining length of the hill as quickly as he could manage. He'd fallen well behind his uncle's group, though, and knew there was no chance of catching up to them. If they'd seen he'd been shot, they'd have surely stopped to try to grab him up; but Squire hadn't called out, not wanting to put them in jeopardy trying to help a lame man who likely had no chance of making it anyway.

But make it he did, somehow, to the bottom of the hill and the flat ground of the salt lick. He tacked west, keeping himself out of direct alignment with the ford, hoping to avoid notice. He thought sure he heard rifle fire from the opposite bank; if the fighting had spread to the other side of the river he was a dead man for certain. Then, shockingly, he saw a number of Indians running from the flatland back toward the hill. Something had rattled them, giving Squire at least a prayer of escaping.

Using the rifle as a crutch, Squire limped along, making steady progress. His eyes darted in all directions, searching for a horse. Nothing. He heard whoops from the hillside, drawing closer; the Indians who'd run had gathered their cohorts for a coordinated assault and were heading again toward the river. Squire didn't look back; he kept pressing forward, biting down the pain that accompanied each step.

Then he heard hoof falls, soft at first but growing louder as the rider closed the distance. Squire's stomach went cold. The sound of the hoofs intensified, pounding in his ears, death itself drawing closer, soon to overtake him, the beast now at his heels. Squire closed his eyes. Then, to his astonishment, the animal bolted past him. The rider pulled back on the reins and the horse turned to block Squire's path.

"Keep hobbling, come on," Samuel Brannon yelled as he leapt from the horse and cupped his hands low to the ground.

Squire, his adrenaline spiked from thinking he was about to be killed a moment earlier, pulled from reserves he didn't know he had and picked up his pace. When he reached Brannon, Squire dropped his rifle, jumped, and placed the foot of his good leg into Brannon's hands as Brannon straightened his knees and lifted with his arms to throw Squire upward. Squire flung his bad leg over the horse and landed perfectly in the saddle. He looked down at Brannon to smile, but his eyes went wide when he saw half a dozen Indians headed their way, on foot, two with arrows notched and ready to fire. Brannon sprang onto the horse, plopped down behind the saddle, and wrapped his arms around Squire's waist.

"Go, go!" Brannon yelled, but Squire didn't need the prodding; he grabbed the reins and turned the horse, making for the ford in a mad dash. The two arrows whizzed by, and Squire knew sure he felt a feather graze his cheek. The horse hit the water and plunged forward, slowed gradually by the increasing depth and current of the river. Both men turned to their right to look behind them, then Squire realized he had to turn left to see around Brannon. They'd put some distance between themselves and the Indians, who were just now reaching the riverbank. Three of the braves jumped into the water and began to wade out, but there was no chance of them overtaking the horse; the concern for the two Kentuckians was getting out of arrow range. Most Indians were more accurate with a bow than with a Brown Bess, quicker at notching arrows than loading rifles, and the longer Squire and Samuel were confined to the river, the longer they made for a good-sized, slow moving target.

Water lapped onto Squire's injured leg. He watched as blood from the wound snaked downstream, the sight of it making him lightheaded; he'd have to tie the leg off to stop the bleeding as soon as they were a safe distance away. He was staring, half dazed, at the rivulet of his blood when an arrow zipped into the water, disturbing it—then another, then a third. Squire blinked to bring his vision into focus, looked back, and saw the three braves who were knee-deep in the river notching fresh arrows. He spun around to see how close he and Samuel and the horse were to the southern bank; not far now, but far enough. There were no militiamen in sight, and it occurred to Squire that he and Brannon were likely the last of them left alive to retreat.

More arrows zipped by, barely missing them, and then only on account of the horse's bouncing as it fought for traction to pull itself from the water. They'd nearly made it.

"Blazes," Brannon said.

Squire turned and saw what Brannon had; two of the Indians who hadn't run into the river had found abandoned rifles at the water's edge. Kentucky long rifles.

The frontiersmen turned and leaned forward.

"Yah, yah!" they both yelled, hoping to badger the horse into picking up speed. Brannon began smacking the animal vigorously on its hindquarters as encouragement, but the silt and sand beneath its feet didn't afford the same traction as solid ground. They heard two shots. Neither of the men, nor the horse, were hit. The Indians would have to reload now, and, by then, the Kentuckians would be well on their way.

An instant later the horse was rising out of the water and up the bank. Brannon nearly slid off. They hit solid ground, and the horse rushed for the tree line at a full gallop. Squire and Brannon laughed.

"Samuel, you surely saved my—"

Squire heard a shot and felt Brannon's arms slip from his waist before the horse was suddenly moving faster. Squire turned and saw Samuel's body bounce once on the ground, then roll to a stop.

The third Indian had apparently found a rifle as well.

Squire pulled back on the reins. The sudden change in message confused the horse, and it took her a second to stop. Squire turned her and rushed back to Brannon. He heard more shots, but they no longer concerned him.

Brannon was on his back, eyes open in a blank stare. There was no blood that Squire could see—at least not yet. Samuel looked peaceful.

Another shot zipped past Squire's head. He looked up. The Indians were crossing the river, the first of them nearly at the bank. A dozen more were running down the hill where the battle had taken place to join them.

Squire took one last look at his friend and neighbor. "Thank you, Samuel," he said. Then he turned the horse and headed into the woods.

FORTY-SIX

Patterson opened his eyes and found he was looking at the sky through a thick canopy of leaves. He wasn't sure how long he'd been out, but he suspected it had only been a minute or two. He hurt all over and couldn't decide if he was more distracted by the new pain at the back of his head from where he'd apparently hit a rock, or from the old pain of his bad lung, exacerbated by the exertion of the day.

He listened for a moment; the sound of the battle was scattered and distant. He stood, mindful of his footing, but even still stumbled on account of his dizziness, and would have had a second tumble down the cliff if he hadn't managed to brace himself against a small tree. He caught his breath and was about to ease his way down the bluff when he heard something rustling through the brush, rushing quickly toward him. He scanned the ground for his rifle, didn't see it, then remembered he'd dropped it several yards back where he started his fall. His hand went to the hunting knife at his waist just as Aaron Reynolds appeared from a cluster of pines.

"Hell, Captain—I've been looking all over for you," Reynolds said.

Patterson let out the breath he was holding. "Where are the others?"

"At the bottom of this damn cliff where we outta be, I reckon," Reynolds said as he hurried to Patterson's side and swung the captain's arm over his shoulder. "No time for loafing, come on, come on."

They started down the slope. It didn't take long to reach the bottom; Reynolds threw himself into a sure-footed skid most of the way, Patterson along for the ride, the captain's feet coming out from under him several times but Aaron keeping him upright. When the incline leveled, Reynolds transitioned from a skid to a hop, propelling them out of the trees and onto the narrow bank of the river. Both men scanned left and right. They could hear shots and yelling around the bend toward the ford, but here, at least, they were alone.

"There," Reynolds yelled as he darted upstream. Patterson looked to where Reynolds was headed and saw a horse wading in the river; it had likely panicked when the shooting started, made its way here, and had now forgotten its troubles and figured on a cool bath.

Reynolds splashed into the water, taking big steps but being careful not the spook the animal, which he assumed was already skittish. He reached it, extended his hand slowly, and petted its neck. The horse didn't flinch.

"Good girl," Reynolds said as he took hold of the bridle.

Patterson had finally caught up and was just starting into the water when he noticed Reynolds was walking the horse back.

"Here you go, Captain," Reynolds said when he reached the shallow water near the bank. He gestured to the horse and smiled, the absence of the tooth lost in the previous night's scuffle quite conspicuous.

"Get on first and help me up," Patterson said.

Reynolds scratched his head.

"No, sir," Aaron responded. "There ain't no ford here. Water's too deep for even a fresh horse to swim two grown men across, let alone this one that's tuckered out. You're the scrawnier of us. Take her and go."

Patterson narrowed his eyes. "Reynolds, I order you to—"

"Shit fire, Captain," Reynolds said, cutting Patterson off. "I ain't the one that can't walk a dozen paces without breathing heavy. I can make the swim, you can't, and the longer you dillydally the worse both our chances, so get on the damn horse!"

Patterson's mouth tightened. He glowered at Reynolds, but the man's logic couldn't be argued against. The captain put his foot in the stirrup, grabbed the saddle, and worked to pull himself up. Reynolds had to help, proving his point; Patterson was pretty near worn-out as it was. The second Patterson hit the saddle, Reynolds smacked the horse on the rump and the animal took off. Patterson grabbed hold of her mane with one hand while fishing for the reins with the other. He found them. The horse trotted and splashed across. When the water became too deep, she began to swim.

Reynolds did have a problem he'd decided against mentioning to the captain, not wanting to sway the man against taking the horse and feeling a mite embarrassed besides; wading into the river as he'd done, his fancy buckskin

303

trousers had sopped up their full measure of water—which seemed to Aaron to be about half the river—and become unbelievably heavy. There wasn't a chance in the world the strength in his legs would hold kicking across the full width of the river with the extra weight. He plodded back to the bank, cussing under his breath. Reaching it, he faced the river to check Patterson's progress; the horse was about half across, in the deep of it. Patterson was looking over his shoulder at Reynolds, a confused look on his face. Aaron stuck out his hand, palm down, and waggled his fingers to indicate to Patterson to keep going, that he was fine, just fine. Reluctantly, Patterson turned; the current was rough this far out and he had to put his full attention on keeping the animal calm and steady and not getting swept off the saddle.

Finally, thought Reynolds. He plopped down in the silt and began the arduous work of peeling off his trousers. It was frustrating to have to do, but at least he had the time; he figured the Indians were good and busy rounding up any remaining horses downstream and wouldn't be heading this way any time soon.

With sizable effort and frustration, Aaron managed to wriggle the trousers down his thighs, then off his right leg. He got them clear of the left, but they hung on his foot. He pulled hard and the foot popped free, the force of it spinning him to the right, causing the butt of the rifle to slam into his left ear rather than the back of his head as the Indian intended. The blow flipped Reynolds forward, and his face hit the ground and scraped against the wet silt. The pain was overwhelming, and he nearly blacked out, but curiosity kept him lucid, and he managed instead to flop to his side and look up to see what had hit him.

Two big Indians stood over him—or at least they seemed big from Aaron's vantage point—one markedly larger than the other. The sun was in Aaron's eyes, so he couldn't see them clearly, but what he could make out suggested at least one of the men was a Cherokee. Good; he had experience with the Cherokee, most of it friendly, and it was always easier to work with what you knew.

The little-big Indian said something to the bigger one; Aaron knew a little of the language, but his left ear was ringing so loudly he couldn't make out the words. Little-Big pointed, and Big nodded and took off in a sprint upstream—searching for horses to snatch, no doubt, although why the big one was taking orders from the smaller Reynolds couldn't figure.

Aaron pushed himself to his knees. Little-Big looked down at him and gestured with his rifle, miming smashing the butt end into Aaron's head again. Aaron lifted a hand and lowered his head to show that he took the man's meaning. *Worthless Brown Bess*, Reynolds thought. *I'm gonna die having my head bashed in by that piece of no-count garbage.* Then it occurred to him that it was probably worse than that, that he'd likely be taken prisoner, tortured, and scalped alive.

He wondered why the Cherokees hadn't fired at Patterson. He looked up, blinked, and through blurry vision saw why; two Indians across the river were riding hard toward the captain from the east.

Patterson's horse cleared the water and was struggling up the opposite bank when he saw them; the Indians were less than a hundred yards away and closing the distance fast. Patterson figured he could just make the tree line before they reached him, then lose them in the woods—if he were lucky.

305

But what of Reynolds? At least one of the Indians would wait here for Aaron to reach the bank. Patterson started running options through his mind but exhausted them quickly; he wasn't armed, but there were rocks enough, he supposed.

The horse was up the bank and on firm ground. Now that he was able, Patterson looked back to check Aaron's progress and saw for the first time that he'd been captured. Patterson stared for a moment and said a prayer for the man. He couldn't be sure, but he thought he saw Reynolds smiling at him. Then a rifle barked and kicked up the dirt a few feet from Patterson's horse. Patterson cursed, which he knew would have given Reynolds great joy had he heard, and bolted for the woods.

Little-Big watched his brethren follow Patterson into the trees. He scoffed, then looked down at Reynolds and chuckled. Aaron felt sure it was on account of his lack of trousers.

He felt water running from his left ear, then remembered he hadn't gotten his head wet, so it probably wasn't water at all. He hung his head to the side. Red blobs dropped from the ear and rhythmically splattered on the ground. He glanced up; Little-Big was looking downstream, watching for his friend's return. Then Reynolds noticed the Cherokee was still clutching the rifle in the battering position, his fingers on the opposite side of the weapon from the trigger.

Aaron slowly laced his fingers together then sprang up, catching Little-Big beneath the chin in a two-fisted uppercut. The force lifted the Cherokee from his feet, and even through the ringing in his ears Aaron heard the man's jaw crumble. Little-Big hit the ground, dropping the rifle. He struggled to stand, head wobbling loosely on his neck, his jaw hanging slack. He coughed, spitting blood and teeth. Reynolds grabbed the rifle, raised it over his head, then swung it like an axe, smashing the Indian on the head, giving the man as good a whack as he'd doled out himself, the force of the blow spinning Little-Big half around as his body went slack and fell.

Reynolds suspected Little-Big was unconscious rather than dead and considered doing him in but decided against it; he'd never killed a man and wasn't sure he could live with the burden of it. Sure, he had fired his rifle several times during the battle, but the smoke was so thick he wasn't sure he'd ever hit his mark, and that was war besides; it was something else altogether to shoot a man already down. Perhaps when the Cherokee recovered he'd remember his life had been spared and might do the same for a white man in the future. Perhaps.

Aaron hurled the rifle, sending it spinning into the river. He sprinted into the water. When it was deep enough, he dove forward and started to swim, fast as he was able, knowing the bigger Cherokee could return at any moment. He felt a fool, but there was no doubting his speed was improved by his lack of trousers.

FORTY-SEVEN

Anne Morgan was tired, scraped, and bruised. She knew to head south and had been guiding herself by the sun, but the density of the forest and her fatigue had run roughshod over her faculties, disorienting her. Still, being lost in the wilderness was preferable by far to being a prisoner of Caldwell and his band.

No sooner had she escaped her captors—running into the thickly clustered trees at the western edge of the battlefield— than she found herself in fresh peril, falling, tumbling over and over until thick brambles brought her to a sudden and painful stop. She sat up, careful not to shift her weight, realizing that she'd run off a bluff hidden by the trees. The brambles were the only thing keeping her from falling to her death.

She looked down.

It wasn't a sheer drop, but it was mighty steep, and the bottom far enough away that she was looking onto treetops. There were plenty of roots and vines that she could use as holds to make her way down though, so long as she was mindful.

She took consolation in knowing the bluff would make it that much more difficult for anyone to follow her; her tumbling had also given her a decent head start.

The slope became less treacherous as she neared the bottom. She increased her pace. Within moments Anne was standing on the narrow riverbank, assessing her surroundings. There was no ford on this side of the hill; she'd have to swim across. Hurriedly, she unfastened her dress, removed it, then stepped out of her petticoat—she was a strong swimmer, but she'd never reach the other side with the drag of the heavy garments working against her and making it impossible to kick with her legs.

Stripped to her shift, she snatched the dress from the ground, twisted it into a tight coil, then tied it around her waist. The petticoat she left. She darted into the river; when the water was up to her ribs, she took a deep breath and started swimming. She couldn't yet allow herself the luxury of leisurely reflection, but, after three days of being force-marched in the summer heat, she was conscious of the spiritual uplift gifted to her by the cool, refreshing nature of the water.

She reached the opposite bank and hustled immediately into the woods. It would have been preferable to pause, catch her breath, and dry in the sun, but the risk of being seen was too great. Hidden within the trees, she stopped long enough to wring out the dress and wrap it around her left forearm. Then she took off, holding the arm in front of her face as protection against the green saplings and branches that snapped at her like whips as she ran. She never slowed or looked back. Her wet shift seemed to snag on every bramble. Luckily, even in the humidity of the Kentucky summer, the thin linen was completely dry when she popped out of the woods thirty minutes later and found herself standing at the edge of the buffalo trace. She listened. Nothing. She proceeded cautiously onto the trail, looked in one direction, then the other. Nothing still. She unrolled her dress, now nearly dry, and slipped it on. As she did so, she caught sight of her bare feet; they were blistered and torn, cut and bleeding, although just how badly she couldn't tell because they were black with dirt. She looked back to where she had stepped onto the trail and saw partial footprints drawn in blood. Well, there'd be no hiding that. Perhaps as she went enough dust would cake her feet to tamp down the bleeding.

She proceeded south down the narrow trail, hewing to the edge, figuring to dart into the trees at the first sign of trouble.

The sun was bright and intense above her, although large trees bordering the trace offered regular intervals of shade. She walked for what seemed an hour, perhaps more. Her mind had become increasingly occupied by her thirst; she'd have to dip back into the woods soon and hope to find a spring or creek close to the trail. Bright as it was, hot as it was, night was coming for her, and she wondered if she could make it to the relative safety of the ruins of Ruddle Station before the sun fell.

She rounded a bend; the trail straightened and she saw a large object lying across it, fifty feet or so ahead. She froze. Squinted. Dead animal most likely. She took a few cautious steps. As she drew closer, it became unavoidably obvious that the shape was a man, lying prone; a white man she supposed from the clothing, although it was difficult to be certain. Frontiersmen had embraced the Indian style of dress out of

310

practicality, and certain of the Indians, particularly the Shawnee, had adopted elements of white men's clothing, blurring any clear distinction.

He didn't move. Was he dead? She inched closer.

Familiarity struck her. She ran and crouched by the man's side. Her eyes scanned the body. Not seeing any obvious breaks, no limbs oddly contorted, she rolled him over. He let out a muted grunt, the first indication she had that he was alive.

"James," she said, brushing his hair from his eyes and placing her hands on her husband's face. James Morgan's eyes fluttered open.

"Anne?" he asked, his voice thin. "Anne. You ain't dead."

He struggled to sit up. She helped him and saw then the huge, dark stain of blood spread across the left side of his hunting shirt. She gasped.

"Just the arm," James said. She made a closer examination and saw he was right; there were holes in the sleeve of the shirt at the upper arm, front and back. The ball had passed through cleanly. She looked back at his face and stared into his eyes. She was afraid to ask but had to know.

"The baby, James—is he safe?" It was more a plea than a question.

James put the palm of his good hand to her cheek. "Yep. Safe with Sally Craig at Bryan's," James said, smiling.

"Thank the Lord," Anne sighed. She felt certain then that God was watching over her family. How else to explain happening upon her husband in this way?

His eyes filled with tears as he looked over his wife; her bare, torn feet, tattered dress, and dirty face. "I rode with the militia," he began. "I had to find you. I had to try. But we were routed and—" He cut himself short and looked at Anne quizzically. "How'd you get away?"

"I ran," she said, and laughed.

Then James wrapped his good arm around her, she hugged him back, and they laughed together.

FORTY-EIGHT

Samuel Boone led the way as the battered band of Fayette County men trudged through the woods back to Boone Station. Samuel had no real authority and none was asked for, but he understood that his name carried the weight of inherent responsibility.

As they'd retreated and crossed the Licking, each man had run as far as stamina and instinct could carry him. Then, once realizing he wasn't being pursued, he'd cut toward Boone Station, hoping to meet up with other survivors along the way. None had interest in returning to Bryan's where they expected the rest of the militia would retreat. It was time to go home.

One man found another, then the two found a group of three, and before long fifteen of the twenty-one men from Boone, Strode, and McGee stations were accounted for. The math of it shocked them; it was near unfathomable that so many of their number had escaped death or capture despite being part of the Fayette company that'd advanced furthest into enemy territory. Still, it didn't diminish their concern for those in their band who were missing, or their sorrow for the dead. Andrew McConnell they'd seen killed. Possibly Squire Boone. Missing were Samuel Brannon, John Morgan, and Israel and Daniel Boone. They hoped the men had escaped and were making their own way. Short of that, they hoped they'd been killed in the fighting; death was a better fate by far than being captured and kept for the amusement of the Indians.

The group of fifteen had five horses among them which they took turns riding. None of the horses were theirs; in the days ahead they'd check for saddle markings and attempt to return the animals to their rightful owners or their families.

As the hours passed and their adrenaline drained, they became increasingly exhausted and dejected. They longed for home and the comforting arms of their loved ones, but their pace was slowed when they considered the devastating news they'd have to deliver to the families of the men who weren't returning.

Peter Scholl took the rear, riding a good piece back. He heard a snap and stopped his horse. Then heard another. Then faint hoof falls, drawing closer. He was about to burst forward to warn the others but spared a moment to look back down the trail and saw a horse rounding the bend. The rider's head was down, his shoulders slumped. Peter recognized him immediately.

"Daniel," he shouted, loud enough for the men ahead to hear.

Peter turned his horse and galloped toward Boone, who stopped and waited. Peter rode up beside him. Daniel looked up; his eyes were red and damp. Then Peter notice the blood that covered most of Boone's shirt.

"Israel . . ." Daniel said. He tried to say more but the words hung in his throat.

The rest of the men rode or ran back to greet Boone, but when the closest, Thomas Brooks, heard Boone speak, he pulled back on his reins and put up a hand to signal the others to stop. The men who could see Daniel's face knew. Brooks didn't want to ride any closer, feeling he was intruding on Boone's private grief somehow. He removed his hat. The next man who still had one did the same, then turned and whispered to the man behind him. That man removed his hat, turned, and passed the news on down the line.

Peter Scholl didn't know what to say. He put his hand on Daniel's shoulder. Boone gave him a weak, tired smile.

"I'm glad you made it, Peter."

Peter burst into tears. Israel was his friend, and the fact that he'd just the other day spoken poorly of him, even in jest, made him feel ashamed.

Boone put his arm on Peter's shoulder. After a moment, he looked up and turned to Brooks.

"And you, Thomas," Daniel said. Then he shifted in this saddle to look past Brooks.

"Charles. Andrew. Ephraim," Boone continued. "John. Abraham," and on through the ranks as the men rode or walked closer to him. These were Daniel's neighbors and friends, men he felt fondness and a responsibility for, and each one living meant one less widow, or a mother and father who still had a son.

Samuel Boone dismounted and rushed to his uncle. Seeing him coming, Daniel swung from the saddle. Samuel threw his arms around him and began to sob. Daniel hugged him. He looked over at Peter.

"Squire?" Daniel asked.

Peter shrugged and shook his head.

Boone and his men continued on to a small creek they knew was ahead a ways, looking forward to a cool drink and an opportunity to wipe the sweat and grime from their necks and faces. They broke through the trees and found John Floyd standing on the bank, the Arabian beside him. How he'd managed to retrieve his own horse amidst the chaos not a one of them could figure, although neither were any of them surprised.

The story circulated later that Floyd, retreating from the battlefield, reached the bottom of the hill and saw a Miami astride the Arabian, riding through the flatland, cavalierly tomahawking white men from the saddle. Floyd strode past a number of riderless horses, the story went, any of which he could have mounted to escape. He picked a tomahawk off the ground, then whistled. Hearing the signal, the Arabian turned and ran to his master. Floyd flung the tomahawk, burying the weapon in the Miami's chest. The man fell from the saddle and Floyd swung up to take his place, the Arabian never slowing.

Most considered the story apocryphal; but for the men who had seen Floyd in action at Blue Licks, it was believable enough.

FORTY-NINE

"Riders!" little Richard Barrow hollered, loud as he could manage in the midst of his coughing fit. He'd just taken a giant swig from his water jug when he looked up, saw the riders and men on foot approaching, and swallowed in a panic so he could quickly sound the alert, sending the water down the wrong pipe.

"Ours!" he spit out between coughs; he didn't want Flanders Calloway scolding him for scaring the entire station into thinking an Indian war party was thundering toward them. He ran across the roof of his family's cabin, down the ladder he'd propped against the side, then bolted to the station's gate, kicking up dust as he went. The two Stinson girls who were keeping watch put down the rifles they were cleaning, jumped up from the log they were sitting on, and swung the gate open. Richard burst through as soon as there was gap enough for him to squeeze past, which didn't take much.

He ran headlong down the trail; it was clearly defined this time of year, flanked on both sides by tall, thick grass. Even at this distance Richard could make out that Daniel Boone was leading the group—he recognized the man's bearing. He pushed himself to run faster. When he was close enough to see the faces of the men clearly, however, he slowed; he was only seven but knew despair when he saw it. Boone dismounted and walked toward him, then crouched to the boy's level and put his arms around his scrawny shoulders.

"Walk back with us, Richard," Daniel said. Richard nodded. Boone knew the boy would feel it was his duty to run back to the station and report what he'd learned, and Daniel wanted to spare him the burden.

The five other riders dismounted and, along with Boone, unsaddled their horses; the animals would be content to graze on the lush grass and have no mind to wander off. The men flung the saddles over their shoulders and walked with the rest toward the fort. John Floyd held back; this reunion wasn't his, and he had no intention of intruding upon it.

By then everyone in the station had gathered outside the gate. Assessing the postures and labored progress of the distant figures, the residents began to fear that the news wasn't good. When the men were close enough to count, that fear was confirmed.

Rebecca stood in the crowd holding little Nathan, her other children beside her. She picked out Daniel straight away, felt a wave of relief, then scanned for Israel. Her relief turned to ice and dropped to the pit of her stomach.

Jemima reached for her mother's hand. "There might be a second group," she whispered. Flanders touched Rebecca's shoulder.

Rebecca tried to cling to Jemima's hope but couldn't get a handhold.

She knew.

Daniel suddenly remembered his blood-soaked shirt. He dropped the saddle and gear, pulled off the shirt, and tossed it into the grass; Rebecca needn't live out her days with the image of him covered in the blood of their son etched in her memory. Then he picked up what he'd been carrying and resumed walking.

Mary Boone, Martha's normally shy seventeen-year-old daughter, couldn't contain herself any longer; she spotted Peter Scholl among the militiamen and ran for him. Martha reached out instinctively to stop her, then realized there was no point in trying.

Mary threw her arms around Peter's neck. Peter, slightly embarrassed, put one hand loosely on her waist and the other behind his back. Joseph and Abraham Scholl stared at each other; they didn't even know their brother was sweet on the girl.

Others followed Mary's lead and rushed up the trail to meet their loved ones. No one asked the men about details or outcomes; the fact that they were alive was the only victory that mattered in that moment.

Rebecca knew there were others in the crowd experiencing heartache. The Morgans. The Brannons. The McConnells. She saw Samuel Boone among the militiamen, but not Squire. She turned to Sarah. Sarah looked at her, tears filling her eyes. Sam Boone took his wife's hand and led her toward their son. Samuel hugged his parents. Before they had a chance to ask, he told them there was yet hope for Squire. He decided not to mention that he'd seen his brother shot.

Daniel paused a few feet from the gate as the other men's families led them into the station. He stared at Rebecca. He'd dropped the saddle but was still holding Will Hays' rifle—

the rifle Israel had been carrying. Emotion caught in Rebecca's throat and she forced it down. She stepped forward.

Daniel stood, stone like; he was using all the strength he had left to keep his grief at bay. His every intention was to remain strong for his wife, and he knew if he moved even a little the grief would flood in and he'd soon be on his knees—so, by God, he wouldn't move a muscle. Rebecca stopped just in front of him, Nathan in her arms. She looked into Daniel's eyes; it was the first time she'd ever seen him truly broken. Each reached up and gently wiped tears from the other's cheek. Daniel tried to speak but couldn't.

They wrapped their arms around each other and let go of all they were holding back. Levina, crying, ran to them first, pulling young Jesse with her. Daniel Morgan and Rebecca followed. Will Hays held Susannah tightly as she sobbed; Israel was her big brother, and they had grown up together. Susannah felt a touch on her arm. It was Jemima. Will let go of his wife, and the two women ran to join their family.

Guilt stabbed at Will, but he knew whatever pang of regret he felt was likely a shadow of Daniel's own. Flanders, carrying guilt enough himself and a child in each arm, walked up and stood beside Hays.

Will gazed across the landscape and noticed for the first time a man standing in the distance. He squinted, then nudged Flanders and pointed. Flanders looked out; his eyes went wide and he turned back to Will. Neither could believe it. Then Will raised his arm and waved for Floyd to come on in.

The rest of the settlers, their heads low, walked silently back into the station; there would be opportunity soon enough to express their condolences. For now, the Boones deserved what little privacy the cramped station afforded.

FIFTY

Friday, August 30

Boone pulled the chair back from the table as quietly as he could manage. It was well after midnight and the rest of the family was asleep. He should have been so himself, but he avoided sleep whenever possible because the first thing he thought of when he woke was Israel and how he'd shamed the boy into riding with the militia and how now his son was dead.

The only break in his despair had come around lunchtime three days after the battle. Two riders approached the station. Flanders, who'd been spending a lot of time on watch, saw them coming and, thinking he recognized one of the men, rode out to meet them. He was right; the man was Monk Estill, the former slave, unforgettable to all who knew him on account of his fine fiddle playing. Riding beside Monk was a nearly unrecognizable, pitiful looking Squire Boone.

Flanders led them into the station and straight to the cabin of Sam and Sara Boone. Every Boone relation who could fit inside the home eventually joined them for the tearful reunion. They encouraged Squire to sit and eat, but he refused—he had something to tend to first. He walked, alone, to the Brannon cabin and told Samuel's parents of their son's bravery.

Not long after the curious residents gathered in the courtyard to hear Squire's tale. He wept when he told of Samuel Brannon and how the man had saved his life at the expense of his own. Samuel's parents wept as well, but their souls also swelled with pride as their neighbors offered them comfort.

Squire had only vague memories of what happened after he escaped Blue Licks. He'd certainly intended to ride directly to Boone Station but was apparently slipping in and out of consciousness along the way, delirious from fever and loss of blood. He woke at one point beside a stream he didn't recognize, bobbing back and forth in the saddle; his horse was pulling to get Squire to loosen the reins so she could lower her head for a drink. Squire figured he must have gotten down and had a drink himself, for when he next came to he was wet from head to toe but in the saddle and not in the least thirsty. Next he knew he was in front of a cabin, Monk Estill and his wife running out the door to catch him before he fell from his horse.

"You think the boy looks bad now, you should have seen him then," Monk told the crowd. "Like death itself, only more pallid and less vibrant. He tipped his hat to my wife, only he wasn't wearing no hat, said he was powerful glad to see me, then tumbled straight into my arms."

Squire woke in a bed in the Estill cabin two days later. The Estills had taken the opportunity provided by Squire's fevered unconsciousness to set his broken leg, which minimized the trauma for all involved. Monk and his wife then nursed Squire to good enough health to make the ride to Boone Station.

After he and Squire had finished their storytelling, Monk stuck around long enough to have a meal at Daniel and Rebecca's home before saying his goodbyes and riding back to his isolated farm.

The next day, word reached Boone Station that it was time to return to Blue Licks to bury the dead.

Colonel Logan and his men had reached Bryan Station the day of the battle and learned for the first time that Todd had led the militia from there in pursuit of the raiders. Even as Logan contemplated what to do next, survivors began to trickle in from Blue Licks; some wounded, all exhausted and downtrodden. Logan questioned each man and soon had a picture of what had transpired; the militia had ridden right into an ambush and been roundly defeated.

Logan determined there was no point in repeating the mistake. The Indians and British were clearly positioned on favorable ground. They outnumbered the militiamen he'd brought with him from the south—hardly fresh themselves after several days of marching—and it was plainly evident that the men who'd retreated were in no shape, physically or mentally, to join a new assault.

So they waited. Then, four long days after the battle, the survivors and Logan's men gathered at Bryan's and rode to Blue Licks. For the second time since coming to Kentucky, Daniel buried a son killed by Indians.

The following day Daniel rode to Boonesborough to speak with April Calloway. Israel's friends and cousins had already told her of Israel's death, but she deserved to hear of the heroism of the man she loved as only Daniel, the man's father, could tell it.

Daniel stared down at the paper, quill, and vial of ink illuminated by the soft glow of the single candle he'd brought to the kitchen table. He realized suddenly that he'd been sitting, unmoving, for some time, lost in thought, frozen by sorrow. He turned his head to look out the window; the sun would rise in a few hours and the world would begin moving, and he'd be forced to move with it at that point whether he wanted to or didn't. Best to face it now, on his terms. He picked up the quill, dipped it, and began.

> *Sir*
>   *A present circumstance of affairs causes me to*
>   *write to your Excellency as follows.*

Daniel felt no ill will toward Governor Harrison personally; the man had barely been in office ten months and had inherited coffers completely emptied by the war effort. Boone understood—as it had been told to him often, year after year, by those in authority in Virginia—that the lack of funds meant Kentucky was on its own when it came to protecting itself. But understanding a thing didn't mean a man had to like it, and Boone now felt an obligation to say his piece for the record.

He began by detailing the events leading to the battle at Blue Licks as plainly as he was able; he knew the governor would see immediately that he wasn't a learned man and had considered enlisting Hays to give the language some polish, but Will hadn't been on the battlefield. No, this was Daniel's responsibility, and he'd do it on his own, polish be damned. He was careful to check his emotions, though, as it was imperative that Harrison have an accurate picture of the situation in Kentucky and not think he was reading the biased ravings of grieving father.

Daniel noted dates and distances, spelled out the militia's basic strategy, mentioned the number of militiamen involved (182 including himself) the assumed number of the enemy, and listed the officers present—with the exception of Floyd.

Before riding for Louisville the day after they'd returned from the battle, John asked Daniel not to mention him in any official correspondence; as far as the record and politicians were concerned, John Floyd was never there. Floyd gave no reason when making the request, and Boone gave no thought to pressing for one. He could tell the man was full of fury, and knew Floyd intended to have words with General Clark to convince him to garrison more troops on this edge of the frontier. Louisville was a vital shipping lane and needed protection, but if the settlements to the east were lost to further Indian invasion, Louisville would have no chance of standing on it own; all they'd worked and fought and died for in Kentucky would be lost.

Daniel also made no mention of debates, bad decisions, or even McGary's actions, feeling it petty and pointless; that they'd foolishly rushed headlong into an ambush was plain in the telling, and assigning blame would smack of dodging his own responsibility for the outcome, which he had no intention of doing. Boone blamed only himself. Had he not lost his temper in a manner that was atypical, had he not allowed himself to be baited by McGary, perhaps he could have succeeded in delaying the militia's advance. Perhaps he could have been more forceful in demanding Israel return home. Perhaps he could never have shamed his son into going in the first place.

Daniel blinked, pulled himself back to the moment, and continued.

> *From the manner we had formed, it fell to my lot to bring on the attack, which was done with a very heavy fire on both sides, and extended back the lines to Col. Trigg, where the enemy was so strong that they rushed up and broke the right wing at the first fire. So the enemy was immediately on our back so we were obliged to retreat with the loss of 77 of our men and 12 wounded,*

The quill had to be dipped after every few words, the excess ink gently tapped back into the vial. It was a tedious process, but did allow a man plenty of time to consider the words he was putting to paper.

> *afterward we were reinforced by Col. Logan which with our own men amounted to 460 light horse with which we march'd to the battle ground again but found the enemy were gone off so we proceeded to bury the dead*

Boone wiped his eyes with his free hand then began again.

> *which were 43 found on the ground, and many more we expect lay about that we did not see as we could not tarry to search very close, being both hungry and weary, and somewhat dubious that the enemy might not be gone quite off.*

He'd come to the bottom of the page. He lifted it from the stack and carefully moved it to the side, face up, to give the ink opportunity to dry.

He stared at the fresh sheet. Now he'd come to the crux of the matter.

> *By this Yr Excellency may draw an idea of our circumstance. I know Sir, that your situation at present is something critical but are we to be totally forgotten? I hope not.*

He requested reinforcements, men he knew would not be coming, before launching into his personal declaration.

> *I have encouraged the people here in this country all that I could, but I can no longer encourage my neighbors nor my self to risk our lives here at such extraordinary hazzards.*

He suddenly felt the letter pointless and almost crumpled it. But he'd gone to the bother, so he figured he might as well see it through.

> *I remain Sir your Excellency's most obedient humble servant.*

He signed it. Perhaps he would ask Hays to look it over in the morning and pretty it up. No, no point in wasting anyone's time aside from his own.

He sat back in the chair, placed his hands on the armrests, and considered pushing himself up but didn't.

He felt a touch on his cheek and opened his eyes; he wasn't sure how long he'd slept but it was still night, although he saw from the window that there was a faint line of red on the horizon. Perhaps there'd be rain today; the land could certainly use it. He hoped it would rain so much that the Licking would rise and swallow up the Blue Licks forever, but he knew that wasn't likely.

Rebecca was behind him, the fingers of one hand placed lightly on his face, little Nathan held in her other arm as she looked over Daniel's shoulder and read his letter.

Daniel craned his head back. Rebecca's eyes were rimmed with red; she'd done too much crying and had too little rest.

"What do you think of it?" he asked, his voice heavy with sleep.

"It's you," Rebecca said, still looking at the final page of the letter. "It's good."

Rebecca placed Nathan into Daniel's arms, then put her hands on her husband's shoulders and kissed the top of his head.

"You misspelled *hazards* though."

Daniel smiled. "I misspelled way more than that, but nice of you not to mention the rest."

She hugged him, her arms around his neck and her chin on his head. She looked out the window as Daniel looked down at their son. He placed the tip of his finger on the boy's nose.

"I think it might rain today," Rebecca said.

Daniel thought on it.

"No," he said after a moment. "I don't think it's ready to just yet."

1786

FIFTY-ONE

Friday, October 6

Boone's heart leapt into his throat, making it difficult to speak. Even without seeing the man's face Daniel recognized the big Indian; he'd lurked in every dark corner of his mind for the past thirteen years.

"Jim!" Boone finally managed to call out in a voice so thick with gravel and anger that he didn't recognize it as his own.

Indeed, Boone shouted with such force that the big Indian heard it from across the village, even through the clamor of the battle that raged all around him. Jim turned, rifle in hand. His eyes hunted and found Boone, on horseback, surrounded by a half dozen mounted militiamen.

"Mind that fellow there," Boone said to his men. "He's the man who killed my son James."

Colonel Logan and his men had been riding for close to a week, a good four days longer and much further into the Ohio

331

country than they'd intended. They'd reached Chillicothe on the third day, as expected, only to find it deserted. They shouldn't have been surprised; the Shawnee had moved the town many times before, and were certain to have done so again knowing this location had been identified.

So the militiamen pressed on, frustrated, tired, and hungry. Riding at the head of one of the companies, Daniel Boone did what he could to bolster the spirits of the men under his command.

In the year following the events at Blue Licks, the British, their cause lost, slowly disengaged from the frontier. Caldwell's group of Butler's Rangers was disbanded; for their loyalty to the British Crown, each man was rewarded with Canadian land along the Detroit River. Retreat and forced retirement didn't sit well with Caldwell, although he felt confident fresh conflicts requiring his skills and expertise would arise soon enough. They always did.

The British withdrawal left their Indian allies fighting a war they were now losing, a war the British themselves had propagated. Indian raids against settlers in Kentucky continued, followed by retaliatory strikes by the frontiersmen, followed by more raids from the Indians. It was a fire destined to burn for as long as both sides insisted on adding fresh fuel.

Little assistance flowed to the Kentuckians from Virginia, despite the constant requests of Boone, Levi Todd, and John Floyd. This didn't engender much in the way of good will for the Virginian government among the settlers, and talk of Kentucky breaking off and becoming its own state was in the air.

Even General Clark had grown frustrated. The Louisville area, which Clark made no bones about considering his priority, was the most supported by Richmond, although slightly more than none wasn't all that much. Clark had come to the conclusion that playing defense was a losing strategy and, acting on his own, launched an offensive into Ohio against the Indian towns, figuring to finally put an end to the conflict. This campaign of Logan's that Boone was participating in was part of that effort.

Boone was no more fond of Logan than he'd been previously, but found now that the colonel treated him more or less affably. The change in attitude was well short of an apology, but it was a turn. Daniel figured fighting against the British and Indians at Blue Licks and losing a son to the cause was finally enough to convince Logan that he wasn't in cahoots with either.

McGary was another matter. He'd signed on to the campaign despite no one requesting it, and he and Boone kept a good distance between them. Although his actions at Blue Licks were widely known, McGary hadn't been busted down in rank or even reprimanded. Boone now regretted his decision to not hold the man to account in his written reports of the affair, although he knew it would have made little difference; Logan had a habit of protecting McGary, though no one understood why. Perhaps he owed McGary a debt, or perhaps McGary held something over the man. Whatever the reason, the result was the same; McGary was like a weed that returned time and again, regardless of how often it was ripped from the dirt.

Boone and Simon Kenton were faring better on the long journey than the other militiamen; they were first of the best when it came to frontiering, with Daniel, now fifty-one, having twenty years on Simon besides. Kenton was also a giant compared to Boone (or most anyone else for that matter), a fearless brawler with a massive chin and the jaw to support it. When Daniel was shot in the ankle during the Boonesborough siege in 1777, it was Kenton who scooped him up, laid him across his shoulder, and carried him to safety through a hail of Shawnee rifle fire.

Finally, scouts rode back to tell Colonel Logan they'd found it—new Chillicothe. Boone had spotted a pack of dogs the day prior and told Logan that if they followed the animals they'd lead them straight to the Indian town. No one contested the notion; everyone on the frontier now knew to listen to Boone when it came to such matters.

Logan gave his orders. Minutes later, the attack was underway.

Big Jim raised his musket. Boone's men sped their horses toward the Indian, but Daniel himself was frozen. Jim fired, as did the riders. Jim's shot hit one of the Kentuckians, throwing the man from his horse. Several shots hit Jim, spinning him hard to the ground.

The five remaining riders bolted past Jim's body, their eyes now on other braves who were darting through the village in all directions and firing at them. But Big Jim wasn't dead. He rose, bleeding, reloaded, and fired a second time. Another Kentuckian fell.

From across the way, Simon Kenton, atop his horse, had just fired at a brave who'd done the same to him when he caught sight of Big Jim at the edge of his vision. Whether Kenton's shot found its mark or not he never knew; he tossed his rifle to the ground the second after firing, jumped from his horse, and rushed toward Jim, pulling his hunting knife from his belt as he went. Seeing him coming, Big Jim struggled to reload but blood from a shot to his shoulder had run down his arm, making his fingers slick; cartridges from his rifle pouch spilled to the ground as he fumbled to get hold of one. Kenton leapt, knife arm drawn back. He landed, plunging the blade into the Indian's chest. Big Jim crumpled to the dirt. He looked small suddenly compared to the mountain that was Kenton, who stared down at the hilt of the knife protruding from Jim's chest, watching to be certain it didn't rise and fall with breathing.

It didn't.

Two militiamen were upon Jim a moment later. They grabbed the body by the hair and dragged it to a sitting position. Then one of the men drew his knife and went to scalping.

All around them, scattered throughout the village, the militia pushed forward, ducking behind tents, trees, and any available cover, taking fire and returning it.

Except for Boone. He sat upon his horse, immobile, watching the end of Big Jim. He found it curious; when Israel was alive, Daniel was often preoccupied thinking of James. Now, when he should be thinking of James, his mind drifted to Israel.

"Fetch my knife when you're finished," Kenton said to the men working on Big Jim as he walked away. He picked up the rifle Jim had been using—a nice-looking Kentucky long rifle. Kenton loaded it from his own kit. It was a certainty that Big Jim had taken the weapon from a settler he'd killed at some point; there was no chance a frontiersman would have traded with so notorious a murderer. Kenton felt justified in reclaiming it.

FIFTY-TWO

Tuesday, December 12

Daniel trudged through the soft, powdery snow. Most of it had fallen in the night while he'd slept, comfortably wrapped within a thick bearskin beside a glowing fire that the snow had extinguished at some point in the night.

He'd risen just before dawn, his spirits high; the colder the winter became, the thicker and more lush the furs. There'd be good hunting ahead.

The boys didn't stir when he'd grabbed his gear—they were heavy sleepers, typical of children in their teen years—so he made no effort to wake them. His trail would be easy enough to follow in the snow, even with it still coming down, and finding him would be good practice for the boys, who were quickly becoming pretty fair trackers.

Jesse and Daniel Morgan had been excited to come along, and Daniel humored them, even though he knew they'd tire of it early and he'd have to come out of the woods long before he would otherwise. Rebecca seemed unusually happy with the idea, whether because she was anxious for the boys to spend more time with their father or just relieved to get them out of the cramped confines of the cabin now that winter had set in, Daniel wasn't sure.

He left camp and set out for the large hill that was close by, wanting to get a sense of his surroundings. It took a bit more than an hour to reach the top. He scooped up a handful of snow, bright and glistening in the morning sun, and took a generous bite to quench his thirst. He was hungry, too, but figured on making the boys hunt for breakfast once they found him.

He tucked his rifle under his arm and pulled his hat from his head to dust the snow from the brim. He gazed over the horizon and, watching the sun claim the sky to the east, took stock. It was a view hard-earned; not by the hike, but by the years of fighting and surviving, loss and sacrifice, blood and treasure that had brought him here.

It is, indeed, a beautiful country, Boone thought.

Then, far in the distance, he saw a thin line of smoke rising above the trees. He traced the tendril from the sky down to its source—the chimney of a tiny cabin in a recently cleared patch of woods, barely visible through the dense forest that lay between it and the hill where he stood.

"Hmph," the frontiersman sighed. *Starting to get a little crowded.*

Then he turned and headed back down the hill, figuring now on meeting the boys halfway.

AUTHOR'S NOTE

Although a real event, certain details surrounding the Battle of Blue Licks as portrayed in this book are invented, bridging the gaps between truths—lost mainly to the passage of time—with the assumed and imagined. What is presented here is not history in the strictest sense; it is story, intended to breathe life into a largely forgotten past. That said, the facts that have survived laced together in such an intricate and interesting manner that there wasn't much point in replacing them with inferior make-believe.

My research was made easier thanks to the Daniel Boone biographies written by John Bakeless, John Mack Faragher, Robert Morgan, and Meredith Mason Brown, as well as Neal O. Hammon's indispensable non-fiction account of the battle, *Daniel Boone and the Defeat at Blue Licks*.

POSTSCRIPT

Simon Girty

Almost twelve years to the day after the events at Blue Licks, Girty was present at the Battle of Fallen Timbers, the last battle of the Northwest Indian War. He was once again in the company of William Elliot, Alexander McKee, and William Caldwell. This time, however, the American forces were victorious, thanks largely to the Kentucky militia led by Robert Todd, younger brother of John and Levi Todd. Girty was later awarded land in Canada for his service to the British Crown, establishing a farm near what is now Amherstburg, Ontario.

Lieutenant Colonel William Caldwell

In addition to commanding a militia company at the Battle of Fallen Timbers, the newly-promoted lieutenant colonel later led a group of Canadian volunteers, now known as Caldwell's Rangers, in several engagements of the War of 1812.

Major Hugh McGary

McGary suffered no official sanction for his role in the disaster at Blue Licks. Four years later, perhaps haunted by his actions and still grappling with personal demons, McGary murdered an American-allied Shawnee chief named Moluntha in a fit of rage, asking the man repeatedly, "Was you in the Battle of Blue Licks?" (Moluntha was not). McGary was stripped of his commission and court-martialed for the crime. His son, Hugh McGary, Jr., later founded Evansville, Indiana.

Major Silas Harlan

General George Rogers Clark was known to refer to Silas as "one of bravest soldiers that ever fought by my side." In 1819, the newly-formed Harlan County, Kentucky, was named in Major Harlan's honor.

Lieutenant Colonel Steven Trigg

Before his death at Blue Licks, Steven Trigg and his wife had a daughter, Mary, named for her mother. Mary later married David Logan, nephew of Colonel Benjamin Logan. Mary and David's son, Stephen Trigg Logan, moved to Springfield, Illinois, where he became the law partner of Abraham Lincoln.

Major Levi Todd

Robert Smith Todd was born to Levi Todd and his wife, Jane, in 1791. Fifty-one years later, Robert's daughter, Mary, married Abraham Lincoln and later served as first lady of the

United States from 1861 to 1865. As it happened, Daniel Boone had led Captain Abraham Lincoln, grandfather of Mary's future husband, over the Cumberland Gap into Kentucky in 1779.

Aaron Reynolds and Captain Robert Patterson

Although lacking his trousers, Aaron Reynolds made it safely home to Bryan Station where he eventually married, took up farming, and joined a Baptist church, after which it was said he only cussed half as much.

Robert Patterson moved north to where the Ohio River meets the Licking and cofounded the port city of Cincinnati, Ohio, in 1788.

The two men remained lifelong friends.

William and Susannah Hays

By all accounts, Will and Susannah lived a passionate—though often tumultuous—life together until Susannah's untimely death in 1800, just shy of her fortieth birthday. Will never recovered from the loss. He began drinking heavily and became quarrelsome. Four years after his wife's death, Hays pulled a rifle on his own son-in-law, who shot him dead in self-defense.

Colonel John Floyd

In addition to cofounding Louisville, Kentucky's largest city, Floyd County was named in John's honor following its establishment in 1800. The Battle of Blue Licks was not, as alluded to in our story, John's first scrape with the British, nor was it destined to be his last confrontation with Indians. Those, however, are tales for another time.

Lieutenant Colonel Daniel Boone

The first Boone biography, written by historian John Filson from in-person interviews with the frontiersman, was published in 1784, right around Boone's fiftieth birthday. The book was an international sensation.

Daniel was elected to a third term in the Virginia legislature in 1791. He packed up Rebecca and eleven-year-old Nathan and brought them along to Richmond. They were in the city the following June when word arrived that Congress had approved Kentucky statehood.

In 1799, at the invitation of Spanish authorities, Daniel and most of the Boone family, including Jemima and Flanders, moved to Spanish-held Missouri. Could be Boone figured Kentucky had gotten too crowded; likely as not, he simply craved a new adventure.

Made in the USA
Middletown, DE
30 October 2023

41497308R00210